"Where are you off to?"

The huskiness in his voice surprised Kyle.

"I—I dunno."

The crickets and frogs ramped up to a crescendo as he debated the wisdom of what he was about to do.

"How many couples do you think sat on this porch, maybe even in this very seat, just as we're doing now?" he whispered, tracing Allison's cheek with his finger. He liked it when she smiled and how the pulse jumped at the base of her throat.

"Hmm. That's over a century and a quarter. Got to be a lot."

"I wonder if they felt the way I do."

Now it was her finger sliding along his arm. "And how exactly do you feel?"

"Happy. Yeah. And...like I'm in the calmest place on earth."

She stared at him, and then she looked away. For a moment, he felt the connection between them break and all his earlier doubts and misgivings begin to flood in.

He didn't want to think about all of that, not the variance, not the house.

Impulsively, he craned his neck to meet her eyes, muttering, "I'm probably going to get slapped for this..."

And then he kissed her.

Dear Reader,

I was blessed to grow up amid sawdust and boards and nails; my mother was the type of woman who moved walls around furniture, not furniture around walls. I took for granted that, once I reached adulthood, I would naturally know how to wire light fixtures, do plumbing and frame walls.

Alas, I'm the least handy person in my family, and at the tender mercy of any contractor willing to put up with me...yet I'm still cursed with a love of old houses and the knowledge of how easy my mom made it look to renovate.

So I empathize with Allison and Kyle as they negotiate not just their growing love for each other, but the crises that arise from the renovation of the beautiful old Victorian in *What the Heart Wants*. No doubt you have your own stories of renovations—and how the true test of a relationship is a good house remodel!

I hope you enjoy Allison and Kyle's story.

Cynthia Reese

HEARTWARMING

What the Heart Wants

Cynthia Reese

ISBN-13: 978-0-373-36706-1

What the Heart Wants

This edition published by arrangement with Harlequin Books S.A.

For questions and comments about the quality of this book, please contact us at CustomerService@Harlequin.com.

Printed in U.S.A.

CYNTHIA REESE

lives with her husband and their daughter in south Georgia, along with their two dogs, three cats and however many strays show up for morning muster. She has been scribbling since she was knee-high to a grasshopper and reading even before that. A former journalist, teacher and college English instructor, she also enjoys cooking, traveling and photography when she gets the chance.

Books by Cynthia Reese

HARLEQUIN HEARTWARMING

6560—SEEDS OF TRUST
6610—A PLACE TO CALL HOME

HARLEQUIN SUPERROMANCE

1415—THE BABY WAIT
1533—FOR THE SAKE OF THE CHILDREN

To strong women everywhere who
don't have "quit" in them...including my two favorite
octogenarians, Eloise Baker and Rose Pierce.

Acknowledgments

This book couldn't have been written without loads of help—first from my terrific editors Kathryn Lye and Victoria Curran and all the Harlequin Heartwarming staff, and from my critique partners Tawna Fenske and Karen Rock. But others pitched in as well: Leah Michalek of the Savannah (GA) Metropolitan Planning Commission's Urban Planning and Historic Preservation Department for her endless patience with my research, Adrianna Friedman of the DeLorenzo Gallery of New York City and her kind help with my research on sculptor Jean Dunand, my sister Donna's continual encouragement, my family's patient endurance of my absence while I wrote and researched, and the cheering from my fellow Heartwarming sister-authors. To all of you, I owe you loan-shark big.

CHAPTER ONE

KYLE MITCHELL DESPERATELY wanted to distract the woman in front of him. He could see the way her lips parted softly, the way her eyes grew wide as they drank in every detail. No, this would not do.

He tugged at Cecilia Simpson's arm—politely, respectfully, but still a tug. "And as you can see on the street on your left, across the road, we have a late Queen Anne style, recently restored—"

"But Dr. Mitchell, I want to know about *this* house. This perfectly gorgeous house."

Kyle heaved a sigh and gave up any pretense of ignoring Cecilia's fixation. He faced the house in question: three stories, peeling paint, lawn a little patchy, front walkway showing some weeds poking out of its hexagonal paving stones.

Who was he kidding? Nobody could ignore Belle Paix. It was the house that had hooked him but good when he'd first toured Lombard five years ago.

Back then, Kyle had hoped to see the inside of the house, convince the owners to renovate it and bring it back to life. Five years later, he'd yet to get more than halfway up the front walk.

Today, on his walking tour with the *Southern Homes* folks, he'd just hoped he could distract Cecilia, not to mention her accompanying photographer. Cecilia was doing a tourism piece on Lombard for *Southern Homes Magazine.* A two-page spread of Lombard's historic section would give an extra-big boost to this year's high season.

No such luck. He might as well get it over and done with.

"Of course you recognize it as a Second Empire—and there's the rare sweeping S curve of the Mansard roof. Plus, you see that the wrought-iron cresting is still intact—that's really rare, because people tended to remove it rather than repair or replace it. Originally, the house would have been a much brighter color than its current pale yellow—newspaper reports of the day said it was a deep canary yellow with four different trim colors."

Cecilia clapped her hands in delight. "Oh, it's so beautiful! It could be such a showstopper! You hardly ever see Second Empire examples in the South. But why hasn't it been restored? It's the only home on this street that isn't."

Kyle decided it wouldn't do to be perfectly, bluntly honest and reveal that the home owner had never responded to a single, solitary invitation to attend so much as one historical society meeting. Or that, when she found out how much it would cost to paint the house in historically accurate colors—five different shades including all the trim paints—she'd harrumphed and said, "Why, thank you, sonny. That's a little more than I wanted to spend."

To his dismay, Kyle heard the electronic click of the photographer's digital camera, after which the man scurried off to the street corner to get a better angle. Right. Just what Kyle wanted *Southern Homes* readers to see, a house in need of a makeover.

He swatted at a bevy of gnats that were swarming around his face. It was late spring in south Georgia, and hot and muggy to boot. But Cecilia had her feet planted firmly on the carefully restored sidewalk just his side of Belle Paix's wrought-iron fence, and she was apparently waiting for him to answer.

"Well? Why not?" she prompted.

"The home owner is elderly, the house has been in the same family since it was built, and she's…well, I'll leave it to your imagination." Kyle looked past Cecilia to see a striking redhead about his age striding down the sidewalk.

The woman, tall and long-legged, in running shorts and a tank top, with an iPod draped around her neck, looked as though she'd just finished a morning walk. As she skirted around the photographer, who was still kneeling as he fired away with his camera, she lifted her dark auburn hair off her neck, apparently as bothered by the steaming temps as Kyle was. He knew all the home owners along this street, but he didn't recognize her.

And he would have if he'd ever seen her before. One look, and he would always remember that face.

Beside him, Cecilia was still nearly swooning over the house, despite its disheveled appearance. "In the same family! All this time? It looks like something off one of those fantastic animated films! When was it built?"

Kyle yanked his attention back to the house and Cecilia. "In 1888—well, that was when it was finished. It was built by a wealthy timber-and-railroad baron as a present for his wife—"

The other woman must have heard him, because she threw back her head and laughed. "A timber baron? A present for his wife? Yeah, right. That's exactly how it went."

Cecilia turned to her. "So it wasn't like that?"

The redhead shrugged as she closed the gap between them. "Ambrose Shepherd was a carpetbagger born to a shopkeeper in New Jersey, and he was determined to get rich. He came south at the right time and made pots of money by getting timber down the Altamaha River, but he was no baron. He married a country girl from Darian, Georgia, during his timber days, and then moved her up here when the railroads started expanding. He always had his eye on making money, Ambrose did, and when he saw that the railroads would make the river obsolete, he invested in the Central Railroad. But when he got to Lombard to make sure the railroad expansion was going like he wanted it to, nobody would receive his country-girl wife. So he decided he'd build the biggest, showiest house Lombard had ever seen."

Cecilia's attention was rapt. Kyle started to interrupt, to say that wasn't exactly historically accurate, and that he'd never heard this version of the story before, when she burbled, "And did they receive her then?"

The redhead's eyebrows lifted. "It got the society ladies in the door, all right—but then they went away and snickered over the idea of anybody spending ten thousand dollars on a house. Not to mention having two indoor bathrooms, or the scandalous idea of a billiard table in one's very own home, and, well…it turned out about how you'd expect."

Cecilia seemed a little crushed that this wasn't the happy ending she was primed for. "Oh. How sad."

"No, it wasn't." The redhead's mouth curved in a wide, satisfied smile. It lit up her face and made her seem friendly and approachable, despite her earlier crankiness. "Davinia Shepherd had no use for the society ladies, and she was pleased as punch that they weren't bothering her."

Now Kyle cleared his throat. "I'm Dr. Kyle Mitchell, a history professor at the college and president of Lombard's historical society. And you are..."

"Allison," she said, offering her hand.

Kyle took it, liking the way her handshake was firm and professional. "That's, ahem, an interesting retelling, Allison," he said. "I've never heard that version before. How do you know so much about Belle Paix?"

She shrugged her shoulders. "Family stories."

"Oh, gossip, then. I thought you had access to some primary sources that I wasn't familiar with—"

"Not gossip." Now the smile retreated, and Allison's chin lifted. "I guess you historical types would call it oral history. They're the same tales my grandmother told me, the ones her mother told her—passed down. Plus there's a set of journals."

"Journals?" Kyle's brain buzzed as the possibility of a new, undiscovered set of turn-of-the-century documents brought up all sorts of ideas. "You have journals?"

But Allison pushed past him and opened Belle Paix's wrought-iron gate. "Sure, Davinia had to do something with her time once she married money and became a lady of leisure. She'd grown up dirt poor, with ten brothers and sisters, so she was used to hard work. But Gran's made it clear that the journals are private, for family only. And as for how I know about the house, I grew up here."

The gate clanged shut, and Allison strode up the walk away from them. Halfway up, she paused and turned around.

"I don't mean to be standoffish, and it wouldn't bother me at all, but Gran doesn't much care for trespassers. You can take all the pictures you want from the street, but she'd be mad if you put so much a pinky toe this side of the fence, okay?"

Allison didn't wait for their reply. Instead, she continued up the walkway, bounced up the steps, paused at the dark mahogany double doors with their arched glass inserts, and swung one open. It soon thudded shut behind her, leaving Kyle tantalized and frustrated. He'd not gotten so much as a peek inside the house, and it didn't seem as if that would change any-time soon.

ALLISON PEEKED OUT the door's beveled glass pane and saw to her satisfaction that Kyle Mitchell and his historical house fans were staying put on the street side of the fence. Good. She wouldn't have to confess to Gran that she'd let an interloper in, although he'd seemed re-spectful enough.

He'd surprised her when he'd said was a pro-fessor. Obviously, professors could come in all shapes and sizes, but Kyle Mitchell landed closer to the more outdoorsy and overtly mascu-line end of the spectrum than the tweed-jacket stereotype. Dark blond hair cut short, tanned, with a big wide smile…

She squinted to spy some more. He was tall—a good head taller than her, so that meant he had to be well over six feet, since she was five foot seven. And yeah, he was wearing a jacket, but it was a navy one that fit him well.

A flying fur bullet zoomed from behind her, probably from the formal front stairs, and landed at her feet, yowling. Allison jumped, still not entirely used to Cleo's ninja ways. The Siamese wound around Allison's bare legs, then must have realized those legs didn't belong to Gran. She backed up, sat down and glared at Allison.

Allison let her heart settle into a more predictable rhythm before attempting to pet the cat, which skulked backward.

"Cleo..." She knelt down and crooned, the way Gran always did with the stubborn feline. "It's been a month and a half. You have to trust me. I'll get Gran back home as soon as I can."

But the cat, from all appearances, remained unconvinced. She turned and stalked off toward the dining room, her seal point tail hiked high with disdain. She would accept food and water from Allison, and sometimes, when she got desperate, would snuggle up at the foot of Allison's bed. But that was only after she'd kept her awake half the night, yowling piteously for Gran.

"Hey! I miss her, too!" Allison called after the cat.

Good grief. I'm getting more and more like Gran every day. This house will send me to the loony bin.

No point in wasting time wondering when insanity would make its appearance. Allison had planned to rip out the carpet in the dining room this morning, and she still had time to get it done before her afternoon visit with Gran.

The carpet was the reason Gran was in rehab to begin with. The seam at the dining room and library had raveled, and Gran had caught her shoe in it.

Allison crossed the length of the long hall, the formal stairs rising above her in a graceful curve. She stood in the dining room doorway, surveying what had to be done.

Before she could rip out the carpet—a Mamie Eisenhower pink design, which Gran had laid in the dining room and library in the early 1950s, after she'd married Pops—Allison had to move a few things.

Starting with Cleo, who'd taken a seat on the dining table and was grooming one long, slender hind leg. The feline paused, gave Allison a mild hiss with no bite to it and succumbed to the inevitable—she knew she wasn't supposed to be on the table. That taken care of, Allison went upstairs to change into jeans and a T-shirt, determined to get the carpet ripped out before she visited Gran.

CHAPTER TWO

AN HOUR LATER, however, Allison was completely stymied. She'd been able to move the heavy, ornate dining chairs, original to the house, and even the table. She'd managed to move the marble-topped sideboard with no disasters, save for scaring one of Cleo's remaining lives out of her when the handcart fell over with a bang.

But the china cabinet, even with all the dishware removed and put on the kitchen table, even with the little Teflon slides she'd bought for the purpose, was not cooperating.

Allison rubbed her eyes and glowered at the hulking piece of mahogany that remained the last obstacle between her and an empty dining room. Who could she call in the middle of the day to help her move the thing?

The phone rang in the kitchen. She worked her way around the dining room chairs and sideboard she'd temporarily shoved into the kitchen, then stretched across stacks of her great-grandmother's 1920s formal china and plucked the phone off its hook on the fourth ring.

"Thomas residence," Allison said, as she managed to rescue a wobbling soup bowl. "Oh!"

"Pardon?" a male voice on the other end asked.

"Sorry, just a disaster averted. I almost broke a J & G Meakin 1920s bowl. Last time I did that I was ten, and in trouble for a week."

A warm, rich chuckle came over the line. "That's good. That you didn't break it, I mean. I'm Kyle Mitchell. We met earlier, I think, if you're Allison."

His voice, still brimming with amusement, made her temporarily forget her bone-deep weariness. She pulled a chair out from the kitchen table and collapsed in it. "Yes. I hope I didn't come across as rude this morning. Some years ago, my grandmother made the mistake of allowing the house to be photographed for a field guide of old homes, and after it came out, she had a flurry of people knocking on her door, thinking the house was open to the public."

"Perfectly understandable. Listen, I just wanted to extend an invitation to you. Our historical preservation society meets once a month, and I thought you might be interested in joining us this Thursday evening."

That voice… Over the phone, with nothing to distract her from its smooth baritone, Allison soaked in its resonance, its hint of good-natured humor. For a moment, she was tempted—not just by his voice, but her memory of him on the sidewalk. Kyle Mitchell had looked friendly enough earlier, and totally unlike her memories of the typical historical society members who'd visited with Gran during Allison's teen years. Maybe it would be nice to meet some folks in Lombard who weren't ten years past retirement age.

The stacks of china and the glut of furniture in the kitchen reminded her of her priorities. "I don't know. I'm a little busy now—Gran's in a rehab facility and I'm trying to get the place in shape for her to come home."

"Oh, well, of course." His voice dimmed with just enough disappointment to be flattering. It made her wish she'd said yes. "If you need some help or advice, just let me know. I love working on old houses."

Allison snorted, startling Cleo, who'd curled up atop the fridge. "You must be a masochist, that's all I can say. Right now I'm trying to rip up old carpet, and really struggling to move a china cabinet. You don't know of any moving companies that would send out someone, do you?"

"Not a moving company…but I'll help. I don't have to teach classes today, so I'd be glad to. I know how heavy those things can be."

"Oh—I wasn't hinting—"

"No, no. Give me ten minutes. That okay?"

"Thanks! I won't say no."

Ten minutes later, she opened the door to see Kyle. He'd ditched the jacket and button-down for a T-shirt that, unlike hers, was clean and dust free. Automatically, she realized what a fright she must look like.

"I've been—"

"Working. No problem. Anybody who does anything on an old house knows it's a dirty job. Lead me to this china cabinet."

But Kyle stopped short in the front hall. He stared up at the ornate cornices and moldings, at the staircase, then craned his neck to see in the front parlor. Allison tried to view the home as he must, but she was at a disadvantage, having grown up here.

He grinned. "This blows me away. A perfect example of a side-hall Second Empire. So often these old houses have been wrecked inside—too many 'modern' improvements." He shook his head.

"Right. Luckily, our family's motto has always been 'If it was good enough for Ambrose, it's good enough for us,'" Allison told him. "Hardly anything has changed."

Just then, Cleo zipped past Kyle with a yowl, and Allison warned, "You'd better watch out. She always makes a return trip."

"Wow. That's—"

"Ninja cat." Allison moved on to the dining room and swept a hand around. "As you can see, one of the few things that Gran did change was to put carpet in the downstairs."

"Get a load of that pink. Now that is pure, bona fide original, Mamie Eisenhower pink."

"Yeah. I don't quite think that shade was what Pops had in mind when he told her to order it—"

"I don't see why not. That was every woman's dream color in 1954." Kyle stepped into the dining room, gawked at the floor-to-ceiling bay window with its intricate cornices, and turned around to take in the space. His eyes lit on the chore before them: the hulking, huge china cabinet.

"Oookay." He shook his head. "That cabinet took a small forest of mahogany to build." He crossed the room and slid his palm against its smooth dark wood. "This is late Victorian? Is it original to the house?"

"Yep. Bought brand-spanking-new in 1888

and shipped all the way from Philadelphia. Like I said, what was good enough for Ambrose…"

Kyle caressed the mahogany, then trailed a finger down the intricately carved panels alongside the breakfront. She couldn't help but notice his large, strong hands, with neatly trimmed nails. They seemed more suited to handling an ax than a professor's red pen.

He glanced up at her, the amusement in his voice now crinkling the corners of his eyes. "They did believe if one carved flower or cherub was good, two would be better, didn't they? When I offered to help, I was thinking of a china cabinet built in the thirties or forties, a colonial reproduction. Maybe I was a bit ambitious and rash in my offer. I mean, I do work out a little, but…"

Ah, yes, the evidence of *that* was right before her eyes. Kyle's T-shirt couldn't hide nicely defined biceps and a well-constructed chest. Whatever he was doing in the way of weightlifting was working well. Allison grinned, glad for his muscles to assist her with this job. "If you can help me move this, I think you can skip working out for a week. Or three."

"So what was your plan? Originally, I mean?" he asked her, his eyes back on the heavy Victorian china cabinet, which was a good eight feet tall.

She walked over to stand beside him. Her hands, too, traced the smooth dark finish. Maybe it wasn't to her taste, but she could admire the craftsmanship that some gifted cabinetmaker had poured into his labors, and she liked how Kyle could appreciate it, as well. "I didn't think I had a prayer of moving it very far, but hoped that I could shift it enough to take the carpet off the nail strip behind it, cut the piece out, then move the cabinet back. Most things I can at least wiggle and wobble. But that critter? Uh-uh."

"It's not fastened to the wall, is it? For support?" Kyle bent to examine the rear panel.

"No. I know Gran has had it moved before—you know, for carpet cleaning. It was a bear then."

He turned around, studied the room again and nodded slowly. "I think your plan is the best one. So how about this? Why don't we start ripping up the carpet, get it all torn out except for under the cabinet, and then use a piece of the discard upside down to protect the floor? That will make the cabinet easier to shift into place, too."

"Ahh." Allison smiled in appreciation. "That's a brilliant tweak to my plan. I was worried about scarring the floor. I have no idea what sort of shape it's in, but I didn't want to add work. However…"

"You see a problem?"

"I'm all for free labor, but you didn't sign on to help me rip out carpet."

"Hey, I'm curious. I want to see what that atrocious carpet is hiding. Unless…are you too tired? You've been moving all this furniture this morning. Maybe you want a break?"

Allison chuckled. "We Shepherd women never tire. We have Davinia's blood in us. If you're game, I'm game. It's not often I get a sucker to help me out."

Soon after cutting, yanking and tugging, they both oohed and ahhed as Allison rolled back a swath of the Mamie pink to reveal the heart pine floor.

"A good cleaning and a coat of wax, and this will be good as new," Kyle said, clearly admiring the dusty but still intact planks.

"And nothing for Gran to trip over." Allison knelt beside him and skimmed the satin smooth surface of the wood with her index finger. "It's definitely pretty. The upstairs floors aren't nearly in this good a shape."

"This is the original? From when the house was built?" After her nod, he said in a low voice, "Almost a crime to have covered this up in the first place."

She frowned and sat back. “I don’t think it’s so bad to make a house your own. I mean, like you said, in 1954 it was every woman’s dream color. Gran didn’t have her own house, and this was her way of making it hers and new and modern.”

“If you’d seen some of the hideous updates I’ve witnessed, you’d understand what I meant,” Kyle said. “At least this was carpet and not permanent. The worst I saw was when someone decided they didn’t like their oak because it wasn’t ‘uniform’ in color, so they poured concrete over it to transform it into a really bad do-it-yourself terrazzo. Didn’t even try to salvage the old floor. Awful.”

Irritation pulled at Allison. She tried to smother it, tried to attribute it to the fact that she’d been working like a dog almost the entire morning and was tired, hungry and dirty. Kyle was helping her. She shouldn’t be annoyed with him.

But then he added, “Yeah, people don’t know what they have with these old homes. They just don’t appreciate them properly.”

“Oh, really,” she snapped. “I know what I’ve got on my hands—a huge old place that’s two times the size Gran needs, filled with plumbing and wiring that are obsolete and that I can’t get anyone to work on.”

He held up both hands. "Easy, easy. I live in an old house myself—a Sears kit home built in 1926. So I know how aggravating living in an old house can be."

She rolled her eyes. "Ha. You've got a house fifty years younger than this one…and think what technological innovations *came* in that half century. Electricity. Plumbing. Real, modern plumbing. And drywall. An amazing invention, drywall."

"Okay. Truce. I can see you love the old place," he said. "Now how about we finish this job?"

"Sorry. I get so frustrated with this house. I want it safe and nice for Gran. That's all. And here I am, chewing on the nice guy who got roped into more than he offered." She couldn't quite meet his eyes. Gran would not have approved of how rude Allison had been. Even when her grandmother was telling someone off, she did it with impeccable manners.

Kyle laid a hand on her arm. "It's okay. People are allowed one meltdown per afternoon when they're renovating a house over a century old. And I'll spot you a bonus daily mini-tantrum, since Belle Paix was built before the turn of the century."

Allison smiled, warmed by his good nature, and patted his hand.

An hour later they returned from dumping the last section of carpet by the side street bin. Allison stood beside Kyle as they stared at the big china cabinet, still in its original place.

"Are you sure," she asked, "you don't have a bunch of historical committee buddies just like you? You know, with strong backs and accommodating ways regarding free labor?"

The corners of his mouth quirked. "Sorry, no. Looks like it's just you and me."

"Good thing we've got a great team approach going, then. Let's do this."

Allison watched, her breath catching, as the ropy muscles in Kyle's arms flexed when he used the hand truck to lever up his end of the cabinet. Would they be able to move it?

"How am I doing?" he asked.

She pressed her hands against her side. "Good—careful! Careful! It's wobbling—not so high!"

Kyle didn't argue, but lowered it. "Better?"

"Yep! Thanks for not arguing—most guys would."

His breath came in a grunt of effort as he walked the end of cabinet the few inches to the carpet strip. "No point. Saving. My. Breath."

Finally, after a few more near misses, the cabinet was on the scrap of carpet. Allison knelt in the close confines between it and the wall to start the task of ripping up the last section. She jumped when Kyle squeezed by her.

"Sorry, didn't mean to startle you. Here, let me give you a hand."

His nearness seemed to cause her fingers to slip. All she could focus on was his scent, clean and crisp and slightly citrusy. She stared down at the carpet and tried to smother a helpless little laugh at how such a small thing rattled her.

"Having trouble?" he asked. Without another word, he leaned over her to tackle the carpet edge. Of course, it came loose without any hesitation, and she felt her cheeks flare doubly hot. "I think I got lucky," Kyle told her.

He was close enough that she could see a nick where he'd cut himself shaving that morning. Close enough to allow her to drink in that divine clean scent of his. Her pulse hammered in her throat.

"I'll take this piece out," she mumbled, and managed to move away to give him—and her stupidly sensitive nose—space.

A few minutes later, the carpet was cleared, and they tackled the china cabinet once more. It landed with a solid thunk where it belonged.

Her heart racing from exertion and stress, Allison wiped her sweaty palms on her jeans. "That thing can stay there for another hundred years as far as I'm concerned," she commented.

"I'll second that." Kyle had collapsed on the floor, his formerly pristine T-shirt now as grimy as hers. "How they cleaned under that thing, I don't know."

"Oh! I forgot to wax the floor under it!"

Kyle lay back on the oak planks, his eyes closed. "I promise, if the floor police come put you in jail, I'll bail you out. That thing is not moving. At least, not by my hands."

"Well, it's not like anybody will see under it. Okay." She joined him lying on the floor, staring up at the coffered ceiling. "Thank you."

They lay there, exhausted, quiet. Every muscle of Allison's body was quivering with fatigue. She wondered if Kyle felt as weary as she did. Probably. He'd had the heavy end.

The clock in the hall let loose a mellifluous series of chimes. "Look at the time. I've got to get cleaned up to visit Gran." Allison scrambled up, adrenaline coursing through her. "If I don't hurry, she'll be in physical therapy, and after that she's too tired for a good visit."

"Let me get out of your hair, then. That is, if I can manage to find as much pep as you have," Kyle told her. "You've worn me out."

She extended a hand down to him. "Least I can do is help you up," she said.

His hand in hers felt strong and capable, but she knew that already from their work together. He certainly wasn't the stuffed shirt she'd thought him, when he'd been on her sidewalk a million years ago this morning. Maybe she should offer him supper one night in appreciation.

Kyle stood, took in the windows and the expanse of the dining room. "I can imagine that I'm back in 1888, and this room is brand-new. Those windows…wow."

"Yeah. Those windows. They're going. I'm getting Gran some double-paned ones that won't leak air like a sieve."

He stared over his shoulder at her, his eyebrows drawn. "You can't."

"Yes, I can. I have the money. A window guy's coming out next week."

Kyle's frown deepened, out of concern, not anger, she thought. "No. We have rules. Ordinances. Any exterior change to a house in the historic district has to be approved. By the historic preservation committee. Didn't you know that?"

"But as long as they look right, I don't really see a problem, do you? I mean, I'm not putting in art deco glass block windows. I'll pick out good-looking ones. Maybe get vinyl-clad. Easier to take care of."

"Whoa, no." He shook his head, then held

up a hand, as if what she'd just said pained him deeply. "No. You can't do that. We have a list."

"A list?"

"Yeah. Of manufacturers to provide historically accurate windows. And no double-paned ones. Plus, these look to be in pretty good shape, I'd advocate repairing them instead of replacing them."

Allison crossed her arms over her T-shirt and surveyed him. "Whoa, yourself. You can't tell me what I can do with my own home—well, Gran's. This house has been here forever. Surely it's grandfathered in."

"These ordinances protect you, protect the value of your home. Trust me, you'd hate what the house looked like with modern windows."

"I hate seeing the power bill every month, that's what I hate. Do you know how drafty these things are?" Allison realized her hands had moved to her hips and her voice possessed an edge to it. She tried to drop the attitude raging through her. Still, Kyle's know-it-all tone irked her.

"I hear that all the time. And my house is the same way. The price you pay for living in a place that has character."

Allison took in the stubborn jut of his jaw. This guy wasn't budging. Surely, though, these rules couldn't be as cut-and-dried as he made them out to be. Surely she could figure out a compromise, a workable solution. The city couldn't dictate that she remain in a house exactly as it was in 1888.

She decided to change the subject. No point arguing about this any longer, at least not today. "I appreciate your help, but I've got to get cleaned up and get out of here if I'm going be on time to visit Gran."

"I'll see myself out. Thanks for letting me help." Kyle's smile was easy, free from the momentary irritation she'd spotted earlier.

"Thank you. I couldn't have managed without you."

He was halfway up the hall, but called over his shoulder, "Sure you could—you've got Davinia's blood running through you, right?"

"Right," she said. The front door closed behind him, and through the beveled glass inset, Allison stared at Kyle's departing back as he strode down the walkway toward the wrought-iron fence.

Well, blast. She was probably in for a fight with the historical committee if he was anything to go by. A guy who thought it was a crime to put down carpet on heart-pine flooring would definitely think vinyl siding—even the very high-end vinyl siding she'd been looking at—was a mortal sin.

CHAPTER THREE

AS USUAL, the old house showed her who was boss. By the time Allison managed to coax hot water out of a cantankerous set of hundred-year-old pipes for a bath in the claw-foot tub, she had managed to shift from on-time-just-barely to well-and-truly-late.

She rushed down the narrow back stairs to the kitchen, all the while making a blood oath to find a plumber. Somewhere, somehow, there had to be one insane enough or broke enough or some combination of both to tackle the old house's hodgepodge of patched pipes, and yank that upstairs bath into the twenty-first century.

How had Gran survived? Allison hadn't remembered the house being so…obstinate. *Okay,* she thought to herself as she pulled out of the drive and made the turn toward Gran's rehab facility, *so houses don't have souls, exactly, but this one sure does have a cantankerous personality.* In the rehab facility, way down the hall from the physical therapy suite, she could hear her grandmother—just as cranky and stubborn as those old pipes had been, Allison thought with a chuckle.

"Young man, in my day, people didn't rush their elders, no sirree! I'm moving, yes, I am, but I don't trust that contraption."

Allison heard the poor physical therapist's low, conciliatory mumble, and in response, her gran came roaring back with, "Why, yes, I do want to go home! I'm doing these exercises, aren't I? My goodness, you are a strong fellow, aren't you? Are you single? My granddaughter is in need of a good husband—but notice I said good, not just any old husband. A girl would do worse to have the wrong fellow than none at all, if you ask me."

Allison paused outside the door to allow her cheeks to cool off from the embarrassment. Her grandmother, huffing and puffing from her exertion, spoke up again. "That girl is a hard worker—a nurse, so you two ought to have plenty to talk about, you being in the medical field. She's given up a big career in Atlanta to come back to Lombard to live with me, so that I can go home. And that's why I'm doing these ridiculous exercises! As if I need to be on a bicycle at my age! Do you know how old I am? I'm eighty-nine! And before I broke my hip, I lived by myself and drove myself and did all my shopping and housekeeping. Oh, but these old bones…What's that? Save my breath?"

Allison covered her mouth to hold back her giggle. Poor fellow. Some people might call Gran standoffish, but once she decided she liked you, you couldn't get her to hush.

Allison decided she'd better rescue the therapist. Sure enough, he looked as done in as Gran when she came in the room. Still, Allison was glad to see her tiny grandmother with her fluffy white hair, pink-cheeked and determined. That was Gran—a tiger when it came to any sort of goal.

I guess I got that honestly, huh?

The therapist called it quits soon after Allison had taken a seat near Gran's stationary bike to cheer her on. "You're doing good, ma'am," he told her. "Let's give you a chance to recover."

"Now, I'm no wimp," Gran assured him. "I've got Davinia Shepherd's blood in my veins, I have. And I've got to get back on my feet. I am determined that I'm going to be strong enough to climb the stairs to my old bedroom. No more sleeping in the library for this old gal."

It took the man another ten minutes to convince Gran of the law of diminishing returns, and that he wasn't going easy on her because "you think I'm some frail old lady." At that point, Allison helped her to her walker and assisted her down the hall.

Halfway to Gran's room, Allison had to tactfully suggest that they take a seat.

"No, no, I'll get there—"

"No, Gran, it's not you. I'm tired out from working on the house this morning. Can't I have a little bit of a break?" Allison didn't like lying to her grandmother, but what choice did she have?

Gran gave her a sharp-eyed glance. "Well, maybe a few minutes. Help me to that bench over there."

Allison noted how Gran blew out a long breath as she lowered herself onto the bench. Yes, the physical therapy had worn her out. Still, she gave Allison a beautiful smile and patted the seat beside her.

"Sit down and tell me what you've been doing to the old place. I can't believe how much I miss it. How many days is it until I can go home?"

"Now, Gran," she hedged. "You know the deal. You work hard on the therapy and I work hard on the house, and when both of us get done—"

"Pish-posh, that house has been standing since 1888. It's tougher than I am. It doesn't need much—just a good airing out, most likely."

Allison rolled her eyes. "No, not much—just

new wiring, a new heat pump, about four tons of insulation, and new windows. And a swimming pool's worth of paint."

"Now, did I raise you to be sarcastic? Oh, heavens, I guess I did. You have taken up my sharp tongue, haven't you?" Gran folded her hand over Allison's, and it shocked her afresh to see how thin her grandmother's fingers were. Lillian Shepherd Bell Thomas had always seemed a force of nature. Now Allison could detect a new frailty—as though her grandmother's eighty-nine years had caught up with her in two short months.

She's much stronger than she was. I have to remember that. The rehab facility wouldn't let her plan on going home unless they thought she would be well enough.

It was as if Gran had read her mind. "Not much longer until I can be home—and don't you worry too much about fixing up that old white elephant of a house, Allison."

She squeezed her grandmother's hand. "I have to do some things, Gran. You fell because of that old place—"

"I *fell* because I was stupid and forgot about that ragged edge on that carpet. I knew it was there."

Allison decided not to rile her with another debate about whether it was the carpet that had tripped her. “Never mind, I fixed it. That’s what I was doing this morning—ripping all that stuff out, and it’s down to the heart pine again.”

“Land sakes.” Gran shook her head. “It’s a wonder with all that fat light wood the place didn’t go up in smoke years ago. I’ll bet it looks pretty. Once I had the carpet installed, I never did like that old mess your Pops talked me into putting in. Too much vacuuming. But he teased me so much about the color, I didn’t want to let him know I regretted it.”

“It was a lovely shade of pink,” Allison observed in the mildest of tones, knowing what the comment would provoke.

Her grandmother harrumphed. “Whatever possessed me to think Mamie pink was the cat’s pajamas, I’ll never know! Thank goodness I didn’t have the money to redo the bathrooms then—else it would look like somebody had spilled Pepto-Bismol over everything.”

In a more serious tone, Allison broached the topic she knew they had to discuss. “Gran, another reason I was late was that I had to talk with the man about installing the chair lift. He came first thing this morning, and that put me behind.”

“The chair lift?” Gran’s eyebrows skyrocketed. “We don’t need to bother with putting in that. These legs will do all the lifting I need.”

She patted her thigh, which was much too bony to reassure Allison. “That’s money wasted. *My* grandmother never had to have a chair lift.”

Allison swallowed and prayed for some patience and more of that tact. “It’s not anything permanent, Gran. And we’ll put it on the back staircase, so it won’t be ugly, like you were afraid of. But it would mean you could come home sooner.”

Gran appeared appeased by this. “Well, now…”

“But…” Might as well say it. “The man told me the wiring needs to be updated before he could install it.”

“I’ll say. Not enough outlets in that house—never were. That’s going to be a bear of a job, sweetie, and pricey, even if you can find somebody willing to tackle it. Why, I’ve had electricians and plumbers not even get out of their trucks when they got a gander of the old place. They knew it was going to be a nightmare.”

“I have some money. And…Gran, I’d like to put in better windows…and maybe some siding.”

“Vinyl siding? Now that’s an idea. I’d looked at some—they got a kind that really looks good these days, made for old houses, not that stuff on double-wides. No more painting to have to contend with.”

Allison let out a breath. She had expected her to blow her top over the siding, but apparently pragmatism had won out. Sometimes Gran would surprise her like that.

Her grandmother's expression soured and the lines in her face seemed to be etched more deeply.

"But it won't get you too far," she told Allison. "Not with the historical committee running roughshod over you, no sirree. Ha. More like the *hysterical* committee. Tried to tell 'em I needed to put siding on the house, to save on painting, but no-o-o. Got to have historically accurate paint, you do. Five colors!"

"I think the siding is probably doable—just a lot of paperwork, maybe talk to the committee members—" Allison stated, but her grandmother broke in.

"You'd better just skip all that, Allie, girl. Because that what's-his-name—Mitchell? Some sort of professor, he is, but he's the head honcho of that committee. He's never going to approve any of that."

"Kyle Mitchell? I met him today—"

"Well, then, you know what I mean, don't you? Surprised he didn't run off the chair lift guy, because they didn't have such things in 1888. They didn't have air-conditioning or penicillin back then, either, but I don't imagine Kyle

Mitchell would like to go back to those days, now would he?"

"I can't believe the committee won't see reason and use common sense," Allison protested. "If I explain the situation—"

"Common sense? That's why I call it the 'hysterical committee.' It doesn't matter what the *committee members* think. It only matters what Kyle Mitchell tells 'em. Nope, I wouldn't hold my breath if I were you, not when dealing with that Kyle Mitchell."

CHAPTER FOUR

KYLE RUBBED HIS eyes and groaned as he took in what had to be the most horrendous response to his essay question on the causes of the Boston Tea Party. "Because they were 'tea'd' off," the freshman had scrawled. To better his chances at getting at least partial credit, he had doodled a drawing of a stick figure in a passable tricorne hat, shoving a crate.

Kyle squinted. Yep. That was steam coming out from under the brim.

The student wouldn't remain a freshman for long with answers like that, Kyle thought. He riffled through the thick stack of exams and saw he still had at least two dozen left to go. If they were all like this one, at least grading them would be quicker than the first twenty-five test papers.

Just appreciate the fact that you're not in Afghanistan like your big brother. Or even herding teenage football players around the state like your little brother. Teaching history is a lot cushier than either of those two jobs. Plus, you could have graded papers yesterday instead of volunteering free labor for Allison.

Ah, but then he wouldn't have been granted admittance to the mysterious Belle Paix. And it was worth every sore muscle and the double dose of ibuprofen he'd gulped down this morning.

Beautiful.

For a flash, it wasn't Belle Paix's intact side hall with its intricate carved banister that came into his mind.

No. It was red hair. Yards of it. And the barest hint of freckles. And how her dimples danced when she smiled.

Kyle yanked his attention back to the next essay question. The hapless freshman had made a better stab at describing the opening battles of the American Revolution, but had still managed to make a total hash of it.

Unbidden, Allison ambushed Kyle's thoughts again. He liked her. And that surprised him, because she didn't seem to appreciate historical preservation in the slightest.

Amazing how one woman could invade his mind. Why, he could almost swear he heard her voice now, floating down the narrow hall that ran the length of the social sciences faculty members' offices. With a determined sigh, Kyle fixed his focus back where it belonged. He was just bored with grading, that's all.

But then a sharp rap brought his attention to his open door. He looked up—to see Allison.

She wasn't in jeans or shorts today. No, today she sported a light summery dress just right for the unseasonably hot temperatures. Her long legs were beautifully punctuated by delicate, strappy sandals that showed off her toned calves.

"Don't look so blown away." Her mouth quirked a bit at the corners as she seemed to smother a smile. "I promise, I'm not here to ask for help moving another china cabinet."

"Good, because I don't think my muscles will cooperate," he admitted. "No, I'm zoned out by these absolute hideous exams I'm grading. I think I should have done a better job teaching the course material."

Allison wrinkled her nose. "It's not your fault. It's the topic. History. Lotta dates. Lotta names. No offense, but history's a dead subject. I never could get interested in people who lived a hundred years ago."

It wasn't the first time he'd been told that. He'd heard it so often that it was the kiss of death for any blind date that his ever-hopeful colleagues kept setting up for him.

Usually the comment inspired a guilty feeling of superciliousness, as if he was somehow wiser than whoever it was talking to him—that and the sure knowledge that no serious relationship could really develop between two people who didn't appreciate the same things.

But Allison...Allison made him think differently. He wanted to drag Allison to the chair by his desk and keep her there until he could convince her that history *was* interesting. History was a story, and he was addicted to a good story.

She, however, seemed fairly convinced already—of the opposite, unfortunately. Kyle bit back a tart response. "Well, if it's not a burning need to hear a good history lecture," he asked, "what does bring you to my corner of the world?"

Allison beamed. "Ah! Thought you'd never ask. Is this a good time?"

"Yes, of course. Have a seat."

She dropped down into the chair he had for students during conference sessions, and gazed around. "Somehow this is not what I expected," she commented.

"Oh. You were thinking that it would be the typical history professor's lair—stacks of papers and books and—"

"Junk," Allison interjected. "It's wonderfully bare. Did you just move into this office?"

"No. I've been chair here for, mmm, about three years now. I just like things neat. Easier to concentrate." He followed her gaze.

The office *was* bare. Yes, he had the requisite diplomas up, and a bookshelf filled with texts and other sources. But he needed the quiet that a Zenlike bareness helped him achieve.

"I was expecting a lot of artifacts. Isn't that what you history folks call them? The detritus you collect over the years?"

"Oh, I have artifacts. See?" Kyle pointed to some shadow boxes mounted on the wall. "My collection of bullets rescued from battlefields. And that center box has political campaign buttons. And then for the prehistory folks, I've got a middling collection of arrowheads."

"My college history professors' offices were a nightmare. Really gosh-awful," Allison said. "But this? This is nice. I like it. Very modern. Very clean. No gewgaws anywhere."

Kyle regarded her for a long moment, detecting an unintentional insult to his profession, but certain from Allison's winsome smile that she had meant no malice. "So…"

"Oh! You must think I'm an idiot. Here I am, blabbering away about interior design choices and wasting your time." Her smile widened. "I stopped by the historical society office. Good thing I went this morning, as it closes at lunch."

"Yeah, we can only afford a part-time secretary." Was Allison thinking about taking up his invitation to attend some of the society's events? Maybe there was hope, after all.

"The very nice lady there...Trish? Yes. Trish. She told me that I would need to see you about some of the paperwork I need," Allison said.

"Paperwork? You don't need to fill out any paperwork to attend a meeting." What had Trish gotten so confused?

"No, no...very nice of you to invite me, and maybe I'll get around to it, but you know...well, yeah, you *do* know that I've got my hands full, what with working on the house and getting it ready for Gran and all. No, a waiver request. I need a waiver request."

"A what?" Now he was the one totally confused. What on earth was Allison talking about?

"There's gotta be a way, right? To request an exemption? From the ordinances? You know, the ones you were telling me about earlier. I looked at the code, and it did say that any exemption was to be made by the city council at the recommendation of the historic preservation committee."

"Wait." Kyle had managed to ground himself back in the present, not distracted by the way the sunlight from the window bounced off Allison's red hair, nor by the way her smile made him want to smile right back at her and say, "Yes, anything, just name it."

"Trish said she wasn't familiar with any sort of paperwork like that. But there has to be, right? I mean, come on, you're a bureaucracy—oh, not *you*, I mean the committee. No offense."

"None taken." That was a tiny fib. But Kyle didn't think it counted against him too much. "Honestly, I can't think—oh. Oh. Wait." He held up a hand. "I know what you mean. Sorry. It took me a minute."

He turned back to his computer and gave the mouse a nudge. The screen flickered to life, and he typed "historical variance hearing request" into the file search. A few whirs from the printer, and he pulled a thick sheaf of paper from the hopper.

Allison blinked at the pile. "That's a lot of paper. I think my application to grad school was thinner."

"Yeah, probably. It's…it's an intensive process," Kyle told her. He decided he'd better not confess that he'd intentionally made the process as hard as possible to discourage people from even applying. It had been one of the suggestions he'd made when the committee had asked him to come up with ways to safeguard the historic section and the tourist dollars the area brought in.

"Okay. So…any pointers?" Allison reached for the application.

He didn't give it to her. "Are you…sure?"

"Sure?" Now some of yesterday's determination slipped by the cheery "I'm game" mask that she'd kept plastered on her face for the past few moments. "Yes. If this is how I have to get a waiver approved…"

"I'm just saying…" Kyle cleared his throat. He glanced down at the application. "This is a request for a hearing. And basically we—the historic preservation committee members—ask that you explain the project, describe how it is at variance with existing ordinances and historical integrity, and then tell why you feel the need to depart from that."

"In five hundred words or less," she joked.

"Oh, no. The, er, more detailed, the better." He couldn't help but glance back at the unfortunate essay response about colonists being 'tea'd off.'

"So I work through all this, and then I get my variance?"

"Not exactly," he said. Why did he feel guilty about this?

Belle Paix would look horrid with modern windows. Allison's zeal for "modernizing" the house reminded him strongly of the man who'd bought his family home. A sour taste rose in the back of Kyle's mouth as he remembered how the new owner had quickly stripped the venerable old structure of its character.

A perfectly good house. Ruined.

"Then what? Exactly?" Her cheerfulness had a distinct half-life, and it was approaching that point fast.

"Then you get your hearing. If the application is thorough and well thought out."

"That makes no sense. Why can't I just go before the committee and explain it? Rather than write it all down?"

Because then we'd have to tell you no. This way, you don't fill out the paperwork, you don't get the hearing and you blame yourself. Not us.

But Kyle didn't say that. He cleared his throat again. "It's a way to make sure you've thought it all through and explored your options."

She harrumphed. "Busywork."

"What?" He hoped that note of guilt in his strangled response hadn't been as evident to her as it had to him.

"Okay. Hand it over. If this is what I've got to do, this is what I've got to do." She stood up and reached for the paperwork again.

"Would you...like me to help you with it?"

"You would?" Allison's face lit up. Her smile was absolutely breathtaking.

That. That is why you offered.

"Sure. On one condition."

She frowned. "What?" she asked suspiciously.

"That you come to the historical society meeting. You'd find it interesting—this month's program's about Victorian homes. And you could share your story about how Belle Paix was built that you were telling me when we first met. That was fun. Entertaining. Our members would love it."

"I dunno," she said. She put a hand to her head as though warding off a sudden headache. "I was really never good at history."

"I promise you won't have to remember a single date. Or name. Except mine."

Allison laughed. "I wouldn't forget the guy who volunteered his elbow grease to help me out."

"So?" Kyle couldn't believe that he was holding his breath in hopes she'd say yes.

"I was planning on painting Gran's room Thursday—I feel fairly confident in tackling the interior paint job on my own, though the exterior, what with three tall stories and all that scraping, well, that's a horse of a different color. Anyway, you did say when you first mentioned it that the meeting was Thursday, right? I have to work this weekend—I'm a nurse on weekends at the ER at the hospital. So…I really need to get some work done at the house."

"I love to paint. And I've been told I'm very good at it. If I help you tomorrow night, and maybe Friday afternoon when my classes are done…then you'd be free Thursday?"

"You don't quit, do you?" Allison gave a bemused chuckle. It made his heart skip a beat.

"I just think…" He looked down at the paperwork. The meeting would be a way for history to come alive for her, to help her understand why people in Lombard were so passionate about protecting their architectural treasures. Not only that, the historic section was an economic engine for the community, bringing in tens of thousands of tourist dollars each year. "I think that anyone who grew up in that marvelous house ought to know about the time the house was built."

"You really don't mind helping me paint? Or…" Allison pointed at the stack of papers he had clasped in his hand "…working through that monstrosity of an application?"

"I really don't mind."

"Okay, then. That's a deal I can't refuse. Wow."

She took the papers from him. He saw her

skim through them, frown in puzzlement and then shake her head. "I really am going to need your help. Half of this reads like a foreign language."

Again, a twinge of guilt assailed him. He'd made the language as opaque as possible to intimidate would-be variance seekers.

And until now, it had worked. Not a single person had ever actually taken an application once he or she had seen it.

But Kyle had a nagging suspicion that Allison wasn't like anybody else he'd ever met before.

CHAPTER FIVE

ALLISON DUG HER nails into the palms of her hands.

Nope. Not enough pain. Her eyelids were still drooping.

Time for the old bite-your-cheek trick, she thought.

She risked a peek at her watch and saw that she'd been trapped in the historical society's meeting room for an hour and forty-five minutes. And there was still no end in sight.

When would this meeting end? Didn't these people have to eat? Go to sleep?

In the front of the room, a petite woman of about seventy with impossibly dark hair pulled tight into a bun fiddled with her bifocals. "No, no, Eunice, we can't possibly plant that particular variety of flower in the public sections of the district," she said. "It is a more modern variety—why, it wasn't around until 1898!"

To Allison's sleep-deprived brain, the woman's shrill, nasal accent drilled into her as insistently as the tools of the trade of any dentist.

So why on earth was she still nodding off?

Okay, so it probably hadn't been the smartest move in the world to soldier on and come to this meeting after she had been called in to work last night at the last minute. She'd managed to snatch three hours of sleep when she'd gotten home this morning, but the lift-chair electrician was supposed to have shown up.

He hadn't. Of course not. That would have broken her perfect record of repair guys who hadn't shown up for their appointments. Five of 'em. No shows, all.

But this last guy? The electrician? He'd sworn that he'd come, that he needed the work. And she'd crawled out of bed much too soon and even showered to make sure she was presentable.

It made Allison demented enough to want to call the guy up in the middle of the night and wake *him* up.

She should have told Kyle that she needed to sleep. But he'd stayed at the house painting until after 9:00 p.m., and he'd been so excited at the prospect of her coming. And then this evening, when he'd stopped by to walk her over to the library, and she'd started to tell him no, he'd been like a kid. Bubbling with enthusiasm about this person he wanted her to meet, and that expert on Victorians and…

And, well, she hadn't had the heart to let him down. She hadn't even admitted to working all night at the ER. Allison was sure he'd think she was making an excuse to wiggle out of the meeting.

He'd done his part. She hadn't thought one historical society meeting was too much to ask for the help he'd given.

Ha. This is worse than any clinical staff meeting I've ever endured. No wonder Gran steered clear of these gatherings!

She stole a look at Kyle, who appeared to be riveted by this minutiae. He'd actually been paying attention, because now he was weighing in with his own opinion.

"Ladies, both of you are right," he said, smiling.

Even in her sleep-deprived condition, the warm tug of his lips and the way his teeth flashed bright in his tanned, lean face sent a zinger through Allison's body.

What a charmer. Those two old gals are eating him up.

And they were—when they weren't glaring at each other. They turned their attention back to Kyle, who continued. "While that particular rose was very popular at the turn of the century—strictly speaking, toward the end of the historic district spending spree—it hadn't been bred when some of our earlier houses were built."

That drew a smile from the lady with the dye job. Kyle's next words, though, elicited a told-you-so grin from Eunice, defender of the 1898 rose. "But who's to say that some of the owners of the older homes might not have added new varieties? After all, none of us are content with the things we started out with. We keep adding new ones, right?"

Just as Dye Job's smug smile soured, Kyle did something that really amazed Allison. He smoothed over the whole thing and left both ladies nodding thoughtfully. "Still," he said, "we can always skip the roses and do a nice bougainvillea instead. Properly trained, it would do quite well, and it was popular and widely available during those years."

I am going to scream. Hot pokers in the eye wouldn't be this bad. How is he enjoying this? Allison made the mistake of catching Kyle's attention. He grinned. Winked, even...no. Maybe that wasn't a wink. Maybe he had something in his eye. Yes. He was rubbing it. Was he was sleepy, too?

Best prescription in the world for insomnia, one Lombard Historical Society meeting. It had been bad enough hearing the featured speaker, who'd droned on and on about trains and the expansion of the Central Railroad.

True, the speaker had mentioned Ambrose Shepherd, and even pointed out Allison at the beginning of his remarks. He'd called on her to stand up as he'd introduced her. She'd gotten quite the golf clap from all these folks in their Sunday-go-to-meeting clothes.

But there was only so much discussion of board feet of lumber and innovations of cold rolled steel and railroad ties that Allison could endure.

And then? When the speaker finished and Kyle opened the floor for new business?

Distinct turn for the worse.

Allison stared with longing at the ice bucket loaded with bottles of soft drinks that awaited the close of the session. The ice had melted, and tiny puddles had formed on the paper tablecloth around the bucket, but even a lukewarm soft drink would still give her a welcome jolt of caffeine.

She barely managed to cover a sneak-attack yawn that caught her unawares. Allison didn't want to hurt anybody's feelings. These people really were passionate about all this history; it just wasn't her cup of tea.

As she lowered her palm, she noticed Kyle

gazing quizzically at her. In a rush, he brought the meeting to a rather abrupt end.

"It looks like we've gotten so excited about our public gardening spaces that we've run over our time. I suggest we adjourn and head for the refreshments."

"But—but we haven't even gone over the list of sources for antique plumbing supplies," one fellow protested.

Now, why didn't we do that first? Allison thought. *Because* that *would have been useful. And maybe to go along with it a list of plumbers crazy enough to work on old houses. Maybe what I really need is a support group for renovators.*

Despite the man's irritation, Kyle assured him that he had just the list for him. By the time he'd promised to get it to him, Allison saw that the majority of the crowd had stampeded to the refreshments table. They hadn't had to be told twice.

Kyle started across the room toward her, but got waylaid by first one and then another attendee. As she held on to the back of the chair in front of her to keep from falling over, she felt a tug on her elbow.

A tall gentleman with a luxurious crop of snow-white hair and a suntanned face peered down at her quizzically. "Well, now," he said, then cleared his throat and began again. "Well, now. Stimulating stuff, no?"

Allison blinked. Lying was not her style, not even teeny-tiny white lies, if she could get away with the truth. "Er, they are very detail-oriented," she commented.

"Got to be," he said with a satisfied nod. "Got to watch every jot and tittle. Don't want any anachronistic details to spoil the effect, you know? And people will try you. They'll test you. Got to hold the line."

"You mean…about the flowers?" Allison asked. It was as if the man could peer into her very soul and know that she was conspiring to slap vinyl siding onto Belle Paix.

"About it all. I'm on the preservation committee. I should know. All manner of wild-eyed schemes come before us. People wanting to paint their Victorians white. Put Georgian columns on 'em. Enough to turn my stomach, I tell you."

Allison's own stomach sank like a stone at the news that this hard-liner was one she'd face at her variance request hearing. If she ever managed to fill out all that paperwork. *Please… don't have any clones on the board just like you.*

"I can see you take this very seriously," she said.

"And well I should! That young Kyle, he's

turned this place around. You ought to have seen the mess this neighborhood was in…well, you can! Let me show you the before-and-after gallery—it's right out in the hall. You'll be astonished!"

"Uh…" She looked down at the man's hand, which he'd wrapped around her arm. Likely planning to take her to the display whether she wanted to go or not.

"Ease up, Herbert, will you? Don't want to frighten her off on her very first visit, do we?" Kyle's welcome voice interrupted them.

"Oh! Kyle! I was waiting for you."

There, that was true. She was. She wanted to be a polite guest and say her goodbyes, and then totter off to her bed.

Herbert shot her a disappointed glance, but covered it up with a good-natured dip of his head. "I'll show you next time, how about? It will be something to look forward to."

"Yes. It will be something," she said brightly.

As soon as Herbert had drifted off to join the others at the table, Kyle said, "You look all done in. Did you stay up late painting after I left?"

"Uh, actually…about ten minutes after you left, the hospital called and begged me to come in. They were short an RN for the ER last night. What could I say? I'm the new kid in town."

"You worked all night? With no sleep today?"

His eyebrows shot up and he shook his head in disbelief. “If I had only known.”

“No, no. I got some sleep. Would have gotten more if I hadn’t had to wake up to meet the electrician.”

“So you’re rewiring the house?” Kyle asked. “Who’d you get?”

“Nobody yet. The guy was a no-show. Let’s face it. He probably Google-Earthed it, saw what a disaster the place was and didn’t bother coming.”

“How frustrating. Listen, I have a list of good electricians who are willing to work on old houses. Let me go grab it for you from the office—no, no, I insist. I have to get that source list for Paul, anyway.”

“Ahem, can…can I come with you? Because I’m really not up to small talk right now. It’s all I can do to get out guttural cave-woman speech. Even the weather is beyond me, as tired as I am.”

He laughed and jabbed his finger toward her, then back at his chest. “You, Jane, me Tarzan. You come.”

“Sold!”

The two of them made their way to the office, where Kyle deftly picked a few sheaves of paper from two pigeonholes. “Commonly requested items—pays to keep them handy," he explained.

"You are just too organized. You make me feel like a complete slob. You know, you didn't spill a single drop of paint last night, and your paintbrush, when you cleaned it, looked brand-new."

"Didn't yours?" he asked.

"Er, no. Mine wound up looking more like one of those troll dolls. I'll probably toss it and buy another."

"I did happen to notice it wasn't a very good quality brush," he said.

"Aren't brushes brushes?" she asked.

"No. A good brush is something to go to war over to protect. Trust me, after you've done all the trim work on your house—outside and inside—you'll have found the right brush for you. And you'll threaten to kill anybody who so much as lays a finger on it."

"Does this violent propensity extend only toward paintbrushes? Or should I be worried about touching other things that belong to you?" she teased.

He blushed. He really, honestly blushed. She hadn't meant anything risqué with her comment, but now could see the double entendre.

"Mainly paintbrushes," he muttered. "I'll give you…fair warning about the other stuff."

To take her mind off her own flaming face and Kyle's awkwardness, she stared down at the pages. "Well, I guess I should be—"

"I'll walk you home. Let me hand this to Paul."

And in a flash, though she wouldn't have expected it two minutes earlier, Kyle's hand was on her back as he ushered her out the society office's front door and toward her house.

"You didn't much care for the meeting, did you?" he asked.

"Really…I couldn't say." *For sure. Because then I'd hurt your feelings, and you seem like a nice guy. Probably you share Herbert's hard-liner approach about historical accuracy, but even so, you're a nice guy.* "Maybe I was too tired to give it a fair shake?"

He didn't say anything for a few steps. The silence stretched between them, interrupted by the sporadic rush of a car barreling down the street past them, and crickets and a dog barking when the car had passed.

"I liked the idea of going over the antique source guides," she said at last. "That would have been really useful. I mean, to someone like me."

"We should do that. Form a group of people who are in the middle of renovating. So many of our older folks have already done their time in the trenches. They've got all their work done, and they tend to be jealous when it comes to sharing information. I hate to say that." He glanced her way, as if to make sure she didn't instantly hate him for speaking so bluntly about the society members. "But it's true."

"Why would they be that way?" she asked.

Kyle shrugged. "Who knows? Honestly? Sometimes I think it's a sport to some of them. Take Herbert, for instance. He's a great guy, really believes in historic preservation, but…"

"Ya know, I kind of got that vibe, too," she said. "But you have to admire people who stick up for what they believe in. One of Gran's tenets, and mine, too."

"He's done a marvelous job with his house. There it is, up ahead."

Allison came to an abrupt stop as she let her eyes follow Kyle's finger. A huge Queen Anne encrusted with all manner of gingerbread trim stood back on a picture-perfect lawn.

"The old Kilgore house! That's his? Wow. Back when I was little, the place was empty and the windows boarded up. My friends teased me, claiming that it was haunted, and that mine was, too. But that one especially."

"Herbert has worked hard on it. He bought it about ten years ago, when he retired. Gutted the whole place and renovated it from stem to stern. He's one of the main ones who got me involved in having the initial preservation ordinances passed."

Allison smothered a snort. It would be someone like Herbert who'd had the idea to make things supremely difficult for her. "I can definitely see that."

"A lot of the neighborhood has changed. You know, in the last three years, we've started drawing serious numbers of tourists, and that's having a huge impact on our local economy. We have walking tours and ghost tours and Christmas tours of homes. Let me take you on—no, I'm sorry. You're tired. I should get you home."

But Kyle's easy company and the sweet scents of gardenias, night phlox and petunias in the cool evening air had banished the worst of her exhaustion. "Really, I'm better now. Why don't you tell me about the ones on the way home?"

"Yeah? You'd like that? It wouldn't…bore you?"

"No. I have to admit, I am impressed with how neat and clean and picture-postcard the old neighborhood looks. It didn't look like this when I was growing up."

"No. It didn't. It was in a sad state. And it's been only in the last two or three years that we've seen real progress. There are just a few holdouts left and they'll—" Kyle abruptly clamped his mouth shut, stopping himself in midsentence.

"Cry uncle? Sell out? Or get with the program?" she teased. "Or...or do you make them..." she grinned and used her fingers to form air quotes "...'disappear'?" she asked in a mock-sinister tone.

"Now, how did you guess what we do with the really stubborn ones?" Kyle said with a laugh.

"It's probably right out of *The Stepford Wives* manual," Allison teased. "A complete reeducation program in the renovation camps."

"No!" He played along with a theatrical gasp, and clutched his chest. "You can't have tumbled to the secret of our success! Why, now I'll have to make *you* disappear!"

But then the next house came into view, and he suddenly grew serious. "Oh, this is one of my favorite stories—this house got rescued from the wrecking ball. Literally."

"That's gotta be one dramatic tale. Sounds like something on TV."

"It just about was. It was horrible, the condition the house was in. Vinyl siding. The wrong windows. A cheap asphalt shingle roof. Oh, and glass blocks in a back bathroom window. Ugh. Walter and Mary, the couple who own it now, found out that some guy had bought the property to make a parking lot out of it. There used to be a—"

"Law office next door, I remember. Really snarly guy."

"Yeah. He's gone. You don't have to worry about him anymore. I disappeared him."

Allison chuckled and punched Kyle on the arm. "Sorry, I didn't mean to interrupt. Go on."

"They bought it. The day the wrecking ball was due to knock it down. And they started, bit by bit, to restore the old girl to her glory."

Allison gazed at the massive Georgian, with its white columns and its side porches. "It's gorgeous. They must have sunk quite a lot into it."

"Labor of love. But they wouldn't have it any other way."

"Kyle..." She couldn't look at the Georgian anymore. She stared off in the opposite direction, only to find that another old house, this time a beautiful Victorian, stood in perfectly restored, accusing beauty.

"Yeah?"

"Not everybody has the money or the time or the inclination to do that."

"Allison..." He took her hands in his. It was an astonishing move that normally would have weirded her out. But it felt right to have him touch her like this, even though they didn't know each other very well. "I know. I know."

"You know…" *About the vinyl siding?*

"How overwhelmed you feel. I've been there. It's okay. You'll get through it. I'll help you. We'll get Belle Paix looking just as good—no, better! Better than all of these. She's the jewel of the neighborhood. And you're going to polish her up until she positively gleams. I promise. It will happen."

She couldn't meet his eyes. To Allison, the earnest honesty in them was as guilt-inducing as the picturesque houses all around them. Instead, she focused on his hands, strong and capable and holding hers.

No. No. You have no idea. If you knew how ridiculous I thought this whole rigmarole is—oh, Kyle. I am not the girl you think I am. All I want is a good roof over Gran's head.

CHAPTER SIX

KYLE HESITATED BEFORE he pushed the tarnished brass doorbell a third time. Allison surely would have come to the door by now. Maybe she'd changed her mind. Maybe the historical society had scared her off. Maybe his little tour last night of the old neighborhood had backfired and left her feeling overwhelmed instead of motivated.

She said she'd see you this afternoon. And there's a car in the side yard.

But the only sign of life that he could find was through the wavy, 126-year-old glass in the mahogany front door: Cleo glaring at him, her blue eyes filled with contempt.

What did Allison call her when the Siamese sprang out in a full-frontal attack every time he walked through the door? Ninja cat? Yeah. No need for a Doberman when you had a guard cat like Cleo.

Kyle stepped back from the door and walked down the porch steps. Yep. The vehicle in the side yard was her little compact car. So she wasn't at the hospital. Maybe she'd gone for a walk? Or she was asleep? He hoped the hospital hadn't called her again last night, because she'd been so tired she could barely stumble up the steps.

He surveyed Belle Paix from his vantage point on the front steps. It was in amazingly good structural shape, really—yes, it needed an accurate paint scheme, and he'd spotted some dry rot in a couple places. But the siding still seemed sound, the windows looked intact, and the wrought-iron porch posts Ambrose had used in lieu of his own heart pine showed only the need for a good scraping and painting.

There were home owners who would kill for a house in this near-perfect shape, where all they had to do was refresh. His own house's renovation had been a scavenger hunt for missing pieces and obsolete moldings or parts.

He glanced at his watch. Still no sign of life. Okay. He pivoted on his heel and headed for the front gate. He'd go pay the water bill and then swing by again to see if Allison had gotten back—

Suddenly, from above him, came a horrendous screeching of long-stuck wood and a shout. "Kyle! Hey! Don't go! I'm coming down!"

He looked over his shoulder and saw Allison framed by the open window above the porch.

Her face was swathed in pale blue paint and something white covered her nose and smeared across her cheek. "I thought you were gone."

"Only in my dreams! Just a minute." But the stubborn window resisted her efforts to close it as vehemently as it had resisted opening a few minutes earlier.

"Sounds like you need a little graphite on that," he called up.

"Dynamite, you say? Bring it on! This old house—" The rest of her grumble was shut off by the sudden cooperation of the window. Kyle could hear the powerful slam reverberate in the afternoon air.

Allison opened the door, a very unhappy Cleo wriggling in her grip. "No, Cleo, you must learn some manners. Nice Kyle, see? No, you cannot bite the guests—or me, for that matter!"

Kyle shut the door behind him, and Allison released Cleo. The cat streaked off with a series of unhappy yowls.

"You'd think I tortured the creature," she said.

"So you were upstairs, then?" he asked. "I wondered if something had happened—"

"I heard the bell, but I was in the middle of something that I couldn't let go of…and so I just crossed my fingers that you'd be patient. Well, mentally crossed my fingers. I had a problem with a wall in Gran's room, but I think I've got it licked."

They started up the stairs. Kyle saw that, unlike last night, Allison had some spring in her step. A few hours' sleep must have put her to rights. He couldn't help but reach over and touch the white stuff on her nose. It was a chalky paste.

"What is this?" he asked, stopping at the first landing to examine his fingertip. "It feels like… not quite wood filler…drywall putty?"

"Yeah, I've got holes. I started scraping, just like you showed me the other night, and all of sudden this huge chunk of plaster came out. I just about freaked, let me tell you. I didn't know what to do. And then I got smart, went down to our friendly home improvement store, and a guy there told me this stuff would fix it right up."

"Wait. He told you to patch the holes? With drywall putty?"

Kyle tried very hard to keep any judgment out of his voice, but what kind of idiot would advise someone to do that?

"Yeah. Seems to be working."

"Oh, no. Oh, no. No, no, no." He took the rest of the stairs two at a time and barreled through the twisty turn of an upstairs hall to reach Gran's bedroom.

It was a big airy room that took up nearly the entire back part of the house. With direct access to the single upstairs bathroom, and plenty of windows, it had probably been Ambrose's master bedroom.

The two interior walls they'd painted stood pristine and the barest shade of periwinkle blue, her grandmother's favorite color, Allison had said. The back exterior wall?

A huge patch of grayish-white putty painted a bull's-eye in the middle of the wall equidistant between the windows. Already Kyle could see signs that the putty was shrinking at the edges, ready to pull away from the hole. Eventually it would dry up, fall out and maybe take an even bigger piece of plaster with it.

"What a colossal mess!" Kyle swore. "Who would do such a thing?"

The pitter-patter of Allison's feet behind him came to an abrupt stop. "I beg your pardon?"

He looked around to see her eyebrows arched and her chin raised a fraction of an inch. Her arms were crossed over her T-shirt.

"Not you. Whatever dumb salesperson told you about this. It won't work. It will just make things worse."

"It won't?" The haughty look was chased away by a crease of worry between her brows.

"There are patches for plaster…but not drywall putty. Fiberglass is a good way…" Kyle walked over to the wall and ran his fingers over the nubby surface around the patch. He checked for the telltale signs—the way paint can feel over failed plaster, the give of the crumbling, damaged material underneath.

Shoot.

He stretched higher.

Double shoot.

"Better get the ladder," he mumbled to himself. Jerking it over from where she'd been using it to scrape, he propped it by one of the windows and climbed up the rungs. Systematically, he began to inspect the wall surface.

"Kyle?"

Not good. He rubbed his face with the palm of his hand and considered how to break the news.

"Kyle?" Allison said again, this time from the base of the ladder.

"Okay. This corner of the house has a northeastern exposure. Back wall here faces north. And the side wall—" He jabbed a finger toward the other exterior wall, which formed a right angle to the one she was working on. "Well, it faces east."

"What does that have to do with anything?" she asked.

"It's Georgia, right? A hundred twenty-six

summers of high humidity and heat, a hundred twenty-six winters of cold wet rain. The temperature difference, over the years, tends to create dampness. And dampness is not plaster's friend. So…probably on every exterior wall, especially in stretches like this, where you've got lots of windows, you're going to have at least some huge sections of plaster that will crumble at a touch."

"Oh. I guess…" Allison eyed the little tub of putty she'd been using. "I guess I'd better buy a bigger bucket."

"Not of that stuff. And this wall—and probably the other? Well, I'd advise carefully ripping out the plaster in the damaged sections down to the laths, and re-plastering it. Big chunks are damaged, so it's going to be a pain to patch. But by ripping out the plaster, you can inspect for structural damage, check the wiring and even put in new insulation."

She stared at him and blinked. "Do what?"

"I know it's overwhelming. I know just how you're feeling, because I had to do the same thing…"

Allison didn't answer. She just sank down onto the paint-spattered tarp on the floor and stared some more. Her eyes went from Kyle to the wall, back to him, back to the wall. It was almost like watching a concussion victim trying to shake off a good case of having his bell rung.

"Can't I just patch it?" she whispered.

Kyle came down off the ladder and knelt beside her. "Trust me. You'll spend more money in the long run trying to patch it. And it won't look right. You'd never get the texture to match."

"I don't *care* about the texture." She banged her palms against her forehead. "Just once. Just one single time, can't even the simplest thing actually be simple? Gran's going to come home soon, and I haven't even managed to repaint her room."

"I know." Kyle patted Allison's arm, not quite sure what to say to her.

She didn't respond right away, so at least he hadn't said anything to aggravate the situation.

"And—and..." She lifted her head. Her eyes glistened with tears of frustration. "I can't do this. I don't know how. And nobody. Will. Come."

"What?"

"Workers. Repairmen. Anybody but you. You're the only one willing to help me. I call people, and they say they're gonna show up, and they don't. Ever. Not even if I offer to pay for the estimate. It's like I'm blackballed."

"Oh. Oh!" Kyle let out a huge breath. "Is that all? Sheesh. That I can help with. That I can fix." He fished out his phone and scrolled though his contacts. Punched a number and smiled to reassure her.

A moment later the ringing stopped and a voice came over the line in a gruff greeting.

"Hey, Jerry! Glad I caught you! I have a restoration job you might be interested in—1888 Second Empire."

On the other end of the line, Jerry whistled. "You mean Belle Paix. You have got to be kidding me. Somebody bought Belle Paix off the old lady? Who are the new owners? Can I see it? Can I come now?"

"Not new owners, exactly. The granddaughter. She's, er, trying to renovate, and has run into a plaster issue. We could use your expertise."

"Just give me five minutes. No. Four. I'll be there."

Kyle listened to the dial tone in his ear and then lowered the phone. Allison's hopeful expression died on her face.

"See. I told you. Nobody."

"That's where you're wrong." He gave her what he hoped was a look of reassurance. After she met Jerry, though, she might not be reassured at all. "He's coming. Right now."

"What? Really?"

"He's...Jerry's a character. Just warning you

ahead of time. He's devoted to old houses, really loves them. I got to know him through my work with the historical society and the preservation committee. He works all over the state, and it just so happens that he's finishing up a restoration on a house here."

The peal of the doorbell resounded up the stairs. It had rung three times by the time Allison and Kyle managed to get to the landing, and Jerry was starting on the fourth ring as she opened the door.

"You're the granddaughter? What's the budget? Where's the architect? Can I see the plans? We can make this old girl shine!" Jerry told her. "I can see the new paint now, and I'll bet Kyle can find us pictures of the front lawn to restore all the shrubbery to what it looked like then— Wow, this place is amazing! She's… Kyle?" Jerry pivoted in the hall, his head craned back. "Do you see that trim? That carving? This is all original. Man. They didn't mess her up, Kyle. They did not mess her up. This is gonna be so much fun!"

Allison furrowed her brow and cocked an eye at Kyle, past Jerry's pirouettes.

Kyle lifted his hand in what he hoped was a "wait, he's not totally crazy, give him a minute" way. "She's in great shape, you are right. Pretty much untouched. Amazing. But…let's start with some introductions. Allison, this is Jerry Franklin, the restoration expert I was telling you about, although he's not always this, er, exuberant."

Kyle shot a warning look at Jerry to stop acting like a kid let loose in a candy store. It had about as much effect as he expected, which was slim to none. "And Jerry, I'd like you to meet Allison Bell. She's the owner's granddaughter."

Jerry grabbed her hand and pumped it briskly. "This is an incredible opportunity. I have wanted to restore this house for years. Years, I'm telling you."

Allison carefully withdrew her hand. "I see. Well, first I should tell you that I don't really have a huge budget, and so I'm trying to keep things as cheap—"

Kyle saw Jerry's eyes round in horror at the word *cheap* and shook his head vigorously to signal to Allison to avoid it at all costs.

"Uh, I mean..." she paused "...as inexpensive as possible. I need to stretch my dollars... and focus on the priorities."

Jerry seemed comforted by that deft shift in Allison's wording. "Yeah, yeah." He rubbed his hands together. "So..."

"So...I have this plaster problem. Upstairs. And Kyle said you could take a look at it."

"Sure. Upstairs." The man was up the stairs like a jackrabbit.

Kyle sighed. "Listen. Don't—he's not usually like this. But he's been obsessed with Belle Paix for years. And he just wants to see her treated right."

Allison lifted her brows. "Yeah. And I just want to treat my very finite bank account right. If this guy thinks I'm a sucker and want to make everything the way it was in 1888, well, you'd better set him straight."

"Jerry is a bit…temperamental," Kyle warned. "If he thinks you're not…well, he's been known to walk off jobs. You don't want to see him angry."

"How does he keep his business then?" Allison asked. "I mean, if he argues with the home owner."

"Ninety-nine percent of the time he's right, and they know it. They try to do it the cheap way, and then have to call him back in. Because…well, because he's a genius, and because he's one of the few contractors in the state who specializes in old homes."

"You're saying…you're saying he's my only hope?" Allison sank onto the bottom step. "Good grief. He probably charges a fortune, too."

"You get what you pay for, believe me. And

with Jerry, you get a lot of experience and know-how. Plus he won't cheat you." Kyle sat down beside her.

"And how do I know you're not getting kick-backs? That the two of you aren't working some kind of scheme here?"

But he could tell from her tone that she didn't really believe that.

Above them, Jerry bellowed, "Who on earth put this stuff on plaster?"

They looked up to see his bright red face hanging over the railing of the landing, the putty gripped in his meaty fingers.

Allison raised her hand. "That would be me. The guy at the hardware store told me it would work."

"Figured. Idiot."

Minutes later, upstairs, Kyle watched as Jerry went through a much more thorough examination than he had.

"Yep. Condensation. I assume that the roof doesn't leak?"

"No." Allison shook her head in response to the contractor's accusatory squint. "That's the one thing that works in this house. It's slate, and it has never leaked a drop."

"Testament to when houses were built right," Jerry pronounced.

She made a harrumphing noise in her throat

and mumbled something that Kyle thought might have been, "you try living in this old place."

Then she schooled her expression and clasped her hands behind her back. "So your advice would be?"

"Tear out. Tear it all out, all the damaged sections. Down to the laths. Replaster it after you check the wiring—probably needs to be brought up to code, and it's easier to do it then. I'd plan on doing every exterior wall up here, but downstairs, you might not have to. I'd have to look. But it's the temperature changes and the way heat rises—that sort of stuff."

"How…much? And how long?" Allison seemed to stiffen in anticipation of a blow.

"I'll get you a bid. But I can tell you, it ain't gonna be cheap. You don't want cheap. Cheap's bad. Cheap is the most expensive way to go. Trust me. As for how long. Well." Jerry rubbed his chin. "First we got to put in the abatement procedures."

"Abatement? For what?"

"Lead paint. That there? It is lead paint, lady. Not the top layer. Probably not the last three or four or five coats. But underneath? Definitely lead. Lots of it. Big believers of it in the 1880s. So we got to contain the dust, and use breathing masks, and then properly dispose of it…that won't take that long. Say, three weeks?"

"Three weeks? Just to get rid of the lead?"

"And the plaster. Might do it in two. But you want it gone. Trust me. And it'll be gone when I'm done. And then we've got it all nice and bare and we can see the ribs of the old girl. Do some checking. Make sure that condensation hasn't messed up the framing. You do get it sprayed for termites, right?"

"Every year. Gran has a contract with a pest control company. She loses the discounted rate if she skips a year."

"Good. Good. So probably no big surprises under there, but I can't promise. And while we've got it out, we can put in some insulation—that'd be real good to cut down on the utility bills, keep the old girl nice and toasty, help with that condensation problem, too. And we'll check on the wiring, of course. No telling how they wired this thing when electricity came on line here. It's probably pretty scary to look at."

"And you'd…you'd do all this?"

"Well, I'd be the lead contractor. I'd subcontract part of it, a job this big."

"Two walls? Is big?"

"No. The whole house. You gotta do the whole house. Wouldn't be right. Like giving an old lady half a face-lift. Or putting in one new hip joint when she needs both replaced."

"Jerry…Jerry." Allison smiled at him. It was, to Kyle, the most angelic, heart-melting smile he'd ever seen. "I don't have that kind of money. And my grandmother, she's in a rehab facility and needs to come home. I don't have a lot of time. So…what's a…"

Kyle could see her lips change from "cheaper" to "work-around" to finally "an alternative way. You know. Out of the box."

Jerry swiveled his head toward Kyle. "Kyle? I thought you said this was a restoration job?"

"You didn't exactly give me time to explain. Can you help her with this? She's trying to do a lot herself."

Jerry's face crumpled. "Dang. Got my heart broke. I thought for sure…"

The three of them stood in silence, with both Allison and Jerry staring at the wall in question.

Suddenly Allison brightened. "Hey! Hey, I know! Why can't I just put in drywall? You know, over the plaster? I could do that, right? Smooth surface. It'd go up quick. No patching. No disturbing the lead. And it would be easier to fix later on."

Jerry practically hissed. Kyle rubbed his forehead again. "Allison," he began.

"I'll have no part in putting drywall in a

126-year-old house," Jerry told her, his back ramrod straight.

"But—but why not? Just because it's not authentic? I can't afford authentic! Not in time. And certainly not financially."

The contractor opened his mouth, started to speak, stopped, started to speak again. Finally, he growled at Kyle, "Tell her. I'm too—too..." He couldn't finish his thought.

"Jerry is saying... Uh, what he means is it's not going to solve the problem. The issue is the unstable plaster underneath. From the condensation. And...if you put drywall up, the plaster may hold. For a little bit. But then it will come down. In chunks. And cause cracks. And mess up the drywall, since the moisture in the plaster is probably still there. But Jerry would put a vapor barrier up when he removed the plaster... Are you listening? You are not listening, Allison. Allison? Where are you going?"

But she had left. She stalked out into the hall. He thought she was going to march down to the front door and throw them out, but no. The footsteps were on the back stairs, not the front, and they were going up, not down.

So what was he supposed to do now?

CHAPTER SEVEN

ALLISON REACHED OUT a hand to steady the Victorian dressmaker's form before the stained linen-and-wire monstrosity toppled. A cloud of dust billowed out and she sneezed. With the form as steady as it could be on its wobbly center pole, she pushed past it and several hulking pieces of furniture to her object.

The window seat.

The cushions released another cloud of dust from their faded damask upholstery fabric when she sat on them.

The little window seat, overlooking the front lawn from the highest point in the house, had been her favorite bolt-hole when she was a kid. For a home ec project in high school, she'd redone the cushions. It was probably the newest upholstery in the whole house.

She inspected the wobbly seams and the clumsily installed zipper with none of the starry-eyed sense of accomplishment she'd had as a sophomore. What was she thinking? She couldn't fix this house, any more than she had any business trying to cover seat cushions.

Allison curled up on the cushions and waited for the reverberation of the bangs of the door. They'd go, of course. They'd bail on her, once they saw she was in over her head, with no money to get out of this hole.

All I wanted to do was paint Gran's room.

Her embarrassment faded with the first flare of anger. What had she expected, anyway? Of course Kyle would bring in a restoration-nut as a contractor—it probably *was* some sort of scheme. Not an out-and-out con, but more paternalistic—an "oh, we know better" sort of deal.

She heard thumps on the stairs—thumps coming up, not going down. Her irritation grew. They were coming up here? To her bolt-hole?

"Go away," she called. Yeah. It was rude. Probably juvenile. No, definitely juvenile, but if she'd wanted to talk, she would have stayed in Gran's room.

A golden ray of sun hit the crest of Kyle's head as it appeared in the stairwell. A pang of regret coursed through Allison—but only for a moment. It was snuffed out by more irritation.

Because obviously he was not listening.

"Allison?" She could see him blinking in

the dim light. He coughed from the dusty air. "Where are you?"

She didn't answer, just pressed back into the recesses of the dormer, away from the window so that he couldn't see her outline against the bright sunlight. The dressmaker's form offered her the cover it had back in her teen years when she'd been escaping Gran's hard-to-combat common sense.

Nevertheless, he stumbled in Allison's direction, following a narrow path through over a century's worth of her family's junk—and they'd been good about throwing things out, it occurred to her. What if they'd been garden-variety hoarders?

He stopped, poking his head into the billiard room. "Wow. Is that the original billiard table? And…oh, this is a mint-condition spittoon—well, not quite mint."

Oh, good grief. He'd never leave, especially if he found Gran's dad's collection of pipes.

"You don't listen very well, do you?" Allison groused.

Kyle turned back toward her, craned his head around the open door, and spotted her at the window. "There you are."

She noticed he didn't answer her question, proving her point about him. She uncurled herself from the window seat. If she was going to have the house to herself again, she'd need to dispense with the evasive action and go for some proactive moves instead.

"Thank you for getting Jerry here," Allison stated in a very formal tone. "But I don't think it's going to work out."

Kyle bumped up against the wobbly dressmaker form. She saw it tilt and start to crash to the floor. Allison leaped to save it at the same time he did, and they wound up in a three-way hug with the mannequin, hands and bodies pressed against each other. Allison was suddenly way too aware of the taut muscles in Kyle's arms…and there was that divine, clean scent that he always wore.

Stupid nose of hers.

"Uh, this is awkward," Kyle observed after a moment. He carefully backed away. "You got it?"

Allison didn't say anything. She righted the dressmaker form and dusted off her hands. Great. In addition to looking like a complete idiot, she now looked like a dusty idiot.

"So," he murmured, obviously unsure what to say to her at this point.

"Yes, right. Like I was saying. Thanks, but…I think Jerry isn't quite what I'm looking for."

Kyle rubbed at his eyes. "Allison…Jerry's just what you're looking for. Believe me. I know he comes across strong, but you have no idea what kind of experience he has in these situations. You'd be a—" He broke off.

"I'd be a fool not to snap him up on the spot? Is that what you were about to say?" Her earlier anger returned, full force. "No, I'd be a fool to turn a guy like that loose on this house. He'll find a dozen different ways to prolong a project. He'd break me."

"He'll get it done the right way, and it will cost you less in the long run—" Kyle started.

She broke in. "You're used to working with rich retirees who come back with plenty of money and plenty of time and plenty of patience, and I'm fresh out of all three, Kyle."

"Allison, you've got it all wrong. Most of the people in the historic district *aren't* rich. They're like you. They struggle to find the money. They borrow it, they scrounge around for grants, they use tax credits… It's hard work, I won't lie, and it's time consuming. But in the end, when they see the finished project, they're glad they dug deep. People—and I say this from personal experience—people don't regret what they *do*, Allison. They regret what they *don't*."

For a moment, he seemed to be fixed on something far removed from the dusty, junk-filled room around them. What on earth had he neglected to do that made him give her that speech?

Whatever memory Kyle was entertaining didn't matter, not now. She had no time to dig for funds that might or might not exist. "It's all well and good for you to tell me what I'll regret," she told him. "But I don't care. I honestly don't care about getting the texture right! Or whether it's a grievous sin to put drywall inside a 126-year-old house! I. Don't. Care."

His quick intake of breath and his glower told her the story. She couldn't have insulted him more if she'd slapped him.

"You don't mean that," he said. He reached out to give her another one of those reassuring pats.

She waved it away. Allison was not about to be soothed, not when she had managed to work herself up into a proper seething fury of righteous indignation.

"Is this what you did to my grandmother? Huh? Did you make this house renovation business seem so overwhelming that she didn't even want to try? That she let it go downhill to the point she got hurt by it? All because you and your kind want to insist on having things perfect! I don't need perfect, Kyle! I need fixed. Fixed, I tell you!"

"Why can't you do both?"

"Why can't you see reality? Get a grip on reality! I have other things besides the authentic texture of plaster to worry about! Really. Believe it or not. Some people have actual, real problems to think about. To solve. Not drywall. Drywall is not a deal breaker for me. And I will find someone who will fix this. Not make it perfect. Not make it authentic. Not worry about what the heck this place looked like in 1888. But just fix it. I just need it…fixed."

There. She'd gotten that off her chest. She felt lighter, freer. As though she were floating.

But then she saw the wounded expression on Kyle's face, and her elation popped and sank like a deflated balloon.

"Yeah. Okay. I get it. I was just trying to help." His tone was clipped. With a quick turn on his heel, he headed back through the collection of trunks and shelves and discarded furniture.

"Kyle—wait—"

"No. Honestly. You've said it all. I'm sorry if I overstepped my bounds."

And then that golden ray of sun lit upon his head again as he disappeared down the stairs, leaving her behind in the middle of all that junk.

CLEO WAS NOT helping matters.

Allison had filled the cat's dish with her favorite food, showed the blasted feline the fresh stream flowing from the bathroom sink before she filled up her water bowl, even tried to pet the cantankerous thing…to no avail.

The cat just kept yowling. She'd yowled in her querulous way ever since Kyle and Jerry had vacated the premises. That had been yesterday afternoon.

Allison sank her head into her hands and poked her fingers in her ears. "I've fed you and watered you and changed your litter. What else could you want?"

The cat yowled again.

"Gran?" Okay. She was officially hearing things now, because she could have sworn the cat had just called Gran's name. In Siamese, of course.

To add to the surreal, the cat suddenly shut up. Cleo tilted her slender, triangle-shaped face and peered at Allison with those piercing blue eyes. Funny, they were the same shade as Kyle's.

Allison yanked her thoughts away from that dead end. She would not ruminate about her regrets one more second.

She was rewarded by Cleo crossing the few feet between them and circling her legs. The cat even purred.

"I miss Gran, too, Cleo. And I know you

haven't seen her for a long time..." Tears pricked Allison's eyes at the whole absurd situation. She'd abandoned the painting job upstairs to research the proper way to patch plaster, and it all seemed beyond her. And here was Cleo, reminding her that yet another warm body was depending on her to bring Gran home.

Lo and behold, the cat jumped up into Allison's lap, Cleo's tail encircling her neck like some sort of mink stole. Cleo reached up and touched a paw delicately to Allison's cheek.

"If you had a magic spot, I'd give you a good petting," she murmured to the animal. "But you're the only cat I've ever known who doesn't like being stroked."

A rapping on the back door sent Cleo streaking for cover. Allison's heart went into double time. Could it be Kyle?

It wasn't. But it was Melanie Hutchins, former partner-in-crime and still one of her best friends in the whole world.

"I come bearing first aid," Melanie told her.

"First aid? Why? I'm not hurt."

Melanie produced a giant Heath bar and a can of Pringles. "I dimly recall that these two items were the only things that got you over Scott Fisher dumping you just before the prom."

"Not the big guns!" Allison stood aside and

ushered her in. "And for the record, I dumped Scott, not the other way around."

Melanie set the Pringles on the kitchen table. "This place hasn't changed since we were in grade school. I keep expecting Gran to yank some warm chocolate chip cookies out of the oven. And about whether Scott was the dumper or the dumpee? Okay, have it your way. But on the phone last night, you sounded about as bleak as you did back then. So…after I sent my twenty-four little heathens to their respective buses, I ditched my lesson plans and about a thousand papers left to grade, made a stop by the first convenience store I came to, and bought provisions." Melanie waggled the candy bar.

"I didn't sound that down in the mouth, did I?" Allison reached for the bar, but Melanie yanked it back.

"Nope. Not yet. Not until I see this disaster of a paint job."

Up in Gran's bedroom, Melanie regarded the patched plaster in silence, then let out a long, low whistle. "Boy howdy, you aren't kidding. And History Boy says all the walls will be this way?"

Allison shrugged. "If by History Boy you mean Kyle, then more accurately, Kyle's buddy Jerry what's-his-name."

"I know some folks who used him. They own the Queen Anne up the street. I thought the two of them would get a divorce over that stupid house."

"Why is that so easy for me to envision?" Allison said. She wandered over to the ladder, still standing where Kyle had left it the day before. She laid a palm on it, wanting to sense some residual warmth from Kyle's hands. He'd made her feel—well, before he made her exasperated, anyway—he'd made her feel as though she wasn't alone.

But really, Allison was alone, and she'd known it all along, because her philosophy was not his.

"So…"

The ripping of paper drew Allison's attention back to Melanie, in time to see her friend opening the Heath bar and taking a huge bite out of it.

"Hey! I thought that was mine!" she protested.

Melanie swallowed and grinned. "I brought two. And you're right. This is definitely the time for provisions. So…are you going to put in drywall?"

"I don't know." Allison banged her head lightly on the ladder. "At first I thought, yeah, why not? Simple, you know? Just rip out all the old plaster and put in drywall…"

"Don't tell me. Don't. You're feeling guilty, aren't you?"

"What?"

"You are actually considering hiring that Jerry fellow because you don't want to disappoint History Boy—oh, all right. Ky-yyle." She dragged out the one-syllable name the way she used to drag out Scott's name in high school.

"Where's that Heath bar? I need it if you're going to go all juvenile on me." Allison headed for the back stairs and the kitchen. Melanie followed close behind. "And, yes, of course I feel guilty. Gran raised me from the time I was three, Melanie. She sacrificed so much for me, took me on when she didn't have to, and after my parents died to boot. Of course I want the best for her—I want it done right. Well, as right as I can afford. And what do I know? I've taken more than one shortcut in the past that turned out to be a disaster."

"What *does* your grandmother say about all this?" Melanie asked, as they negotiated the tight turn of the back stairs.

Allison came to a halt and looked over her shoulder. "Uh, she doesn't know. I haven't fessed up yet."

Melanie took another bite of the candy and

chewed thoughtfully. She swallowed, but didn't say anything for a long moment.

Allison had almost given up on whatever was weighing on her friend's mind, and had turned to take another step, when Melanie asked, "So what's the worst that could happen if you did? Fess up, I mean."

Contemplating *that* scenario required sustenance from Melanie's provisions. It might even call for the entire can of Pringles. So without replying, Allison double-timed it down the remaining stairs.

She'd popped the top of the Pringles can—oh, that had to be one of the most satisfying sounds in the world—before she'd formed her answer. "Gran won't yell. You know that. It's not her way. No, she'll just ask a ton of questions that she clearly already knows all the answers to, just to make you ponder and reponder the error of your ways. By the end of any of her postmortems, while I clearly know what I *should* have done, I feel like I've stewed in a mortification soup for a couple of hours."

Melanie licked a smear of chocolate off her fingertip. "She doesn't mean to mortify you. She's simply trying to make you—"

"Think. I know. Didn't I live through that with my teen years? But why do I feel like I'm fifteen again? It's this house! Moving back here has transformed me into this indecisive kid who couldn't make a decision if her life depended on it. And that's not me, now. I mean, I'm a trauma nurse. I'm paid to make the hard decisions fast."

"And you still make the hard decisions in the ER, right? But living with a parent—or a grandparent who was practically your parent—is hard as an adult. You have to renegotiate boundaries that sheer geographical distance enforced for you before."

Melanie's rambling jargon made Allison's head hurt. "Oookay. You've had one too many staff development units on childhood behavior. And chewing over this is not helping."

Melanie dug around in her purse and produced the second Heath bar. "Chew on this, then. It never fails."

"And then, I promise, even though Gran had already warned me about Kyle, and she's going to be horribly disappointed about my screwup and the delay it's going to cause to her coming home..." Allison let her teeth crunch into the sweet chocolate bar, and chased it with a salty potato chip. She chewed, sensing peace and well-being from all those simple carbs flowing to her brain. "...I'll go confess all to Gran."

CHAPTER EIGHT

THIS WAS SO not a good idea.

Kyle knew it. He should stay well away from Allison and her grandmother and even that crazy cat. And most of all, he should stay away from Belle Paix.

Through the spring sunshine, he stared at the rehab facility where Lillian Thomas was staying.

The architects had tried to make it look like a home, with its wide porches and rockers, the end porch pillars covered in English ivy. A plethora of blooming flowers exploded from planters along the main walkway and window boxes on each of the long, double-hung windows.

And it was only a detail freak like him who would become irked that the Georgian columns didn't go with the Queen Anne shingles, or that the shutters were too narrow for the wide windows. Worse still, the windows had those plastic inserts for mullions, not individual panes.

His nitpicking irritated even himself. He was

reminded of Allison's plea for pragmatism, and her accusation that his pursuit of perfection—well, the preservation committee's, anyway—had been so discouraging that Lillian Thomas had put off needed repairs.

And that was why he was here. To apologize. To offer his help—as pragmatic as possible.

Couldn't possibly be because you're too chicken to tackle Allison head-on, right?

Out of the car, his feet crunched on the pea gravel path. He wasn't fired up about nursing homes—correction, rehab facilities—and he wasn't at all sure Allison's grandmother would even see him. But he could stick his head in after he'd visited with a former historical society member who'd just moved in.

"Hey! What are you doing here?"

The sound of Allison's voice froze him in his tracks. Slowly, he pivoted on his heel.

"Allison." Kyle could think of nothing else to say. His guilt at the planned end run around her—and that's what he'd really been up to, when he was honest with himself—closed his throat.

Now that she'd hailed him, Allison seemed as unsure about what to say as he was. She closed the gap between them. He couldn't help but admire the light yellow dress she wore and the way her red hair caught the late spring sunlight. More than that, the blush that faintly lit her cheeks made him think she was just as embarrassed as he'd been to see her.

"I—I should apologize for the other day—" she began, just as he, too, stammered out an apology.

They laughed. "You go first, I insist," Allison said. "A lady always likes to hear a guy say he's sorry."

"I should have known better than to bring Jerry in without properly preparing you—and you're right. Belle Paix is your house—well, your grandmother's house—and you have your priorities. And I didn't respect those."

Allison gazed out at the long, wraparound porch. "I acted like a brat. It's just…overwhelming. That's not an excuse, just a statement of fact."

"Old houses have a way of bringing out the worst in anybody. And don't worry. I've seen far worse." He didn't add that, while he had seen worse behavior over the years, it hadn't bothered him as much as Allison's wholesale rejection of historical authenticity as a worthwhile goal.

"Got to be a happy medium out there, don't you think?" she mused.

He bit his tongue before saying that happy mediums produced a mishmash of architecture like the rehab facility behind him. "It's a question of priorities," he said instead.

"Right." She gave him a flint-eyed look of suspicion, and seemed to know what he was thinking. But in the interest of peace and accord, she, too, apparently was choosing her words with care.

For a long moment, neither said anything. Awash in the sounds of the rehab facility even from where they stood at the front door—the squeak of wheelchair brakes, the beep of the keypad by the main entrance, an alarm buzzer insistently going off—Kyle realized that the thin patina of "home" for the residents couldn't be maintained for more than five minutes. He thought again of Lillian Thomas.

"So you're here to see your grandmother?" he asked.

"Yes. To, er, tell her about the latest disaster." Allison's lips compressed in a wince of anticipatory pain.

"She's not that bad, is she?"

"No. No, not really. I just…don't want to disappoint her. You've met her, right?"

Kyle rubbed his mouth. "Not—well, not exactly. I mean, if you…"

"Yes?" Now Allison's eyes lit up with amusement. "I can spot a 'Gran' story a mile away. Give."

"Well, if you have to know, the extent of our acquaintance has been the one time she stopped by the historical society to get a paint scheme approved, and she practically laughed me out of my office. And the only other times…er, does being run off the property twice count?"

Allison threw her head back and laughed. "That sounds like Gran on a bad day. You must be terrified of her."

Not so much that I wasn't planning on trying to see her. Yes. To apologize.

"I wouldn't say terrified," he muttered. "Just…learned to keep a respectful distance."

"Let me guess…you wouldn't have even come here if you'd known you might run into her, right?"

"Not…not exactly. Actually, she's why I'm here."

The friendly expression on Allison's face evaporated into suspicion. "You? Were coming to see Gran?"

"Yes. I thought—" Kyle broke off, ran his finger around a shirt collar that suddenly felt too tight in the warm sun. "Well, I was planning on seeing another member of the historic society who's here as well, and I thought I'd just stick my head in and—"

"Bug Gran." Allison's words were flat.

"No, not…not bug her. I just wanted to properly introduce myself. And to apologize."

"Apologize? For what?"

At that moment Kyle was given a brief reprieve, as a staff member in pastel scrubs wheeled a resident along the path between them. When he looked back, he saw that Allison was still regarding him with confusion.

"You know," he said, "what you were saying the other afternoon. I thought you blamed me for your gran being here in the first place."

"No. Yes. Maybe. If you just wouldn't make it so hard to get something done!" Allison's brows drew together over eyes that Kyle realized looked as gray-green now as a stormy ocean. She blew a long corkscrew curl out of her face with a sigh of exasperation. It settled right back where it had been, and Kyle suddenly itched to tuck it behind her ear.

"It's not me, it's the—"

She glowered. "If you say the historical committee, I'm going to bean you on the head. We both know that you *are* the committee, so don't go hiding behind it like the man behind the curtain, oh great Oz."

"You make it sound like the ordinances are a bad thing, but they're there for a reason, Allison—"

"Right. To make it impossible for normal

people to repair a house that just happens to be square in the middle of a historic district." She rolled her eyes.

"That's not true. That district generates jobs and income for lots of residents. Lombard depends on tourist dollars. And your neighbors need the protection to their investments and their home equity that the ordinances provide."

She put her hands on her hips and scoffed, "Admit it. You wouldn't give two figs about Gran's house if it were a 1980s suburban ranch, now would you?"

The truth of her observation about his interest in Belle Paix stung. Still, he had to defend what he'd helped to create. "Normal people can renovate old houses—there are all kinds of funding options for preserving and restoring old homes—and that's one thing I'd like to talk to your grandmother—"

"Good. You wanted to talk to Gran? Well, let's go talk to her. Maybe you can explain to her how she and I are going to be able to afford to fix the mess I've made. And maybe she'll see *you* and blame the whole thing on you and not me."

At the prospect, Kyle's stomach did a strange flip-flop it hadn't done since he'd turned in his doctoral dissertation. "I don't—if you think—"

"No, sir, buddy, you're not backpedaling

now." Allison tucked an arm in the crook of his elbow and proceeded to drag him to the front door of the facility.

"But—but are you sure? I mean, you seem so angry—"

They'd reached the door by now, and Allison let go of his arm and punched a code into the keypad. It suddenly occurred to him that he might not have been granted access to begin with had it not been for Allison.

"Seem? Just seem? Kyle Mitchell, you have a lot to learn about me if I just 'seem' angry."

They stepped into a large room filled with badly done Victorian reproduction sofas covered in the wrong print for the era the sofas were supposed to be copying. The detail grated on Kyle's nerves. But before he could even swallow the remark he knew he shouldn't make, Allison stopped and gently guided a rail-thin old lady holding a teddy bear back in the direction she'd come from.

"Now, Mrs. Brennan, you know you can't go out there without a staff member—"

"But Teddy! Teddy needs some air!" Mrs. Brennan protested. She held up the bear in agitation and tried to push past Allison, to make it to the door before it swished shut. As the safety lock clicked into place, she let out a fiendish yowl that sent a tremor down Kyle's spine.

"Mrs. Brennan, it's okay…" But the woman wasn't paying the least amount of attention to Allison, focusing her energy instead on sounding as though she'd been tortured.

"Should I go get a staff member?" Kyle craned his head this way and that to find one, to no avail.

Allison shook her head. She patted Mrs. Brennan, then leaned down close to the bear. "What's that, Teddy? What? Your head hurts? You wish—you wish what?"

Mrs. Brennan stopped in midshriek. She bent her head closer to Allison's and Teddy's.

"Oh! You needed a little quiet, huh, boy?" Allison said to the bear. She glanced up at Mrs. Brennan. "Fancy that. I think he wants a nap."

The old woman's features twitched with irritation. "That's not what he told me! He said he wanted a lemon cookie."

And with no further words, Mrs. Brennan and Teddy about-faced and headed off, presumably in search of a snack.

"Wow. I'm impressed. You're really good at that."

Allison shrugged. Dealing with Mrs. Brennan had apparently drained her of her earlier hostility. "Comes from years working in an ER. You just have to know what's important to people."

He cleared his throat to fill the sudden and awkward silence that had sprung up between them, punctuated only by the squeak of rubber-soled shoes and shuffles of residents along the facility's halls. "So your grandmother…she's been here how long?"

Allison closed her eyes. Was that guilt on her face? Did she blame herself? "Too long," she answered. "She was supposed to be here for three weeks after her surgery…and then she got an infection that delayed her therapy. If I'd only come home… But no. I let her talk me into checking her into a rehab facility, instead of taking a leave of absence and coming here to take care of her myself."

"You're here now. That's all that matters."

Kyle's words, delivered with a calm purposefulness he hadn't even known he'd felt, seemed to reassure her. She gave a decided nod of her head. "Yes. Yes, I am. And I intend to get her home as quickly as possible."

Allison strode off down one of the halls, the printed skirt she was wearing billowing in her wake. Kyle hurried to catch up with her. The determined tilt of her chin told him not to bother talking for now.

Besides, he needed to plan his words with Allison's grandmother. His palms broke out in a sweat at the thought of Allison listening intently to the conversation, and he realized he hadn't thought out a script.

And based on his other disastrous encounters with the woman, Lillian Shepherd Bell Thomas was not someone with whom you just sashayed in and tried to wing it.

Allison came to a stop in front of a door. Her eyes glittered with almost malicious amusement and challenge. "Any last words?" she quipped.

As unobtrusively as he could, Kyle swiped his palms against his pants. "You're enjoying the prospect of this, aren't you?"

Her smile widened. "Immensely. But you asked for it. So I see it as self-inflicted agony."

From inside the door came a thin, high voice that still exuded a tone of peremptory command.

"Are you two going to stand out there yammering all day or come in like well-mannered, decent folk?"

Kyle took in a deep breath and swept his hand toward the door. "After you."

Allison's eyes glittered some more. They really were the color of a raging ocean. "Right. Hope you're ready for her."

And she pushed the door open and walked on ahead of him, leaving him standing in the doorway with a decided compulsion to run in the opposite direction.

CHAPTER NINE

THE ROOM WAS brightly lit from a huge window with drapes drawn wide. For a moment, the transition from the artificial light in the hall to the afternoon sunlight almost blinded Kyle. He blinked. Then he spotted Allison bending low over a wing chair in the corner.

She straightened to reveal a tiny old lady with a back so ramrod erect she could have been a statue. Kyle recognized the woman at once and was surprised to see that, despite surgery and a stay in the rehab facility, Lillian Shepherd Bell Thomas was still in fighting form.

"Gran, this is Dr. Kyle Mitchell—"

"Not another doctor, Allison! I've had my fill of 'em!" the woman snapped. "Unless he's signing my discharge orders, he can go." She made a shooing gesture toward the door.

"Er, I'm not that kind of doctor, ma'am," Kyle said. He crossed the room and stretched out a hand. "I'm a professor. Of history."

She took his hand, but didn't shake it. No, she used the gesture as a way to keep him close and peer up at him. "You! You're that man from the historic preservation committee, the busy-bodies who gad about, telling people how they have to paint their houses."

"I am on the historic preservation committee, yes, ma'am." He glanced over at Allison, to find her lips twitching with barely concealed amusement.

The old woman harrumphed. "Well, best I recollect, you're a little long-winded. Why don't you pull up a chair so I won't get a crick in my neck?"

It wasn't a request. It was an order. Kyle reached for the closest chair he could find, remembered his manners and offered it to Allison.

Out of the corner of his eye, he saw Lillian smile. It was a tiny hint of a smile, but a definite mark in the plus column.

A minute later he was perched on the only other piece of furniture for seating in the room—a tiny, undersized stool from the little vanity table. On it, he felt clumsy and oaf-like, but the one remaining spot to sit was on her bed, and somehow that didn't seem proper.

"So you've been annoying my granddaughter," she announced.

"Uh, no, Mrs. Thomas—"

"Call me Gran. All of Allison's friends do—

well, did, before she moved out. Not, of course, that you and Allison are friends. Or are you?"

Gran's eyes, clear and blue in a crazy-quilt of wrinkles and crow's feet, assessed him. He pulled his gaze from hers to Allison's, who regarded him with a fair amount of trepidation. It was as if she was beginning to rethink the wisdom of bringing him to beard the lioness in her den.

"So? Are you or aren't you friends?" Gran prompted.

"I don't know," he confessed finally.

"Honesty. I like that. Too many young men would have tried to bamboozle me with a 'we don't know each other very well' bit of moonshine."

Kyle was shocked by the breath of relief that he expelled at her approving smile. "Thank you," he responded.

"And what brings you here to see me?"

"Well, first of all, an apology."

She drew back to stare at him intently, gripping the head of her walking stick with long slender fingers. "My goodness. What have you done that you require absolution and forgiveness? And from me of all people?"

He cleared his throat. "Allison seems to think…" He stopped, feeling Allison's annoyance with him roil off her in waves. "She believes that part of the reason you landed here is because the ordinances the city has passed made it overwhelming for you to tackle some needed renovations."

"Did she now." Gran's dry chuckle and acerbic glance toward her granddaughter told him he wouldn't be making any brownie points with Allison with his previous remark. "Let me put your mind at ease, then. I blame no one but myself for being here, young man. I knew that carpet was raveling, and I didn't have it fixed. True, to have that white elephant of a house painted in 'historically accurate colors'—" she laid a heavy, sarcastic emphasis on the words "—would require a small fortune that I don't have. But the last I heard, you and your fellow busybodies weren't inspecting the interiors of houses, isn't that correct?"

"That's true. Unless someone asks—"

"And no one in her right mind would." Gran's interruption dripped with finality. "Because?" Now she turned to Allison.

It was her turn to squirm. "Gran?"

Her grandmother tsked. "I would have supposed you'd have learned your lesson by now, Allison. Maybe it's because I was a teacher for so long. No, the reason you don't invite busybodies in where they're not required is of the 'if you give a mouse a cookie' school of thought."

"Oh! Right. You have no idea how right you are about that, Gran," Allison muttered darkly.

Gran gave a crisp little nod of satisfaction and touched her hand to her hair, silver but impeccably coiffed. Her fingers slid down to finger her necklace, an ivory double strand of pearls at her neck. Kyle was no expert when it came to jewelry, but he could tell heirlooms when he saw them, and knew she had been wearing those pearls for decades.

"And?" Gran prompted.

"And?" he repeated, thoroughly confused. Had she said something he had missed?

"You said, 'first of all,' when you sat down. Unless you are careless with your words—and for all your foibles, I don't think that is the case—you had something else on your mind," she stated.

"You're…you're very observant."

"When you get to be my age, Dr. Mitchell, it's pretty much all the fun one is allowed." She settled back against the wing chair and crossed her legs primly at the ankles. "Besides, the last time we talked, you were much more long-winded and beat around a bush or two."

The last time…that was when he'd approached her in her own front yard, an impulsive stop to follow up her visit to the historical society office for a variance on paint schemes. It had not gone well.

"Yes. Fine, I'll try to be more concise, then. As I understand it, you and Allison are concerned with the amount of money that it will take to repair Belle Paix—"

Gran's face lit up with a broad smile. "Do you know, so few people call the house by its proper name these days? They haven't for years. I expect they don't even know it has a name. Belle Paix. Ambrose called it that, you know, before he even dug the foundation. He stood on that property and looked around and thought that such a vantage point was worthy of the name Beautiful Peace. He was fool enough to think that a fancy French title would give his nouveaux riche money a touch of class."

"I take it that it didn't?" Kyle ignored Allison's restless stirring in her far more comfy chair. If the old lady wanted to talk, he could bear this uncomfortable perch.

"I should say not! His first mistake was rebuilding on a lot in the moneyed section of town, where a favorite pillar of the community had had the misfortune to lose a house to a fire. It wasn't Ambrose's last mistake, but he was too much of a Yankee to understand Southern ways. My great-grandmother Davinia never could set him straight on that account," Gran said.

"He built a fine house, though."

"Nothing much wrong with Belle Paix even after a century and a quarter," Gran agreed. "So you tell me—why can't I go home yet? I want to sleep in my own bed and in my own bedroom."

Beside him, Allison groaned. She put a hand to her forehead. "Gran..."

"There's nothing wrong with a woman wanting to die in her own bed, Allison! You wait until you're eighty-nine and see how you feel. Of course, if you don't get busy getting married and starting a family, you might not have a granddaughter to come and visit you." Gran reached over and patted Allison's knee.

"I think..." Kyle decided he might as well pay his dues to Allison. "Mrs. Thom—" When he saw Gran frown, he corrected himself. "Gran. There's a slight delay in getting you back home. When we started painting your bedroom, some of the plaster began crumbling."

"Oh, never mind that." Gran waved airily. "Just stick it back in the hole and put a dab of automotive Bondo over it. It does that all the time. If you were a hundred and twenty-six years old, you'd feel entitled to fall apart a little yourself."

"No, Gran. He's right...it's, uh, more serious than a patch job. I think..." Allison sucked in a deep breath and squared her shoulders. "I think it will need all of the plaster taken down and maybe drywall put up."

Kyle whipped his head around in shock. "Oh, no! You can't take all the plaster down—you'd lose out on some of the tax credits you might get if you apply for some funds available to home owners of historic properties," he told her. "What Jerry meant was that you'll have to take out all the damaged sections—"

Allison's mouth dropped open in surprise. "But that's crazy! It would be so much simpler to rip everything out and put in new drywall. I thought it through last night, and that's the easiest—"

"No, no. See, you have to leave as much of the structure intact as possible if you're going to be eligible for—"

Suddenly a loud whistle pierced the air. Both Kyle and Allison jerked around to stare at the unlikely source of such a brash noise: Gran.

"Not exactly ladylike, but it was the only way I could ever get the attention of the rowdiest children on the playground back in my day," Gran commented. "Now. Enough squabbling. What is this problem? You, Dr. Mitchell. Use those verbal skills you so obviously possess, and keep it brief, young man."

So Kyle told her about the extent of the damage and Jerry's recommendation.

He could have sworn she shrank a little. No, more than a little. She sagged against the chair, her age momentarily revealing itself. Her eyes fluttered shut and her fingers gripped the polished stone of the walking stick so hard that he could see her gnarled knuckles turn white underneath their age spots.

"Well." Gran opened her eyes once again. "We can dispense with the tax-credit nonsense."

"But why?" Kyle asked. "It's a good way to offset some of the expense you and Allison would incur—"

"Good for some people. But not for me. No." When Kyle would have protested further, she raised one finger, and suddenly he felt as though he were six years old and he'd been very naughty. "You're an intelligent man. So think this through."

"Gran…for once, can we just dispense with the Socratic method and you just *tell* Kyle what the issue is?"

But Gran didn't let her gaze leave Kyle's face, even during Allison's aggravated outburst. "And what would be the benefit for him? Remember, caterpillars that don't struggle don't make it. Embrace the—"

"Struggle." Allison banged her palm on her forehead. "I know. I know. Embrace the struggle. It's kind of hard not to embrace the struggle, Gran. Right now, that old house feels like an anaconda, squeezing the very life out of me."

"I can't say I haven't felt that way on occasion myself, my dear. But after all, we have Davinia Shepherd's blood running through our veins. Now, Dr. Mitchell, my granddaughter's bought you some time to contemplate the error of your logic. Have you spotted it yet?"

If he'd been a butterfly at the pointy end of a collector's pin, Kyle could have felt no more desperate and trapped. "I haven't, no. It's a great program, designed to help home owners—"

"Ah, but not all home owners. First of all, I'm on social security and my pittance of a teacher's pension. How much tax do you think I pay?"

Kyle considered this. "Not much, I'd guess, but the credit rolls over for several years—"

"Years?" Gran's laugh pealed out. She reached over and patted Kyle's knee this time. "Young man, only an optimist would give me years. I have months if I'm lucky, and I'd better not hope for more than weeks or days. No, no!" She waved off Allison's protest. "I'm not saying I'll die tonight. But probabilities are probable for a reason. I'm guessing that I certainly won't be around to earn back a sizable tax credit. No, sir, Dr. Mitchell. Your tax credit is designed for much younger home owners, not a tough old bird like me. No, it's made for spring chickens."

"Oh, Gran! You shouldn't be so fatalistic," Allison said. "Why, didn't your own mother live to be over a hundred?"

"That she did. Of course, she never broke her hip, but then she made it through childbirth without anesthesia and antibiotics, so I guess we're tit for tat. Still, back to the subject at hand. If the plaster has to go, the plaster has to go. But let's not pussyfoot around trying to save plaster that will just crumble in the next few years anyway, certainly not for a tax credit I won't be around to use."

Kyle thought about the craftsmanship in that 126-year-old plaster, how it had been lovingly applied all those decades ago by a man who understood the material in a way few workers in this day and age did. The thought of it being gone and no longer a part of the house wrenched at him. But…

"You have a valid point," he said. It felt as though the concession had been torn out of him.

"I always do, young man. I always do. Allison will tell you that. Now, I'm not as young as I used to be, so that entitles me to a nap before that awful business they call supper. You two go on now."

Kyle could recognize a dismissal when he heard it. He scrambled to his feet and placed the vanity stool back in its rightful place. "Yes, ma'am. If it would be all right, I'll stop by and talk to you some more. I'd like to hear stories of the old days. It would help me in planning my lectures on local history."

Gran shrugged. "As you please. But Allison will warn you that I tend to blather on once you get me started."

Allison stood, too. "We'll get you home soon, Gran. I promise. I'm working hard on the house."

"It doesn't have to be perfect, Allison. Don't let this fellow hornswoggle you into thinking it does. Just give it a good cleaning and call it enough. Oh! And one other thing. Are you working this weekend? No, no…not this weekend. Friday week, that's the one."

"Not that I know of, but my schedule could change."

"Good! The man with the tomatoes will be coming that Saturday."

"Gran! I don't have time for tomatoes—"

"Tomatoes wait on nothing and no one, Allison. You know I always put up tomatoes, without fail, every year. The one concession I've made to my old bones is that I buy them instead of grow them. But maybe next year you can start the garden plot up again."

"Gran…you didn't order very many, did you?"

"About what I did last year. That should just do us…after all, there aren't many jars of tomatoes left in the pantry, are there?"

Allison's shoulders slumped in defeat. "No. I used the last one the other night for supper."

"Excellent! I calculated just right, then. However, with you home, perhaps I should increase my order—"

"No! Gran! You were well last year and able to help, and it nearly killed me—"

"Nonsense. Kyle here will help you. Won't you, Kyle? After all, you like experiencing historical things, don't you? Something as anachronistic as putting food by should appeal to you."

He jumped, startled that he'd been pulled into the middle of their squabble. "Uh, sure. I'll be glad to help. Though I admit, I've never done any food preserving."

"Nothing to it," Gran said. "I'll come home that weekend—they've told me I could have the equivalent of a weekend pass, aren't they generous." Her lips twitched with sardonic amusement. "Allison, what's that face you're pulling? You should have the business with my bedroom done by then, surely. Because naturally, I'll need to supervise you young people, as Kyle here has said he knows nothing about preserving. Besides. Nothing like two people in a kitchen together to see if they're compatible, is there? Now, off you go! I need my beauty sleep."

CHAPTER TEN

THE DOORBELL PEALED long and loudly for the third time. Fumbling with the sash on her robe, Allison stumbled out of her bedroom, around piles of debris and enough plastic tarps to give a person claustrophobic nightmares. A fine powder of dust lay everywhere; she could swear she felt it grit between her teeth.

Gran's room, the back stairs and the sole upstairs bathroom were temporarily blockaded with plastic and tape in a vain attempt to keep the demolition dust at bay. Allison made her way down the front stairs, saw no one at the front door and groaned.

Next she negotiated the back hall, past the yards of plastic and duct tape that encased the rear stairs. The doorbell pealed again, this time longer. She double-timed it, clenching her teeth and feeling again the unmistakable grit of construction dust between them.

But she dared not complain, fearing Jerry would halt the construction process, invoke more stringent lead abatement procedures, and another week would be wasted.

Through the glass pane of the kitchen door, Allison saw the man of the hour—Jerry the contractor, with a box in his hand. And—Kyle?

Her heart rattled in her chest at the sight of him. What was Kyle doing here? She put a hand to her hair—not movie bed-head, elegantly tousled and inviting. No, more along the lines of a rat's nest.

Jerry she couldn't care less about. In the past week, he'd been showing up at the crack of dawn and staying until nearly eight o'clock in the evening with his crew, so he'd seen her at her worst.

But Kyle? Especially when he appeared nattily turned out in a blazer and slacks, ready for his first lecture? No, for him, she wanted to appear fully in control, ready to face the day, ready to go to battle again over that variance paperwork he still hadn't helped her with.

She swung the door open. "Jerry. I thought we agreed. Not before 8:00 a.m.?"

He barged through the doorway past her. Kyle slipped in behind him, hardly daring to look her in the eye, the rat.

"Yeah, Miss Allison, I know, but I found this, see? And I wanted to get yours and Kyle's thoughts on it!"

Allison closed the door and swung back around to face Jerry and whatever lovely surprise he had for her this morning. “Found what? A miracle that will fix Gran’s bedroom and bathroom before this weekend? Oh, and the kitchen…I really, really need the kitchen back together before Friday, Jerry. You promised. I have Gran’s canning to do, and she won’t budge. She wants to sleep in her own bed and her own room and put up those blasted tomatoes.”

Beyond him, huge holes were gaping in the plaster of the back kitchen wall, barely hidden by translucent plastic that did a poor job of keeping even more construction dust out of the few meals Allison had been able to cobble together.

“Yeah, yeah, we’re working on it! We got it!” he assured her. “Everything’s great!”

Everything was not great. It seemed as though Gran had been all too right: give a mouse a cookie—or Jerry a pinky-toe access into the house—and life turned into a disaster. First he’d discovered that the wiring indeed needed reworking—surprise, surprise—so now throughout the house were huge gaping holes where the electrician had been pulling new wire. And then, oops, the plumbing in the upstairs bathroom had been jarred and sprang a gusher of a leak, and lately Jerry had been obsessing over the match of the plaster finish in Gran's room. He'd redone it three times now.

And she was stuck with him. Because Jerry had been the only one who would deign to work on the house. If only Gran hadn't been so insistent on coming home for a visit this weekend—to can those tomatoes!

"What is this? One of your brainy ideas?" she growled at Kyle.

He shrugged. "All I know is that he wanted me to come look at it with you before 2:00 p.m., and I have classes and meetings all day. This was the only time I could come. Sorry. He told me you wouldn't mind."

"And you believed him?" she muttered, then sighed. "Okay, Jerry. What is it?"

He had set the box on the kitchen table. "Found this online through a buddy I know in Chicago, and he sent me part of it, told me to let him know before two o'clock today if I wanted the rest. That's FedEx's last pickup for his shop. He'll ship it next day to us." Jerry whipped open the box and yanked out a dusty, dirty faucet.

Allison blinked. "Jerry."

"I know. Incredible, right?" He looked from her to Kyle. "Amazing. I didn't think there were any to be had!"

Kyle whistled. He took the faucet from Jerry,

turning it over in his hands. "No! It can't be! Is this—Allison! Can you believe this?"

A slow, righteous anger boiled up within her at being awakened with just three hours of sleep after working the night before on the variance paperwork. "No. I can't."

The flat tone of her voice caused the two men to jerk their attention from their find to her. "You don't know what this is?"

"It looks like a secondhand bathroom faucet. Kind of interesting detail, what with all that leaf design embossed into the spout, and I'll bet an incredible pain to keep clean."

"Allison!" Kyle seemed to take her description of it as near sacrilege. "This is a faucet design that could be original to the house. And it's a mixing tube design—one single faucet, not a hot and cold one. For the time, it was a luxury model. See? Solid brass!"

Jerry took it back and rubbed the spout with the tail of his T-shirt. The metal did give up a somewhat brighter gleam.

It did little to brighten anything else for Allison, though—including her mood.

"Original. Great. So that means it's a 126-year-old faucet. Just like the one I have. Already. That I hate. Because it leaks. And I can't get parts to fix it. Terrific."

"Uh, Miss Allison. About that faucet in the

upstairs bathroom. I kind of…well, it sort of…" Jerry closed his eyes and compressed his mouth in pain. "When we were taking everything apart yesterday, it sort of…"

"Gave up the ghost," Allison finished.

"Yeah. Yeah, it did. So I never would have thought we'd be able to find another one—and really, this is authentic, but a much better faucet than you had. Plus, with a few fixes, it'll be as good as new."

"No. No." She sank into a chair and wished like the devil that she didn't have to unplug the toaster to put on the coffeepot. But the way Jerry had things rigged up, she had only one safe working plug in the kitchen right now. "It's okay. Send the faucet back. We'll just get a brand-spanking-new twenty-first century faucet. Okay? One that doesn't require washers or obsolete parts."

"No!" Kyle protested. "This is part of the character of Belle Paix! You can't just slap new stuff in willy-nilly."

"I can. It's my house."

"No. It's your grandmother's. And remember? What's good enough for Ambrose?"

"No. No, no, no, no, *no*." Allison straightened up. She fixed Kyle with a glare. "I'll bet I'd have to pay three hundred dollars for that hunk of junk—a hunk of junk that I doubt even works."

"But my buddy…he's got the match for the tub…and even a showerhead—" Jerry protested.

"No. That's final. It's pretty, but you and Kyle won the plaster wars. I get to win this one. I want new plumbing. Shiny, brand-new, fresh-out-of-the-box plumbing for that bathroom. Don't you see? It was a sign. The universe is telling us that I have permission to have new bathroom fixtures!"

"Uh, Miss Allison. You don't understand. The bathroom sink? With all that pretty hand-painted flowers in the china bowl? You know, the one-of-a-kind that you're not gonna find anywhere else?"

"You didn't break *that*, did you?" Her heart stopped in her chest. Gran loved that sink. Allison had heard her ooh and ahh over it as long as she could remember. That was one reason Gran had never redone the upstairs bathroom.

"No! You think I'd be standing upright if I broke something like that? I'd be dead in a funeral home…you'd be at my visitation!" Jerry protested. "No, it's okay. But, see…modern fixtures…they don't fit the holes."

Allison wanted to shriek in frustration. What little money she had saved was evaporating fast in the week since she'd turned Jerry loose on the house. She knew what he was going to say next, his favorite, favorite line.

"Let me guess," she said. "This is my only option."

He nodded. "Yep. 'Fraid so. But aren't you glad I found it? Now we can save that bowl that your granny is so fired up about. She called me the other day, after you told her that I was doing work on the bathroom, and made me swear a blood oath I wouldn't take that sink out. I gave her my word."

Allison stood up, made her way to the extension cord, unplugged the toaster. Plugged in the coffeemaker. Grabbed the carafe and headed for the sink. Halfway there, she realized that she had to get water from the downstairs bathroom because there was none in the kitchen. Joy of joys.

For a long moment she just stood there, in the middle of the disaster of a kitchen, gripping the empty coffeepot and trying hard not to cry.

Kyle closed the gap between them and gently took it from her. "Let me guess. No water in the kitchen."

"I'll get it fixed," Jerry blustered. "The little bathroom works. But hey, I gotta go now! Gotta make sure that my buddy will ship the rest of this!" And he was out the kitchen door with a bang.

Five minutes later, Kyle was handing Allison a steaming mug of coffee and smiling at her where she sat, defeated, at the kitchen table. "It gets better," he assured her.

"I'm broke. I'm tired. And Gran keeps harping on those tomatoes. I need to be working every extra hour of overtime I can in order to afford my new Jerry habit. Are you sure you and he don't have some sort of scheme going to trick me out of my savings? Because if you do? Just a fair warning, it's below the minimum balance. Frankly, I'm at the red alert stage."

She took a drink of her coffee and felt immediately cheered. He'd known that she liked lots of cream and lots of sugar. When had he learned that?

"It happens. Happened to me. But if you can make it through this, just think. Belle Paix will be beautiful, just like she looked when Ambrose first turned the key in the door."

"No. No, she won't. You know why?" Allison rose from her chair and sorted through a basket of papers on the counter, which was cluttered with canisters and baskets Jerry had had to move to work on the electricity and plumbing. She retrieved the variance paperwork and slapped it down in front of Kyle on the scarred oak kitchen table.

"What's this?" he asked.

"The variance request application for the changes to the exterior. The paperwork you said you'd help me with? Well, I stayed up until four this morning filling it out."

He thumbed through it, skimming its contents. "Allison..."

"And you know what? You are going to help me get it passed. Yes, you. Because you know why? You sicced Jerry on me. And Jerry has spent all the money I didn't have in the first place—money I might have been able to scrape together to paint this house in historically accurate colors—and I checked, Kyle. I keep hearing quotes of fifteen thousand dollars to paint this house. I'd do it myself, but it's so huge it would take me forever. Plus, the rental fees on the scaffolding to reach the third story would cost me nearly that much. No, *you* are going to help me get this variance approved!"

Kyle rubbed his forehead and chewed on his bottom lip. "It doesn't work like that, Allison. You know that. I've told you. The committee—"

"Hang the committee! This house is falling apart. I have to paint it, at least—and I could put Hardie Board or vinyl siding on for the same cost. Anything but having to face this exorbitant bill again in ten years! But okay, I'll meet you halfway. Let me paint it with two colors, and I'll drop the request for the vinyl siding. Because I have *no* money."

"Why not borrow what you need to do the job right? It's a good investment," he told her. "Think of it like this—a renovation loan would be cheaper than rent or a house payment on a much smaller house that doesn't hold nearly the same sentimental value. This house has been in your family for how many generations? You should want to be a good steward and use top-quality—"

"Borrow? Kyle. I'm still paying off student loans! Not to mention a car payment, and it's not like I aim to mooch off Gran! I took a ten-grand pay cut to move back down here to take care of her, so I'm not really able to float a loan right now. Besides, I've got nothing to put up for collateral. It's Gran's house."

"Well, then, Gran can borrow it against Belle Paix, and you pay it back for her."

"Are you insane? Gran won't ever take out a mortgage on Belle Paix. She didn't do it for my college education, and that was really important to her. No. Her dad nearly lost this house in the Great Depression, and they sold eggs—sold *eggs*, Kyle—to pay off a mortgage he took out back then. She has definite ideas about debt, and they don't include putting a lien on Belle Paix."

He shook his head. "That's a really shortsighted view. This is an investment. You have no idea how many people would be willing to take that risk for a house of this caliber."

"I'm not one of 'em. And neither is Gran. So." Allison pointed a finger at the packet of papers he was thumbing through. "You fix that. You get my variance."

He stood up, his chair scraping against the kitchen's wide plank pine flooring, which Jerry had just unearthed this week. "If I do that, Allison, if I recommend that you go with a historically inaccurate paint scheme for the jewel of the neighborhood…it sets a precedent. And it's not fair. What about all those home owners who have gone to the trouble and expense to make sure they comply with the ordinance? Not only does this tell them that they could have done without it, but it also affects their house values."

"So you're telling me you won't do this? You won't recommend approving my request?"

"I'll look at it. But…if I tell you that it wouldn't pass, well, you'd better not put in the request, because you can submit only one application per project a year, and then you have to wait a full twelve months."

"That's crazy!" Allison exclaimed.

"No. It's designed to preserve the sanity of the committee, so we're not peppered with request after request on the same project. Lots of preservation committees have the same rule."

"I don't care. I'm out of money, I can't borrow any and Gran won't, so it's up to you. You can fix this. You can help me see my way out. Those people? They'll listen to you. I know it."

He wasn't really paying any attention to her words, though. He was dragging himself to the back door. He stopped as he opened it, and glanced over his shoulder at her. "I said I'd look through it and give you my opinion before you submit it. But I can already tell you, based on a quick scan, that it's not going to fly."

CHAPTER ELEVEN

ALLISON STRAIGHTENED UP and heard a pop as she released a crick in her neck. Her knees ached from crouching down on the floor to paint Gran's bedroom baseboard. There had to be miles of it left to go, and a fancy molding atop it to boot, but she'd been curled up like a pretzel for what seemed hours.

Directly below her she heard a loud clang and the sound of Jerry's favorite swear expression, "Jumpin' Jehosaphat!" which had amused her to begin with. The idea that a contractor wouldn't curse in this house was a novelty, given all the swearing the house had wrung from almost every repairman who'd ever stepped foot across its threshold.

But in the past week and a half, she'd realized that Jerry uttering "Jumpin' Jehosaphat" preceded "It's your only option."

She sighed and put down the paintbrush. A glance around the room gave her some small measure of comfort: the walls were finally patched and plastered to Jerry's satisfaction, and she had a coat of primer on them. Behind those walls lay new wiring and insulation "to keep the old girl's ribs warm," Jerry had said, and he wasn't talking about Gran.

It was amazing and a bit irritating how Kyle and Jerry talked about this house as though it were a person. To them, the house was never an "it." The house was either "Belle Paix," uttered in reverent tones, or "she" or "the old girl" or, for Jerry, on a particularly bad day, "the cranky old dame."

Allison couldn't figure out whether the fact that they personified it as a woman was what bothered her or whether it was that they treated the house with more respect than they sometimes accorded her. In a fight over what was historically accurate or what Allison preferred as a pragmatic fix, she often felt the house won.

And her bank account lost. The little nest egg she'd saved over the years was down to a pittance, and the outside of the house hadn't yet been touched. Well, that wasn't strictly true—she'd caught Jerry scraping down one of the cast-iron porch posts, but she'd put a stop to that pretty quickly.

And Kyle? He'd made himself scarce after that set-to they'd had the other morning. She'd caught Jerry and him putting their heads together a few times this week, but Kyle always had some excuse to rush out the door as soon as he saw her.

Was it that he knew he should help her with that variance, but was too chicken to recommend it to his committee? Or…

Did he just decide he didn't much care for her?

Maybe he never had. Maybe the only fascination Allison held was the key to Belle Paix's front door.

Now really, what should she have expected? It wasn't as if she had time for any sort of relationship. She was here for her grandmother. What's more, Kyle, with his exasperating ideas of "doing right by Belle Paix," drove her nuts. Pragmatism was the thing. Good old-fashioned horse sense.

And Kyle needed it by the boatload.

Cleo hissed and erupted from her perch high on a ladder in the corner of the room.

Allison stared up to see the feline stretching out in a graceful downward cat yoga position. At least Cleo didn't seem to mind Jerry. It was almost as if the blasted cat knew they were closer than ever to getting her Person home—at least for a visit.

"That's right, Cleo. We both need a break." Allison reached over and tore off a strip of plastic wrap to protect the paintbrush, then laid it aside. “I’m taking a walk, and I don’t care if I am covered in paint. This room has waited twenty years for a new paint job. It can wait another twenty minutes.”

Downstairs, she found Jerry muttering over the installation of new subway tiles behind the kitchen counters, the old ones having been damaged as he’d made holes to access the wiring. It was 7:30 at night, but he showed no sign of heading home.

“Jerry…your crew has left you. Don’t you think you ought to call it a day?” she asked.

“Nah, I’m okay. Besides, this here? This is on the house. I can’t leave the old girl like this, with her tile half done. I get this in for you tonight and you can grout it first thing in the morning. Save you some bucks if you do it yourself.”

Allison didn’t know where his sudden economies had come from in the past few days, but he’d begun to suggest little things she could do to help speed his crew along. She’d learned a lot—like how backbreaking and tedious grouting bathroom walls could be. Her right hand and fingers had ached so much afterward that she’d been reduced to a leftie for a day and a half—not a good thing when you were pulling a busy weekend shift in the ER. Now it looked as if the kitchen walls would be hers, too.

Oh, well. She appreciated every nickel he saved her, even if she secretly suspected he hoped she'd spend it on some other project to "tickle the old girl's toes."

"Er, okay. I need some air. I'm going to stretch my legs for a few minutes. I'm about halfway through with the baseboard in Gran's room."

"That plaster finally matched up, hey?" But his grin was short-lived as he went back to the current irritation at hand. "Jumpin' Jeh—"

She left before he could tell her what her latest only option was.

Outside, the air was warm and muggy, even this late in the evening. Despite that fact, she walked briskly, heading away from downtown to the newer part of the historic section.

Most of these houses were smaller than those on the main drag, and newer by a few decades. They'd been built probably in the thirties or forties, around a park, with neatly groomed yards and picket fences.

Allison could imagine wives in dresses with nipped-in waists and flared skirts setting out pies to cool on the wide kitchen window ledges, men in crew cuts wielding push mowers to keep the lawns lush and manicured, girls in dresses and penny loafers running away from brothers chasing them with frogs or spiders.

Some of the houses were like Gran's, just a touch sad and neglected. But most were breathtakingly restored to perfection. They sat back on their perfect lawns and practically glowed in the twilight, set off by the lightning bugs.

Allison saw one house that just took her breath away—a smart white two-story, with blue shutters. A pair of window boxes on the upstairs windows and another perched over the front door spilled sunny yellow marigolds, orange nasturtiums and dark purple petunias. She marveled at the green thumb the home owner must have, for the rest of the yard was just as beautiful.

The house was one of those with a white picket fence, complete with still more petunias running rampant alongside it. Out front, by the door and its peaked gothic dormer, a wooden bench seemed to invite guests to walk up the brick path and have a seat.

And if it was too hot to enjoy the bench, a person could most likely sneak under the covered porch and have a snooze on the enameled glider. Really, Allison could have believed she'd been swept back in time to the 1930s.

The flawless restoration made her envious and restless at the same time. This was what Kyle had been talking about when he'd gone on and on about historical accuracy. Now that she had seen the real thing, the house next to it, despite its neat exterior, didn't hold a candle to it.

Those folks sank a fortune into that house, she thought, trying to ward off a wave of despair. If she got her variance, Belle Paix would always be missing that little something extra—something that an accurate paint job would do for it.

Oh, for a cool twenty grand to be able to have Belle Paix painted the way it should be. If it weren't such a huge old white elephant, it would cost only about half that. But that's what she kept hearing from every contractor—if a painter even bothered to bid on the job.

Could she paint it herself? No. She'd considered that notion already and had to dismiss it. The project was definitely one for the pros.

Sighing, Allison started walking again, past the house, to circle the rest of the park. From one of the houses drifted the delicious smell of someone's supper on the grill, and her rumbling stomach reminded her that she'd taken time to grab only a piece of cheese and bread for her lunch.

"Hey! Allison!"

When she heard her name, she stopped, turned around. Yes, it was Kyle. He stood on the covered porch, his hand cupped around his mouth as an impromptu megaphone. She blinked. With his dark pants, crisp white shirt and cropped hair, he fit perfectly with the rest of the house's ambience.

She took a few hesitant steps back toward it. Kyle loped down to the gate and threw it open. "I saw you through the patio doors. Did you need to see me?"

"Uh, no, I was just taking a walk. To stretch my legs. So…this is your house?" she asked.

Of course it was. She should have known from its immaculate exterior that it was Kyle's.

"Yeah." He turned and regarded the house with evident pride. "A 1926 Sears kit house… kind of rare, actually. The model was Glen Falls."

"It's gorgeous. I love your window boxes."

"I cheated." He winked. "A local nursery guy helped me with them—he picked out all the flowers that would do well. I'm not much of a gardener, I'm afraid."

"Ha. My cheat would have been to take the window boxes down," she told him.

For a moment, he frowned, as though trying to figure out whether she was joking or not. "Just kidding," she said.

His face relaxed into a smile. "Ah. Would you…would you care to see the inside? I've bored everybody here in town with tours. Can I inflict my house pride onto you?"

"Sure," she said, but her uncertainty must have shown through.

He took her by the elbow. "Come on. If you're worried about getting back to your current project, it will still be there, waiting for you."

She tugged away from him. "How'd you know I was in the middle of a project?"

"The paint in your hair and, uh, everywhere else was an excellent clue," he told her.

"I have paint in my hair?"

Kyle pulled a curl tipped in white primer to show her in the fading evening light. "Yep. But it will wash out. Now your jeans—that might be a different story."

She stared down at the paint-spattered pair of jeans she was wearing and laughed. "These? They are beyond saving. I've actually started recycling them so I don't ruin another pair," Allison confessed.

"Smart girl," he said. He hadn't released the lock of her hair, though, and his nearness unnerved her. Then, his lips still quirking upward at the corners, he tucked the curl behind her ear, his fingers slipping along her cheek.

She shivered and reflexively covered his hand with her own. Kyle froze and raised an eyebrow in surprise.

She couldn't help it; all she could concentrate on was the texture of his skin. These weren't a professor's hands. A callus or two and a muscular leanness saved them from the softness she'd learned to associate with men who did little but push a pencil. And these weren't from tennis or handball or squash…no, these hands had wielded shovels and hammers.

"Can I have my hand back now?" he asked.

"Sorry. You just— I…" Allison decided that she should just shut up before she humiliated herself any further. "I'd like to see your house. Give me the nickel tour."

So he led up her up his herringbone-pattern brick path and opened the front door with a flourish. "See what being totally obsessed with a house can result in? I warn you, you may run away screaming."

She stepped across the vestibule and under an arched opening into a perfectly quaint center hall with stairs leading to the second floor. Down the corridor she caught a glimpse of another room—a study, she deduced, based on the big desk in front of a big window.

"Like I said, this was a kit house from Sears. The original owner ordered it from the 1926 catalog, and put it together himself, with the help of his brother. Cost him just over five grand. which was a pretty significant sum in those days."

"But this is beautiful! I thought Sears kit

homes were tiny things…I mean, didn't they have to be, in order to have them shipped?"

"No. There are even bigger homes that Sears sold—the Magnolia, for one, a large antebellum type with huge columns. They didn't sell as many of them as they did the smaller ones that you've heard of, but Sears was a big player back then. The company did a lot to standardize expectations. Before, you got whatever your local builder was willing to do, with not a lot of recourse. But once they had to compete against Sears and other catalog dealers…well, the local guys had to step it up a notch. Come on. I'll show you the rest."

The living room shouldn't have surprised Allison, but somehow it did. It wasn't girlie in the slightest, but wasn't the stereotypical man cave, with oversize leather couches and faux wood paneling. In one corner sat a grand piano, smaller than Gran's, but very respectable. The room was well lit by French doors, one pair at the back of the house, leading to a screened-in porch, another at the front, obviously how he'd spotted her.

And the room looked…new, but old at the same time, like a 1940s magazine ad.

Then it hit her. "No electronics! Where's the big screen TV? C'mon, you're a guy. You've got to have gadgets."

Kyle laughed. "Very observant. Yep, I do. I like my college football—I admit, I'm pretty much an equal-opportunity ESPN sports junkie, as well, when I'm not working on something." He crossed over to the wall near the front French doors and touched a hidden switch on what looked to be an old-fashioned hi-fi console. A good-sized flat screen slid up. "I just couldn't bring myself to spoil the effect by putting the television on the wall. So when my brother was on leave and here stateside—he's in the military—we rigged up this console table. Neat, huh?"

She gawked at it, realizing the hours of work that must have gone into hiding an anachronistic device like a television. Shaking her head, she didn't bother to smother the chuckle of disbelief that escaped her. "You *are* nuts. Did you know that?"

"That's what Pete told me. Why buy a flat screen if you can't show it off like art, huh? But this was the only room where I went to that trouble. The others…well, see for yourself."

They headed upstairs. As she followed him, Allison asked, "So how long did it take you? I mean, it looks perfect, so it was in pretty good shape to begin with, right?"

"Oh, you have no idea. It had this awful vinyl siding on it that had to come down, and someone had closed in the screened porch to make another bedroom." They had reached the top of the stairs, which ended at a window with a generous window seat.

"Up here are all the bedrooms," Kyle began, and then he must have seen her blushing like crazy.

What on earth has gotten into me? Allison resisted the urge to fan her flaming face. *I'm acting like an idiotic middle schooler. Of course he doesn't mean anything at all.*

Kyle sank down on the seat's upholstered cushion. "Tell you what. You go on and poke around all you want. I'll wait here. Holler if you have any questions."

Allison discovered more back-in-time rooms, complete with twin beds in one, antique furniture and simple coverlets. Tucked in out-of-the-way places were touches of modern life—digital alarm clocks, a stack or two of magazines—all of which, she had to admit, really did ruin the effect.

She could tell Kyle's bedroom at a glance, even if it was as neat as a pin. A little more tailored than the other rooms, it sported a big stack of DYI magazines, and history books on the bedside table. The attached bathroom, fitted out with enough old-fashioned ceramic fixtures and black-and-white floor tile to choke a goat, held more clues. The toothpaste and toiletries on the sink attested to the fact that, yes, this was his.

Allison let her fingers slide over a shaving brush beside a razor and a mug. The brush was damp, a testament that he really did use the silly old thing. She had a sudden image of him swathing his face with foam, then running the razor through thick, fluffy drifts of lather.

Jerking her hand back from the brush, she quickly headed to the hall, where Kyle patiently awaited her.

"Ha. I'm surprised you even allowed a digital alarm clock on the premises," she teased.

He sighed. "My brothers insisted the retro-look one I had in there to begin with went off in the middle of the night. I have to say, the digital ones are easier to set."

"Aha! So you do admit that modern life has its benefits!" she said as she took the first step back downstairs.

"Uh, I guess. I would miss ESPN," he allowed.

"So how long did you work on this house?" she asked, once downstairs and standing in the dining room, with its dark, antique furnishings.

"I'm still working on it. You know old houses. You fix one thing and something else goes wrong."

"Tell me about it. I'm one 'jumping Jehosaphat' from bankruptcy," Allison muttered darkly.

"Ouch. I should have warned you about that," Kyle said. "Those Jehosaphats are pretty expensive. Here, come into the kitchen. I've saved the best for last."

She pushed open an honest-to-goodness green baize door to see another rarity in modern homes. Tucked into a little slice between the dining room and the kitchen was a butler's pantry and a dining alcove with a built-in table under a window.

"They loved those little guys in the twenties," Kyle told her as she slid her palm over the table. "I'll bet it was a way a mom could have five minutes of peace at breakfast time—stick the kiddies in here, kiss the hubby goodbye and have herself a nice welcome cup of coffee with a dollop of solitude."

"It's so cute!"

"And tough to find a replacement. I thought I was going to have to rebuild a modern version. One of the previous owners had yanked it out and put a washer and dryer in here. At least the butler's pantry was still intact."

Allison rolled her eyes. "You took out a washer and dryer to replace a table, just to get things back to the original state? Dare I ask how you wash your clothes?"

"All in good time, all in good time. The kitchen awaits. If you think this is cool, the kitchen will knock your socks off."

So she pushed open another green baize door and gasped. "Oh. My. Word. This looks…this looks like Gran's!"

And it did, down to the checkerboard tile floor, the simple enameled cabinets, the single-basin sink. Unlike Gran's, though, the counters on either side of the sink were the same subway tile as the backsplash underneath the pair of windows above it.

"I did concede to a modern stove, only because my budget ran out before my wishes," he told her. "But…look, I even found the little swing-out seat that goes under the sink." He demonstrated. "This was where the lady of the house could rest her aching feet and back as she fixed supper."

"Oh, so cooking was only women's work?" Allison asked archly, taking a seat on the metal stool for a trial run.

"Heck, no, not always. My granddad cooked way better than my grandmother. She said so herself. And he taught my brothers and me what we know about cooking, because my mother didn't know how to boil an egg. Grandpa said if a man could learn to cook, hunt and fish, he'd never go hungry. No, when I refer to the lady of the house, I'm just going by the probabilities and the custom of the day."

Allison whirled around on the stool's slick red surface and took in the room. "I have to say, even though it looks like Gran's, it feels fresher. Newer. And brighter—plus you have a real, honest-to-goodness vent fan and—is that a French door fridge hidden over there? Honestly, I wish Gran's was tricked out this nicely. I've always hated cooking in it. I'm not looking forward to all those tomatoes."

"Couldn't talk her out of it, huh?" he asked.

"Nope. Not one whit. I'm to pick her up Friday afternoon and the tomato man will be by Saturday morning. With all. Those. Tomatoes."

"So what time do you need me there?"

Allison did a double take. "Huh? You're really going to help? I mean, I know it's a Saturday, but aren't you teaching summer classes?"

"It's a light load this semester, and I said I'd help you. I know nothing about preserving and canning, but then I knew nothing about carpentry when I found this house. They were selling it for fifteen grand, you know? Can you believe that? A four-bedroom house for a steal, even if it was in pretty bad shape."

"It's not now," she said wistfully. "It's beautiful now."

"And so will Belle Paix. Trust me. You feel overwhelmed and burdened and about to throw in the towel, but…"

"No buts, Kyle. Let's face it. You had years to tinker with this house, with nobody depending on you. I've got to get Gran's place in shipshape condition in the next short while. Her long-term care insurance is maxing out fast, and she wants to save some in case she needs to use it again. So it's not her just being impatient and cranky—though honestly, she has every right to be that way with me."

"Hey. Use a little perspective. You're getting the important things done, right? It may not be completed when she comes home, but you'll have safe wiring and better insulation and a chair lift for her. Not to mention you've saved her beloved bathroom sink."

"The chair lift won't be installed until next week, so I have no clue how I'll get Gran up to her room. And that sink cost me the better part of a grand in antique plumbing and repair kits. Talk about jumpin' Jehosaphats," Allison groused. "But if she's happy…"

"See? And she'll be happy. So you'll be happy. And little by little, you'll save a bit more money and do another project—"

"I have to get it painted or put siding on it before it really starts to rot, and those windows… the cold just cuts through them in the winter—"

He knelt in front of her. "Breathe. Take a good deep breath." When she just glared at him, he cajoled again. "Come on. Take that breath."

He put his palms on her shoulders, and she could feel the warmth of them through her T-shirt. She wondered if this exact same scene had played out before in this old kitchen, a 1930s harassed wife—in a dress and not paint spattered jeans—being reassured by her husband.

Only Kyle wasn't her husband. He'd drive her crazy if he were. Consoles to hide television sets, for goodness sake. Tearing out a perfectly good washer and dryer to put in the original built-in dining table. What utter nonsense.

"Okay, okay, I'm breathing—" she started. But suddenly she wasn't. Suddenly she was fixated on Kyle's mouth and how close it was, and how she could bend down and kiss him and hope he'd kiss her back. And on the heels of that thought, it seemed as if Kyle was leaning forward, almost, almost…

And just when she could have touched her lips to his, he pulled back. Stared up at her.

Then, without a word of explanation, he

shot to his feet and brushed his hands together. "Well, there you have it! The grand tour. Care for a glass of lemonade?"

CHAPTER TWELVE

KYLE RAISED HIS knuckles to Gran's door, chickened out and dropped his fist by his side. He was at the point of turning to beat it out of the rehab facility when he pictured Allison's confused and hurt face the previous afternoon.

Right after he should have kissed her.

She'd wanted him to. He'd wanted to. It should have been simple—you meet a woman, find her attractive, ask her out on a date, things progress…and then a kiss just comes naturally.

But not like this. You didn't kiss a woman when you knew you had to tell her no—and not just a simple no to a simple request.

The "no" Kyle had to tell Allison was in answer to what she thought was the solution to her problems, to her dream of bringing her grandmother home.

In fact, he'd just finished reading through her disaster of a variance request when he'd spotted her on the sidewalk. He'd thought it a perfect time to talk to her, to try and convince her not to submit it.

When Allison had been so blown away by his house, it felt like serendipity. Unlike any of the few women he'd dated seriously in the past, Allison had seemed intrigued by the house.

Maybe, he'd thought, he could show her rather than tell her. Maybe if he could show her that even big projects were doable, and that the reason his house worked was the care he'd put into it…

Or maybe you just wanted to show off, he told himself.

He couldn't dodge Allison forever on that variance request. If she turned in a copy to the committee office, that was that. They would have no choice but to turn her down, and then she would be stuck with a badly peeling paint job on Belle Paix for another year.

Because he just couldn't, in good conscience, recommend anything but a flat no to Allison's proposal.

He'd had a frank, honest talk with Jerry, telling him to cut out the worst of his excesses and giving him strict orders to help Allison contain costs. Kyle had hoped she would be able to use some of those savings to go toward a proper paint job. And he'd really talked up searching out grants and low-interest renovation loans and tax credits with Allison…

Only, she seemed determined to pay for the

whole project out of pocket, limiting herself to what she could afford to do for Belle Paix. She refused to consider any other sort of funding.

Time for plan B, he thought, then squared his shoulders and rapped on Gran's door.

"Come in!" she called. When she saw him, she nodded approvingly. "I knew you'd be back."

"Like a bad penny," Kyle told her.

"Well, think of the crick of my neck, young man, and grab a chair. This time you can have the comfortable one. You look as though you have something on your mind."

He yanked the armchair around and sank down onto it. "I do, actually. It's about Belle Paix."

"Allison tells me my bedroom's almost done. Says it's a nice periwinkle blue. That's my favorite color, you know."

"I do." For a moment, he didn't say anything, then cleared his throat and began. "I know the house means a lot to you. You were born there, right?"

"I was. Actually, the first Shepherd descendant not to be born there was Allison's father—he wound up being delivered at Dr. Masterson's hospital. Torn down, now, more's the pity. A parking lot for the post office, I think."

"Yes. Before I became chair of the preservation committee, or believe you me, it wouldn't have happened. Not on my watch."

"You are a zealous sort, aren't you? I do believe you would have stood in front of the wrecking ball yourself."

Kyle laughed and recalled more than one protest he'd been involved in during his college days. That was something else most women he'd dated didn't get. "You know, you might be right. But in all my work, I've never seen a house like Belle Paix."

Gran closed her eyes, breathed a sigh and nodded. "She's something, isn't she?"

"That she is. I'm glad Allison has been able to get some needed work done. It's really stabilizing the physical structure."

Gran's eyes fluttered open and she gripped the knob of her walking stick. "Pish-posh, Kyle. You're beating around about a dozen bushes here. You've got something on your mind besides what Allison's doing right. So spill it. I'm eighty-nine, not guaranteed another minute on this earth."

"Well…yes, ma'am, then. It's her variance application. She's put in a request that we waive the requirements for historically accurate exterior paint…and historically accurate windows…and historically accurate clapboard siding."

"Sounds sensible. But I told her not to bother

with that rigmarole because you were bound to shoot her down."

"Ma'am, all due respect, but if she made all those changes, you wouldn't be coming home to the Belle Paix you left. And you know it."

Gran's reply was a stony silence. She fixed him with an ice-cold glare from those brilliant blue eyes.

He rushed to fill the silence. "And besides… it's not up to me. I couldn't approve those changes even if I wanted to."

Gran waggled the walking stick in his direction like a giant, oversize pointer. "Ah! Now we're getting to the heart of the matter. 'Even if I wanted to,' indeed! Let me guess. You want me to talk Allison out of eminently sensible changes so you won't have to tell her no."

"It's not me telling her no—"

"Now, now, don't equivocate and dissemble. That's beneath you. You have to admit that you hold a good deal of sway over that committee. And you could ask for a waiver in the interest of one octogenarian who survives on a fixed income. They'd be inclined to listen to you."

"The ordinances are very clear—"

"And very wrong-headed. Allison shouldn't have to use her savings to fulfill your fantasy of how a perfect historic neighborhood should appear. I believe I told you before, when we had our difference of opinion on a quite similar variance request, that yours was a rich man's game."

"She could borrow the money. *You* could borrow the money. Think of it as an investment—" Kyle started.

But the old lady's nostril's flared and her lips thinned as she thumped her walking stick, nearly hitting him on the toe in the process. "I will not. She's already sacrificed enough as it is. You know, she had the opportunity to go to work with Doctors Without Borders? And she put it off to come live with me. That's what she was saving for, to be able to afford to help those less fortunate."

Kyle sucked in a breath. Why had Allison never shared this with him? Maybe because, in her mind, her grandmother was worth the sacrifice? "Ma'am, I had no idea. That's—that's impressive."

"And now..." Gran shook her head and stared down at her lap. "She's spent it all on Belle Paix."

Kyle reached out and laid a hand on the old woman's shoulder. He wanted to reassure her that Allison's sacrifice wasn't in vain. "Ma'am...there's a reason people say something is safe as houses. Investing her savings in Belle Paix is just that—savings—"

"Young man, might I remind you, the only way you get a return on a capital investment is if you liquidate that investment. And I don't want her forced to sell Belle Paix when I'm barely cold in the ground, just to get her money out. Because Lord knows, I don't have anything else to leave my granddaughter. You know what a forced sale means—you get a pittance of the value of the house if you can't wait for the right buyer."

Kyle massaged the nape of his neck. "There has to be some way—some compromise."

"The definition of a compromise means *both* parties are giving up something," she said tartly. "Allison and I are giving up our funds…so what will you put on the table?"

The chair, a cheap Queen Anne reproduction with a plasticized finish that might be easy to clean, but still irked him, creaked as he shifted his weight. "I don't know. There's nothing I can give. Nothing except my experience and my willingness to help."

"Help?" The yelp came from behind him, not from Gran. "Kyle! What are you doing here?"

He swiveled in the chair and saw Allison glaring at him from the door. Apparently it hadn't closed all the way, and she'd been able to push it open without a sound. "Oh, hi, Allison. I…I was just—"

Gran broke in with what seemed to be her trademark smoothness. "Coming by to see if I need a lift home. And I just might. Folding myself into your car puts me in mind of a pretzel. Kyle, what sort of vehicle do you gad about in?"

Allison did not look a bit convinced, and his needing a few beats to answer Gran's question didn't improve matters. "Oh, I have a pickup. It might be hard for you to get in, though."

"Is it one of those monster trucks with the huge wheels that you need a ladder to climb into?" Gran asked.

"No, no, just your garden variety truck with a crew cab. It's handy for hauling things."

At least the mention of his pickup served to distract Allison from her earlier suspicions. "For instance, a gas pump to haul around with you," she muttered. "Trucks like that guzzle fuel. Just another reason I have no business in the DIY arena. Gran, his truck's going to be too hard for you to get into. My car's not so bad."

Gran began scooting to the edge of her seat and readying herself to rise. "Well, Kyle, you'll help Allison get me home, now won't you? And have supper with us?"

He heard Allison's intake of breath and couldn't translate it. Was she hoping he'd say no?

"Oh, Gran, I'm sure he has better things to do," she interjected before he could answer.

Though he couldn't figure out what was going on in Allison's head, her grandmother was no mystery whatsoever. He could see a clear expression of "don't even think about saying no" in her eyes that had probably steered many a kid in the right direction during Gran's years of teaching.

"Actually, I'm glad to help," he said, and was gratified by the barest dip of Gran's chin in a nod of approval. "I'll help you get her settled in your car, and then I'll follow you to Belle Paix, how about that?"

"And supper, of course," Gran said. Now she flashed that same "don't even think about it" look Allison's way.

Allison struggled and failed to hide a grimace of exasperation. "About supper, Gran… I wasn't planning on cooking a big meal. I wanted the kitchen ready for tomorrow and those tomatoes. You know, you could just stay here and I'll get those tomatoes put up on my own. You've shown me how."

"Nonsense!" Gran planted her walking stick in front of her. "Then I'd miss all the fun! I might as well buy tinny-tasting canned ones from the grocery store if I don't have a hand in canning them myself. I'm not so long in the tooth that I can't pull my weight. Now, Kyle, if you'll just take my arm…"

To Kyle, Gran's biceps had the fragility of a bird wing. He was terrified that if he squeezed it too hard, he'd leave bruises, or worse yet, snap a delicate bone in two. And his heart practically froze in his chest when Gran wobbled in his none-too-steady grasp.

Allison jumped in to right her grandmother, and huffed again with still more exasperation. "Kyle, I've got this. Honestly, you're just getting in the way. I have a lot more experience transferring patients than you do."

He stood back and watched. Yes, it wasn't a question of strength, but skill. Now Gran rose steadily on her feet, the walking stick firmly planted beside her, her back arrow-straight.

"Nothing like getting old bones aright, now is there?" Gran muttered. But she smiled with grim triumph. "I might not be the most graceful girl anymore, but I have dispensed with the walker."

"Gran, it might not be a bad idea for you to take one home—" Allison began.

"On the contrary, it would be a very bad idea. A person must get around under her own steam, Allison. Independence is a habit, you know. Besides…" she winked in Kyle's direction "…I won't have a chance of catching Harvey Culpepper's eye if he sees me using a walker…and he's the only man in this place with all his teeth *and* a decent head of hair."

If she'd meant to shock her granddaughter, she'd failed. Allison just chuckled. "Okay. You win. Tell me where your overnight bag is, and we'll sally forth."

Gran's walking stick lasered in on a black overnighter that stood at the ready by the door. "That nice nurse's aide has it all packed for me, along with a packet of my medicines for tonight and tomorrow," Gran stated. Then she turned her attention back to Kyle. "Be a dear and grab it, please. And don't dilly-dally. You're so young and handsome that if you walk right beside me, Harvey might think you're after my money and be a bit jealous. Nothing like shaking the sugar tree, now, is there?"

CHAPTER THIRTEEN

ALLISON STUMBLED DOWN the back stairs, grateful that she could use them again and would save her at least a few steps as she answered the kitchen doorbell. She hadn't even had a chance to yank her still-damp hair back into a ponytail before the tomato man arrived.

She couldn't catch a break. Either deliverymen never showed up in the first place, or they were an hour early, she groused to herself.

But it wasn't a man bearing a crate of tomatoes awaiting her at the kitchen door.

It was Kyle.

Her heart fluttered at the sight of him until she sternly ordered it to stop. She opened the door, revealing the lanky figure, clad in jeans and a T-shirt and looking ready to work.

"You are an early bird," she said. "I didn't even hear your truck."

"It was such a gorgeous morning that I walked," he told her. "And I figured, as much trouble as we had getting Gran upstairs, you might need some help getting her back downstairs this morning."

He was right about that, as much as she was loath to admit it. The night before, Gran had insisted on stopping at her favorite Chinese take-out place, never mind the loads of sodium that would not be good for her blood pressure. They'd eaten out of the cartons at the dining room table, a first that Allison could recall. Usually her grandmother insisted on plating up even fried rice on her fine china.

Gran might have been flexible about the dishes, but she wouldn't budge on her bedroom. It had taken both Kyle and Allison considerable time and effort to help her upstairs.

To Allison, though, once she heard her grandmother's "ooh!" of pleasure, it had been worth it. The rest of the house might still be a disaster, but Allison had forcibly put that out of her mind and vowed to concentrate on finishing Gran's bedroom and the upstairs bath.

Gran had slid her hands over the periwinkle walls, the fresh white molding, the coverlet on the four-poster bed. Then she'd sagged down onto the mattress beside a contented Cleo, curled up at the end of the bed.

Gran had exhaled sharply. Her mouth had trembled a bit, until she'd compressed it tightly and closed her eyes. Then she'd breathed out again and opened her eyes.

"Thank you. Thank you both very much," she'd murmured. "Why, I—I wasn't sure if I'd ever see this room again."

It had been all Allison could do not to burst into tears. She knew that when it came time to take her grandmother back Sunday, to finish her prescribed physical therapy, she would cry coming home, just as she had the first time she'd visited Gran.

Now, this morning, the memory of Gran's pleasure brought a huge lift in Allison's spirits and reminded her why all this trouble was worth it. It was for Gran.

"Uh, yeah, thanks," she told Kyle. "I heard her moving around a few minutes ago. Why don't you get a cup of coffee and wait here while I go check to see if she's ready for company?"

"Point me to it," he said.

She turned in the direction of the coffeepot. It was empty. "Oh, no! I forgot to turn it on last night! I meant to…I set it on a timer—"

"I got it. You go check on Gran. I think I can—whoa! This is the first time I've noticed, but that's a Chambers stove, isn't it?" Kyle walked over to the big hunk of junk Allison had kicked more times than she could remember as she was learning to cook.

"Yes. It is. And Gran can't bear to have it replaced."

He ran a hand over the enameled surface and gave her a quizzical look. "Why on earth would you have it replaced? What's wrong with it?"

"According to Gran, nothing. But it is the most aggravating, infernal device to cook on. What I wouldn't give for a smooth top electric." Allison reached past him for the coffee canister, surprised again at the sinewy muscles in his arms as she brushed against him. She nearly dropped the canister, but managed to save it, just as Kyle grabbed for it, too.

"So." Her face felt hot. "Clumsy."

"Too many late nights," he said.

She smiled at his joke. "You bet."

He took the coffee from her. "Go on. I've got this. Unless you're particular about your coffee."

"All right—hey, let the tomato man in if he gets here, okay?"

"Will do."

Upstairs, Allison found Gran dressed and ready, beaming at her bedroom.

"Cleo and I have decided that I'll just stay here and not go back," she announced, stroking the cat. The Siamese gave Allison a smug know-it-all smirk before snuggling closer to Gran. "It's much nicer at home, even if I wouldn't see Harvey as much. Besides, his son took his keys away. Can't go on a date with a man who doesn't drive."

"Oh, Gran. I wish you could stay. And in a very short time, you *will* be home. But they made me promise to have you back so you could finish your therapy. Besides, after we put up all those tomatoes, you'll enjoy a break and being waited on hand and foot."

"Pshaw! I don't think so. It's fun for maybe a week, and then you just itch to do something for yourself. But it's always, 'why, no, Miss Lillian, you can't do that,' and 'careful, Miss Lillian, you'll hurt yourself.' Might as well put me in a wad of that bubble wrap. Has he brought the tomatoes and the beans yet? I heard voices."

"No, that was Kyle—wait! Beans? What beans?"

"Just a few handfuls of green beans. He offered them to me free of charge. Said they'd dry up on the vine if we didn't take them. No reason to let them go to waste."

"Gran! Speaking of handfuls—we'll have our hands full of tomatoes today."

She waved off Allison's protest. "Pish-posh. Anybody who can't can a few tomatoes and beans, well, they need a lesson. So you're going to help me down those stairs? I tell you, your lift chair might be just the thing once you get it installed."

"If I ever do… Just a minute. Kyle is here and is going to help us—"

"Oh, good." Gran grabbed her walking stick and pounded it on the floor, startling the cat. "That'll bring him running. It's what my grandmother did whenever she needed us. Worked a treat, I tell you!"

It really did bring Kyle running. He appeared at Gran's doorway after pounding his way up the back stairs. Allison found herself at once irritated and impressed that despite his haste, he wasn't the least bit winded.

"Ready?" he asked.

"Oh, yes," Gran said. "Are the tomatoes and beans here?"

"Brought 'em not five minutes ago. Two bushels of tomatoes and a bushel of green beans. That sound about right?"

"Why, no!" Gran frowned. "There should have been three bushels of tomatoes. Two bushels will barely get us started. That won't even be fifty quarts."

Allison thought about all the painting and spackling and caulking and sanding that still needed doing, not to mention laundry. She'd hoped for a single bushel of tomatoes, not a mountain.

"Gran…really, fifty quarts of tomatoes is a lot for just the two of us."

"I was planning on sharing them with some of my friends at the center."

"Oh, that's sweet, but we'll have plenty to share," Allison assured her.

"Plus, we have to share with Kyle here. After all, he's graciously agreed to help us."

"We'll have more tomatoes than you can shake a stick at. One pint per meal would be more than enough for either me or Kyle, probably both. But…" Allison took in her Gran's disappointment and prayed her next words wouldn't come back to haunt her. "If you're not happy with the yield, I'll can get some more for you next week."

Gran sighed. "If you insist. I still think, since we have everything out already, it makes more sense to…"

But Allison was ushering her to the door as tactfully as she could, and then they began the arduous process of getting her downstairs. Allison had a sneaky feeling that her grandmother had not told her doctors at the center that she would be managing stairs…but then again, since they hadn't outright prohibited the activity, maybe they thought it was good therapy. Or more likely they thought Allison would have better sense than to let Gran tackle a steep flight of stairs in a rickety old Victorian house.

She appreciated Kyle's calm, step-by-step approach to the staircase and then the tomatoes. He set Gran to work snapping green beans, and then somehow magically managed to convince her to can the beans whole—something Allison had never been able to con her grandmother into doing.

Meanwhile, he started washing the tomatoes, while Allison began sorting the ones suitable for blanching.

Kyle in the kitchen, she found, was as good a helper as he was with a paintbrush. He did argue with her about the most efficient method of doing something, and it aggravated her when Gran would wade into their squabbles and suggest that she try Kyle's suggestion. It aggravated Allison even more when he hit upon a way that actually did work better.

By 10:00 a.m. the kitchen looked as though a bomb had gone off in a produce stand, with dribbles of tomato juice here and there on the white enamel cabinets and yellowed marble countertops. Allison had long ago given up on keeping her T-shirt clean and had resorted to wearing one of Gran's aprons.

Still, the pressure canner was loaded, locked

and starting to steam with a full quota of green beans. The first batch of tomatoes was coming out of the water bath canner, and the second batch was progressing. She was beginning to see light at the end of the tunnel—or maybe it was light from a volcano, as hot as it was in the kitchen.

The kitchen had begun to heat up as the first huge, hot-water-bath canner went on the stove. Now, Allison's back was sticky with a film of perspiration. She noticed how Gran's face was entirely too pink to suit her. Even Kyle, usually cool, calm and collected, had become more short-tempered.

Allison swiped her brow with her forearm and gave up. "Let me go see if that air-conditioner needs turning down," she said. "It's really getting hot in here."

"Nothing compared to what it was before we had that unit put in, I tell you," Gran called after her. "Why, Kyle, I could tell you stories..."

Which, Allison thought, was what her grandmother had done all morning long as she'd supervised the two of them—kept Kyle entertained by telling stories from years past. It had kept Allison entertained, as well. She wished that she'd thought to tape her grandmother's tales. They were always interesting, usually funny and sometimes even a little eyebrow-raising.

Allison walked to the front hall, where the thermostat to the ancient central unit was located. No wonder they were hot—it was nearly 80 degrees in here. It had to be a half-dozen degrees hotter in the kitchen at least. But…

She noticed that the thermostat was set to a reasonable 72. So why wasn't the air coming on?

She bumped it down first to 68, then to a snowball-ejecting 65. Nothing. The air refused to come on.

Allison threw back her head with a groan and kicked the baseboard. "No!" she moaned. "No, no, no, please, please don't do this to me, not today!"

Kyle came into the hall. "What is it?"

"The air-conditioner is broken. It won't come on."

"Huh."

"Huh? No—disaster, not huh."

But Kyle was already fiddling with the device, peering first at the numbers and then removing the cover to reveal its innards.

"Why now? I mean, I know it's ancient, but couldn't it have lasted one more day?"

"Shh," Kyle said. "Let me think." Then he

looked over at her. "Where's the unit? On the roof? Behind the house?"

"In the backyard. It's a heat pump Gran had put in fifteen years ago. Maybe twenty. It's probably a goner."

"Is there a window near it? Go stand there and tell me if it makes a sound when I call out, okay?"

She frowned. "You can fix this?"

"Maybe. Maybe not. But before you spend a fortune on a Saturday emergency call, let's see." He grinned.

Her spirits sank as she heard nothing coming from the machine when he signaled to her a few minutes later. She was halfway back to him when he called, "Hey, can you turn off the breaker to the heat pump?"

"Uh, sure. Wait! Gran! You can't lift that!" She had spied her grandmother trying to lever a basket of green beans from the pasta pot they were using to blanch them in. Allison dashed to remove the basket to the sinkful of ice cubes, and switched off the burner on the stove. "Just wait for a bit, okay? Let me see about the air-conditioner."

"Young woman, you are treating me like a two-year-old—" Gran protested, but her complaint was interrupted by a shout from Kyle.

"Allison?" he called. "Got that breaker off?"

"In a minute!" she yelled back.

The breaker off, she hurried back to Kyle. "Off. Wait! That looks dangerous—"

He was deftly wrapping the bare ends of two wires together, without gloves or electrical tape or even so much as a pair of insulated pliers.

"Don't worry. I know what I'm doing. My dad was an electrician and my brothers and I helped him in the summers. See? The power's off, and besides, it's low voltage. Might give me a tickle, but it won't kill me—got it! You can turn the breaker back on, and we'll see what happens."

She flipped the switch, and to her joy heard the familiar, welcome groan of the air-conditioner coming on.

"You fixed it!" she cried jubilantly as she raced back into the hall. "Yay you!"

He shrugged. "No big deal. It's your thermostat. Tell you what. I'll run get another one and replace it, one of those programmable ones that will save you some money. How about it?"

"I'd love you forever," she told him. And then realized the words that she'd used. "Er, you know what I meant..."

"Gotcha." He snapped the cover back on the thermostat. "It won't hurt it to run like this for a bit, just until I get back. That way the house will have a chance to cool off."

"Thanks. I—I really appreciate this."

"I know." Kyle winked. "You'll love me forever."

And then, before she could say anything, he was bidding goodbye to Gran and stepping out the door. Allison stood there, thinking how much easier the world was when you had someone in your corner.

And maybe Kyle would stay in that corner… maybe he understood that she needed that variance. After all, he saw how much this place meant to Gran, how much she wanted to be home for good.

CHAPTER FOURTEEN

"I'LL NEVER LOOK at a tomato the same way." Kyle groaned and rubbed an ache in the small of his back as he collapsed on the bottom step of the front stairs.

He hadn't felt this tired since the early days when he was renovating his house. His feet hurt, his hands hurt, his body felt as though it had been pummeled from head to toe.

A metallic "pop!" echoed all the way from the kitchen, and then another. The sound elicited a grin from Allison. "That was quart number thirty-one and thirty-two sealing," she told him. "Beautiful sound, no?"

"Pulverizingly close to angels singing on high," Kyle muttered. "What time is it? And how on earth are you still so chipper?"

She was beyond chipper, actually. Usually it was Kyle giving her pep talks, but now it was Allison whose face was wreathed in smiles. She grabbed him by the hand and tugged. "Almost midnight. C'mon. The sound will travel up the stairs and keep Gran awake."

"And you know this how?" He pushed himself off the stairs and stumbled for the living room. "Oh, whoa. I'm not even close to being clean enough to sit on Gran's chairs."

"The front porch, silly," Allison told him. She opened the door and led him outside, where the air had finally cooled off.

Kyle collapsed onto the wicker love seat and pulled Allison to sit beside him. "Now spill. What's your secret energy source? And let me guess, you sat on the landing and eavesdropped on all of Gran's conversations."

"Uh, not all of them. Just the ones that concerned me, and only until I was about, oh, twelve or so. At that point, I figured I knew it all, anyway. The back stairs are even better, though, because I could hide just beyond the landing, and I was closer to the kitchen."

Kyle let the velvety night air soak into him, listened to the quiet of a small town put to bed for the night. Beside him, he sensed Allison's high energy subside into something more calm and restful. "You've always lived here? With your gran, I mean?"

"Yeah. Well, not always. My parents were killed in a car accident in 1987, when I was almost four, and that's when I came to live here. I don't even remember them. Gran and Pops were the only parents I ever knew, and he died when I was in high school."

"Had to be hard."

"Oh, yeah—Gran was sixty-three when she took me in, and Pops was five years older. My father was almost forty when I was born, so I came along late in everybody's life. That's why—well, Gran could have said no, you know?" A tremor shook Allison's voice, and she bit her lip. "She could have arranged for an adoption. I mean, the way I understand it, the family and children's aid people urged her to do that because she was so old at the time. Old! Sixty-three seems young now that I see Gran at nearly ninety."

That explains the tight bond between them, Kyle thought. "The Gran I've come to know would have never turned her back on her family," he said. "I'm sure she never even considered it."

"That's what I mean. She practically blessed those bureaucrats out when they advised her she and Pops should give me to a young couple. At least, that's the story Pops told me when I was an ungrateful twit of a teenager. And I get it now, the sacrifices she made. She raised one child on her own—Dad—after my biological grandfather died in World War II. It wasn't until my dad was five or so that she remarried. And then, boom! At sixty-three, she had to grieve for the loss of her only son and start raising a grandchild?" Allison shook her head. "She's tougher than I ever could be, Kyle. And she deserves to be able to come home. She's fought to keep this house through all manner of catastrophes, and I aim to see she lives out her last days here, and that they're warm and comfortable."

There was an edge to her voice, a challenge that Kyle could not mistake. She was thinking about that variance.

He pictured it, the thick stack of paperwork that Allison had painstakingly filled out. He'd started to circulate it around to committee members in an informal way, trying to get a read on any compromise they might be willing to give. But already he had heard from at least two members that they thought the same way he had… Belle Paix deserved to be treated right, and any substandard renovations would serve to damage not only the home's value, but the neighborhood's character.

Plus, there was the question of precedent. If the committee allowed this, some other person, for less noble reasons, could take the committee to court and have a good chance of getting the entire ordinance thrown out.

It irked him that never before had he gone to this much trouble with a variance request. He really shouldn't be doing what he was doing—legally, it could get him into a bind. But it was for Gran.

No. It's for Allison and *Gran.*

For now, Kyle chose to ignore Allison's not-so-veiled allusion to the topic. "You're making progress," he assured her. "You're pretty much down to the cosmetic part—you know, repainting the kitchen and all the rooms where the plaster had to be knocked out for the wiring."

She tipped her head back and stared at the porch ceiling…which Kyle had noticed just minutes earlier was peeling. "I hadn't planned on the expense of painting all the rooms, you know. This is really eating into my funds. And the outside… If I don't do something with the exterior of this old place, dry rot will set up. It can't wait much longer."

Again, Kyle tried to distract her from the tough challenge that posed. "So what color are you going to paint the kitchen?" he asked.

She slid a squint-eyed glance his way. "I'm sure you have a historically accurate suggestion."

Kyle chuckled. "As a matter of fact…"

"I knew it."

"Well, it was something Gran said in one of her stories tonight. She said the kitchen was buttercup yellow, remember?"

"That, according to her, was my great-grandmother's favorite color."

"It was actually a very popular color in the twenties and thirties…and that kitchen is early 1930s from the look of it, not too much older than mine. I am just blown away by how it's still intact."

"Yeah, well, if it was good enough for Ambrose," Allison muttered. She stretched out her feet on the table and groaned.

"You'd rip it all out, wouldn't you? Put in new cabinets and granite countertops and a smooth top electric range and a chandelier, something straight out of a big-box DIY store's dream kitchen catalog."

She sat up and twisted in the love seat to face him. Her eyes seemed full of uncertainty. "I don't know. Maybe. But is that such a sin? I mean, after all, Ambrose used the latest technology and design when he built this house in the first place. It was shockingly modern for its time."

"But it was new. Sure, if you're building a house from the ground up, go modern if you want. But it's going to look dated really quickly, whereas your grandmother's kitchen…"

"Just looks sad." Allison propped an elbow on the back of the seat, then dropped her chin on her forearm.

"No. Tired, maybe. I'll grant you that. Still, the new subway tiles look great."

"Do you know, Jerry worked for nearly two hours to match the new grout to the old stained grout? You can't even tell what's new about it." Allison shook her head in amazement. "In the time he took with that, he could have put a coat of primer on at least one downstairs room."

"Sure, but now it doesn't look patched. And those marble countertops may be yellowed, but they're worth a fortune."

"I realize that. I really wouldn't gut it, you know. I don't think, anyway. At least the cabinets are okay, really. The drawers stick, but I kinda think I'd miss it if they didn't. Still, Gran could use a new fridge—that's not original, so you'd let me get by with replacing that, right?"

"You could get those decorative doors and do a built-in, and it would—"

"No. Absolutely not. You can't have ice and water through the door with the decorative doors. And I like my ice and water through the door."

"You don't have it now."

Allison sat upright and folded her arms across her chest. "But I did, and I know what I miss."

"Okay. But at least get stainless steel, all right? It tends to blend in better than the other finishes."

"Wow." She blew a raspberry and waggled her eyebrows. "Next you'll be telling me it's okay to ditch the stove."

"No! That's a Chambers! And it works fine. How many quarts of tomatoes did we can on that thing?"

"Let's see…with the extra bushel the guy brought later, we wound up with sixty-seven. Of which Gran says you get a third."

"Can I just come here and eat them? They'll taste better cooked on a Chambers stove," Kyle quipped.

She made a move to swat him, missed and fell against him. For a moment, Kyle's breath went out in a whoosh as he felt her weight against him. When she made a sudden move backward, he held her gently in place.

"Hey. Where are you off to?" The huskiness in his voice surprised him.

"I—I dunno."

The crickets and frogs ramped up to a crescendo as he debated the wisdom of what he was about to do.

"How many couples do you think sat on this porch, maybe even in this very seat, just like we're doing now?" he whispered, tracing her cheek with his finger. He liked the way her lips were quivering with a half smile, that the pulse jumped at the base of her throat.

"Hmm. That's over a century and a quarter. Got to be a lot."

"I wonder if they felt like me."

Now it was her fingers on his skin, sliding along his arms to his shoulders to lightly hold him. "And how exactly do you feel?"

He closed his eyes to concentrate on his answer. Talking about feelings was never easy for him. He could describe events and people and complicated political theories, but feelings? He needed to get this right.

"Happy. Yeah. And…like I'm in the calmest place on earth." He opened his eyes again.

She stared at him, then looked away. In an instant, he felt the connection between them break and all his earlier doubts and misgivings begin to flood in.

He didn't want to think about all that, not the variance, not the house. In the darkness, he could pretend the Victorian was perfectly painted, that the rattan in their seats didn't need recaning, that Allison fully "got" his yen for historical accuracy.

So, impulsively, he craned his neck to meet her eyes, muttered, "I'm probably going to get slapped for this," and kissed her.

And she kissed him back.

And then she didn't. In one frenetic move,

she was up on her feet, her arms clasped protectively around herself.

"It's late. I need to go check on Gran." Allison bit her lip and rushed on. "Thanks for everything. I really appreciate your help today… and on that variance, too. I need to get a move on, you know."

With that, she left him on the front porch. The door thudded softly behind her, the lock clicked with a loud squeak and the crickets started up again.

But at least she hadn't slapped him.

CHAPTER FIFTEEN

ALLISON STARED UP at a ceiling brown with age as she lay in the huge antique bed. The morning sun streamed in the bedroom's windows and at least gave the dingy ceiling a charming touch of sepia.

Ha. There was nothing charming about this house.

No, that wasn't true. She loved this place, but it required so much dedication and sacrifice. And she was afraid that she didn't love it quite enough.

That's why she had jerked back from Kyle last night. That, and the way he'd hesitated again before he'd kissed her. Because if he had doubts and she had doubts, well, maybe it was best not to push things.

And of course she had doubts. It wasn't simply about Kyle's unbending need for historic accuracy. It was that, deep down, she knew she'd never have that same need. Even last night, as they'd sat there, they hadn't talked about life and goals and dreams. They'd talked about refrigerators and paint.

What happened when the house was done and they no longer had anything like that to talk about? And done to her specifications, not to Kyle's? Because she had a feeling he could tinker with Belle Paix forever.

Belle Paix. Now he was rubbing off on her, and she was even calling the house by its fancy French name.

She threw off the covers and was about to bounce out of bed with a loud thump when she remembered Gran across the hall.

Gran hadn't stirred. Maybe she was still asleep? They'd kept her up awfully late.

Tiptoeing across the hall, Allison peeked into her room. There her grandmother lay, serenely curled up in a ball, her breath moving through her tiny body in that huge old bed that was even bigger and chunkier than Allison's. Cleo raised her head from her place at Gran's feet and blinked. Leave it to Gran to have the one ninja guard cat in the world.

Satisfied that she was sleeping okay for now, Allison slipped back across the hall and pulled on jeans and a T-shirt. She'd fix Gran a good breakfast, if that cranky old Chambers stove would cooperate, and maybe take her out for a late lunch before she had to get her back to the facility.

Downstairs, Allison reviewed with satisfaction the rows of jars full of tomatoes and green beans on the shelves. It looked as though they had all sealed, and later today she could move part of them to the pantry and the rest to the daylight basement downstairs. At least she could mark one item off her to-do list.

But behind those rows of jars, the kitchen, with its patchwork of new plaster repairs against the tired old painted plaster, stood ready to remind her that loads of work still needed to be done.

And fast, if she wanted to bring Gran home to at least a finished interior.

Sliding a finger across the battered finish of one of the metal cabinets, Allison wondered if they would need sanding before she painted them. The proper thing to do would be take them out and have a cabinetmaker spray on the finish. That way, it would be a smooth and professional job, just like new. She'd bet Kyle or Jerry could tell her the name of someone who could restore the cabinets to their original state.

Arrgh. Now she was *really* thinking like Kyle. No. No more depending on him, because Gran was right. If you gave a mouse a cookie…

Allison slammed the cabinet door with more force than she'd intended, and it clanged shut.

No. She'd just paint them with a roller. After all, that's how Gran had done them for years. Quicker, cheaper and easier. Done, done and done.

The wall phone rang, startling her. As she crossed over to grab it, Allison instinctively glanced up at the ceiling to check for sounds of Gran. Sure enough, as she spoke a hello into the mouthpiece, she heard stirrings from upstairs.

"It's Kyle. I was just thinking that maybe you needed help with Gran?"

Allison clenched her teeth. She so wanted to tell him that she could manage at least one thing without him bailing her out. But pragmatism ruled.

"That would be great. I think I hear her moving around upstairs."

"I'll be over in a few minutes then." And he hung up, not really saying goodbye. Was his tone a touch cool? Definitely there was a standoffish awkwardness there.

But hey, she had been the one to leave him on the porch the night before. Allison shook her head to clear it and crossed to the bottom of the back stairs.

"Gran?" she called. "Do you need help?"

She heard her reply but didn't quite get it. So

she tramped up the steps, to find her putting the finishing touches on her hair.

"Gran! You've already had a bath? You could have called and I would have helped—"

"Don't need any help. I do just fine by myself. It was nice to be back in my old tub. There's something lacking in those plastic tub surrounds. Never feels substantial under your feet." Gran used a powder puff to give a final dusting to her face. "There. I am presentable to the world again, as presentable as eighty-nine years will allow me."

"Okay…well, Kyle is coming to help you back downstairs."

"That's a fine young man, Allison. A very fine young man."

Allison began making Gran's bed, and in the process disturbed Cleo. "Don't start."

"Start what?" Gran had turned on the vanity stool and taken up her walking stick.

"You know very well what I mean." Allison fluffed up a pillow sham and began to toss the multitude of Gran's pillows back on the smoothed coverlet.

"I just observed that he was a fine young man. You don't agree?"

"Certainly I agree. But I can sense a bit of matchmaking happening, Gran, and I don't have time for that."

"It's not like I'm drawing up a marriage contract," she mused. "But since you brought up the topic, then, yes, I will say you could do far worse than Kyle Mitchell."

"We are complete opposites, and you know it," Allison told her. "He wants things to be picture perfect, and I just want them to *work*."

"You seem to have managed to work with him this far."

"Because I'm an idiot and I let him and Jerry talk me into things that I know waste time and money."

"Somehow I doubt that, Allison. I know you. You research things to death in your drive to make the best decision. Tell me you haven't tried to find a less expensive or better alternative to any of the choices you've made here."

Allison exhaled and frowned. "You know me too well."

"I know the dark circles under your eyes mean that you're working too hard and spending too much time on the computer, too little time sleeping."

"I...Gran—" What could Allison say? If she told her about the red-alert status of her finances, that her own money was just about gone, it would only worry her grandmother. And she wasn't about to hit Gran up for more money for this old house. "You win. I'll spend less time surfing the web and more time getting my z's. I'm going to start on breakfast, okay? Do you mind waiting up here until Kyle gets here?"

"Not at all. Kyle is usually very punctual."

Downstairs, Allison and the Chambers stove had come to an understanding by the time Kyle rang the back doorbell. She had the bacon sizzling and the pancakes cooking as she let him in.

"Gran's ready upstairs. Just let me take out the bacon and finish the last of the pancakes," she said.

"I never thought I'd say this," Kyle said, "but you're right about the chair lift. It will give Gran a lot of freedom to enjoy the house."

Allison nearly dropped the strips of bacon she was taking up. Wherever Kyle had ditched the standoffish guy on the phone, she was glad of it. She liked having the old Kyle back. "Oh! Yeah. I just wish they'd been able to get in here and have it done before this weekend." She set the plate of bacon on the counter and turned her attention to the last two pancakes on the griddle.

"So all you've really got left inside to do is the painting?"

"Ha! Really? All? Do you know how big

these rooms are? And all the ceilings need doing first—ten-feet-high ceilings."

"I do a mean paint stroke," Kyle told her. "And I have a spare extension roller."

"I'm surprised. I figured you were a brush guy all the way—if they didn't have it in 1929, then you wouldn't deign to use it."

"I can be pragmatic." He leaned over and filched a piece of bacon. "Yum. See? I told you a Chambers stove cooked better than its modern cousin. Don't you think?"

"I *think* we'd better get Gran downstairs before either you eat all her bacon or her pancakes get cold." Allison used a lid from a saucepan to cover up the bacon, and reached overhead to the pot rack for a colander, which she turned over the pancakes.

"Neat trick," he said. "Keeps the heat in but lets the moisture out."

"Wow. You sure are affable today. Let me guess—you're just flattering me, aren't you?" she asked.

She'd been teasing, but did a double take as Kyle's face paled. His mouth tightened, then eased into a forced smile. "Flattering you?"

"The bit about Gran's chair lift, and the bacon…" She trailed off. She stared at him, wondering if she was hypersensitive because of the night before. Yeah, she probably was, but to ask him point-blank about it—would just be that much more awkward. "Wait, I get it," she tacked on in a forced jovial tone. "You're hoping to get breakfast, aren't you? From my Chambers stove?"

Kyle seemed relieved that she'd let him off the hook. He chuckled. "Got me in one. Somehow a granola bar doesn't come close to pancakes and bacon. Let's go get Gran, and after that, maybe I can find my paint roller and help you out with some of those ceilings."

KYLE HOISTED THE six-foot extension pole over his shoulder and toted it to his pickup. There. He had his favorite trim brush, his best scraper and the extension pole. No more dawdling. He needed to head back over to Belle Paix.

But man…what if this didn't work?

He slammed the tailgate shut and leaned against the back of the truck. Fishing out his phone, he punched in a number. "Herbert? This is Kyle Mitchell."

His fellow member of the historic preservation committee replied, "Thought you might be calling after that email I sent you."

"Yeah. I figured your take on the Belle Paix variance request would be like mine."

"You knew it when you sent it to me, Kyle. Quite frankly, I'm surprised at you. You usually wouldn't even waste my time with something this far off from the ordinances."

"I know. But listen, Herbert, Mrs. Lillian is in a tight spot. She's our oldest resident, and she's on a fixed income. I've gone over the idea of loans and tax credits, and she's right…neither option really fits her needs or gives her any benefits."

Herbert cleared his throat, and Kyle could picture him squinting in concentration on the other end of the line. "I agree. It's a bad thing. A terrible thing. But we've worked too hard—*you* have worked too hard—and Lombard has come too far. You know that."

Kyle rubbed his eyes. "She's an old lady, Herbert. Surely we've got to have a little flexibility in those ordinances."

Herbert cleared his throat again. "Seems to me, Kyle, that you aren't as concerned with Mrs. Lillian as you are with Mrs. Lillian's granddaughter. I mean, I've never known you to have trouble saying no to anybody else. There was that young couple who bought that arts and crafts bungalow, and you were as tough on them as you were me. And I'm glad you were, for my part, because you really pushed me to make my house a showplace. This neighborhood is what it is because you didn't let your emotions get in the way. People are depending on you, Kyle.

Not just property owners, but the folks who depend on the tourist trade. You know what you've always said. People don't come to visit an almost-restored old house, they—"

"Come to visit a perfectly restored house," Kyle muttered. He hated being stabbed with his own pitchfork. Was Herbert right? Was Kyle just going soft because of the pull he felt toward Allison? "I know. I know. I guess I am letting my emotions get in the way. But I feel as though maybe we have one shot here, that Belle Paix is as close as it will ever be to getting those repairs it needs."

"If there's just one shot, then we'd better hold their feet to the fire. Because they're not going to be a bit interested in putting money into a proper paint job if they've spent half the amount they'd need on a bad one. Sure, a proper paint job will cost, what? Well, my house is almost as big as theirs, and mine cost me eight grand."

"Yours didn't have the complicated paint scheme, Herb. You know that. Adding those extra colors—plus the fact that Belle Paix is a freaking big house—that doubles the cost right there. She's talked about trying to do it herself—"

"Ha! I tried that. You can't do that with these big old barns. Better to bring the professionals in here with a full crew and get 'er done."

"I agree," Kyle said. "But what if we gave them some time? Say, they put the main color on this year, and then next year, when they'd saved up some money, they could do the trim?" Now Kyle felt as desperate as he had when he'd asked his dad, "It followed me home, so can we keep it?" about the stray dog he'd wanted to adopt as a kid.

And just like his dad, Herbert came back with a reasoned, logical answer he couldn't refute. "You know why we put a time limit in place, Kyle. Heck, you were the one who suggested it as a means to keep people from *saying* they were going to do a proper paint job and then not ever finishing it. And it would cost more money in the long run if somebody was doing a piecemeal job. You *know* that."

"Yeah. Yeah, Herbert, you're right. I've just got to—"

"Do your job. Let us all do our jobs. And the best advice you could give Allison—or Mrs. Lillian—is to not submit that variance request. Because all we can do as a committee is turn it down. And then we won't be able to hear another request on that project for a year."

"You're preaching to the choir, Herbert. I've already—"

"Well, then, I'm glad to hear it. Would you listen to that? That's my grandkids coming in!

Gotta go, Kyle. Don't worry. They'll figure it out."

Kyle put the phone back in his pocket and groaned. He'd been hoping, even though Herbert would be the toughest nut to crack, that since the man was closer to Gran's age than anybody on the committee, he would bend a little.

But maybe Herbert was right. Maybe Kyle was letting his emotions sidetrack him from what was best for the community.

No, what he needed to do was what he'd planned this morning after he'd read that email: persuade Allison that she couldn't afford *not* to do proper renovations on Belle Paix's exterior.

He could do it. He could sell her on it. After all, hadn't he and Jerry convinced her to do the more in-depth renovations on Belle Paix's interiors?

Yeah, right. You conned her into doing renovations where she had flexibility, and now she's got no money to do the ones she has no wiggle room on.

But this was Belle Paix. Herbert was right. Belle Paix didn't deserve anything less than to be properly renovated and restored, and neither did Lombard's historic neighborhood. So Allison would just have to be more open to looking at grants and tax credits and other sources of funding. Maybe Gran could deed the house to her, so she'd have the collateral to borrow against it.

And Kyle? He'd have to dig just as deep to convince her to borrow the money in the first place, especially since he knew what dreams she'd already given up to come home to Belle Paix.

CHAPTER SIXTEEN

ALLISON WATCHED THE mixer shake the can of paint, with bleary eyes. How many gallons of ceiling white did that make? Ten? Twenty? Her neck felt as though she were working on her millionth gallon.

The machine shuddered to a stop and Curtis, the clerk she'd gotten to know really, really well over her thousand gallons of paint, released the can. With a quick, practiced hand, he opened the lid, swiped a smear on the top and pounded the lid back on with a rubber mallet.

"You need any more tarps? More rollers?" he asked her, handing her the can. "How about some more stirrers?"

"Toss me a handful of those sticks. And, yeah, what's another pack of rollers, huh?" she asked bleakly.

"Okay!" He slapped a stack of stirrers and a three-pack of rollers down on the counter. "On the house, 'cause, hey, you're my best customer here lately. How much more painting you got left to do?"

"Oh, just a few million square miles to go."

"Now, I've been thinking, when you get started on the outside, I can see it—a nice yellow, right? With a deep burgundy, and hunter green for the main trim—those complementary colors will make it pop, right? Can you see it? And then to tie it all together, for the relief trim, how about, say, black and a shade darker yellow—almost a beige, but not quite? See? I've been pulling some swatches for ya."

He yanked out a piece of paper with the five color swatches taped on it. "Looks good, no? That old house will be making the cover of *Southern Living* next year, you wait and see."

Curtis appeared so pleased with himself. She stared down at his work with dismay. The colors looked great...honestly, it was almost as if he'd read Davinia's journal about what the house's original paint scheme had been. How long had he worked on this? Did he maybe get a commission from all the paint he'd sold her?

"Oh, no, no, I'm sorry, Curtis, but I won't be going with such an ambitious color scheme. I've got a variance request submitted to the historical society. But, hey, I like the yellow. And the historical society will probably nix my request for vinyl siding or Hardie Board—I kept that in there so they'd have something to say no to, and they'd feel like saying yes to going with a two-color paint scheme. So maybe we could do something with that…and the green. The green for the trim?"

Curtis blinked, his confusion evident. "But he said…"

"What? Who said something?" Allison felt her skin prickle with awareness, and the wire of the paint can's handle bit into her fingers as she clenched it. "Did Kyle Mitchell put you up to this?"

She'd thought Kyle had been up to something. He'd been way too generous with his labor, entirely too willing to hang around and let her natter on. Even as she'd appreciated all the help, she'd felt sucked in, as if he was trying to charm her into doing things his way.

"Kyle? Nah. It wasn't him. Shoot, I haven't seen him in ages. No, it was something Herbert told me. He said he'd seen your proposed variance request and that you were going to withdraw it because it wasn't historically accurate and didn't have a prayer getting passed."

"He what?" She set the can down with a thud. "You mean they've already had the hearing on it? Without me there?"

Now Curtis looked as though he'd stepped on a land mine and didn't quite know how to get off. He threw up his hands. "No, no. Believe me, they do up a variance request hearing right—you'd be there, of course. What I thought was—well, I must have misunderstood Herbert, that's all."

"He's seen my variance request?"

"Yeah, informally. You know, a lot of times they do it like the Supreme Court does their big cases—they circulate it around among themselves until they get a consensus. Before it's all official."

"That doesn't seem particularly legal."

"Well, h…most people don't even bother with the hearing, truth be told. They just do what the historical committee tells 'em. Not much point trying anything otherwise."

Fury rattled through Allison. "Someone needs to show this blasted committee that they can't just order people around to their liking. They shouldn't be able to bully home owners into going into heaps of debt just so that the neighborhood will meet their impossibly high standards," she fumed.

"I dunno. I really couldn't complain. It's been great for our business," Curtis pointed out sheepishly.

"I'll say." She didn't bother to keep the sour note out of her voice. "And for the contractors and the subcontractors and the bankers, too. But what about normal, everyday folks? I mean, my grandmother's eighty-nine years old, and this is the only home she's ever known. She didn't choose this house—it was the one thing her parents left her when they passed away. So why should she be penalized because it sits in a certain square mile of the city?"

"You're not the first person I've heard say all that—and more," Curtis allowed.

"Well, I must be the first one who's willing to take on that committee. I'm not going to let them intimidate me." *Or*, she thought grimly, *sweet-talk me into something I know better than to do, and that's what Kyle's been up to. Debt is debt, and I can't afford it.*

"No, plenty of people have complained—a few have even shown up at city council meetings. But, Miss Allison, you got to understand, these are official laws on the books—they have been for years. It would take the majority of members of the city council to repeal those laws. And with the historical society such an influential organization—I mean, nobody wants to upset little old ladies, you know? Well, you got a goose-egg's chance of getting those laws repealed."

She let his words sink in. "What did you just say?"

"You got a goose egg's—"

"No, before that."

"The historical society. It's made up of a

bunch of little old ladies who really know how to work the city council—"

"Nobody wants to upset little old ladies. That's what you said." She smiled grimly, feeling a calm purpose sluice over her. "And you're right. So let's just see how the committee reacts when people hear how they're trying to force a little old lady out of the last of her savings, hmm? Is the newspaper office still on Douglas Avenue? Because I need to know where to send a letter to the editor."

EN ROUTE TO the newspaper office, Allison tried Kyle's cell phone twice and got voice mail. When she dialed his office number, she reached the department's administrative assistant, who told her that Kyle was in class and had two meetings back to back after he finished up with his last lecture.

"I can put you through to his voice mail or I can take a message," the woman suggested.

Allison debated over the choice and decided she didn't want to leave a long and rambling voice mail, or try to explain why she was so angry to someone who had nothing to do with the historic preservation committee. No, Kyle's assistant wasn't the louse, he was.

Allison discarded both options. "I'll call him later," she told the assistant.

"Can I get your name again for our phone log? And I will certainly let him know you called."

Allison grudgingly gave the information, then clicked off and stepped out of her car. The newspaper was in the heart of the downtown business district, housed in a two-story brick building on a corner, imposing pilasters flanking the doors and Greek friezes over the tall windows giving the structure a serious, intimidating look. She pushed through the heavy glass door into the lobby.

Behind the counter, a woman in her early twenties with a bored, put-upon expression, hot-pink streaks in her short blond hair and a nose ring in her left nostril glanced up from her cell phone. "If you have a subscription complaint, I can't help you. I'm just covering the desk for someone who's grabbing lunch."

"No, no subscription complaint. Why did you think that?" Allison asked.

"You look as mad as a wet settin' hen, as my granny used to say. If it's not that, then what is it?" The woman set down her phone and propped a hip against the granite counter, her eyes alight with a sudden curiosity.

"How does a person go about getting a letter to the editor put in the paper?"

For a moment, the curiosity dimmed in the

woman's eyes. She fingered the tattoo of an infinity symbol on the inside of her left wrist. "It should be typed, 250 or less words, and contain no libelous statements or personal attacks. Also, you have to provide your name and address as well as a daytime telephone number and a photo ID for verification purposes. Oh, and it needs to be in by lunchtime forty-eight hours before the date you want it to appear, so that we can verify the identity of the writer."

Allison scribbled all this down on a notepad from her purse. "And the address? Do I have to mail it, or can I just drop it by?"

"You can drop it off here, or if you don't mind scanning in your driver's license as an attachment for proof of identity, you could just email it. Say, what are you so heated up about? Because I'm a writer here, and there could be a story in it. I mean, Wilson—that's the editor—said I had to stay here for the afternoon unless a hot story came up. So I'm pretty jazzed at anything that might give me a chance to get while the gettin's good."

Allison couldn't believe her good fortune. "There just might be. What would you say if I told you that an eighty-nine-year-old woman on a fixed income and in a rehab facility was being forced to choose between not painting her house or going into debt to paint it the 'proper' way?"

"I'd say...hmm..." The reporter tapped a rhinestone-encrusted lavender fingernail against her chin. "I'd say she's most likely having a run-in with the hysterical society, and that it's high time those rich old dudes got their comeuppance. Oh, and also—" she extended a hand to Allison "—that my name is Gwen Chapman and I'll be happy to hear you out if you don't mind waiting for me to grab a camera and run to a drive-through for some lunch." And then she picked up the phone on the counter and punched a number. "Hey, Wilson, I got a story, so I'm leaving, okay?"

GWEN SPUN AROUND in the living room of Belle Paix and took a bite out of her hamburger. "So you actually grew up in this mausoleum? Man. What a bummer. But I've got to admit, it must be nice for, like, you know, Halloween parties."

"Yeah, it's got atmosphere," Allison agreed. She saw crumbs gathering like snowflakes on Gran's old Turkish carpet, and tried to hide an inward cringe. "Uh, can I get you a plate? You know, we could go sit down in the kitchen or dining room for you to eat—"

"Nah, it's okay." Gwen waved her off, another flick of hamburger bun floating to the carpet as she did so. "Burns more calories if you eat standing up. Besides, if I eat while I talk, we won't waste time. And it sounds like your granny doesn't have much time, does she?"

Allison nodded. "Right. She wants to come home as soon as possible so that she doesn't run through her long-term health care benefits… you know, in case she needs to use them again."

"Plus, I mean, like you said, she's eighty-nine. My granny was about fit to bust a gasket when we had to put her in a swing bed after her hip surgery. Kept talking about never seeing home again."

Her word choice gave Allison an uneasy pause; Gwen didn't sound like any writer Allison had ever talked with.

"So how long have you been a reporter?"

"Oh, about six months. Wilson has me doing obits, believe it or not, and me a magna cum laude. I think he just likes seeing Little Miss 4.0 having to do scut work, ya know? But this story…" Gwen's smile made her face seem a little harder, a little older. "It's got everything. Well, everything except sex, but you can't have it all, now can you? It's David and Goliath, the average Joe against city hall, the—"

"I get the picture." Allison's doubts roiled around in her stomach. She had been hoping for any reporter who would listen, but she felt somehow repelled by Gwen's open, in-your-face agenda to launch herself out of the obits.

"And little old ladies. Who can't help pulling for sweet old grannies, ya know?" Gwen had found the grand piano, where Gran's collections of photos stood. "This her? With you?"

"Yeah. That was a few years ago at my college graduation, but she hasn't changed much."

"She's cute as a button," Gwen observed, and set the silver-framed photo back down on the piano with a cringe-inducing thud. "I'll need to talk to her, and maybe we can get her home to have a picture…I know! In front of those peeling front porch posts!"

"Uh, I'm not sure how Gran will feel about—"

"Or we could just have her at the wrought-iron gate, with the house looming behind her—it would make great lead color! And symbolism, too—the place is an albatross around her neck, kind of, or this huge weight on her shoulders."

But Gran had never felt that way about Belle Paix, Allison thought with a pang. The house had always been something worth working to protect, to save.

Allison's cell phone rang. She glanced down, saw that it was Kyle. "Excuse me…I've got to take this."

"No problem. I'm just gonna poke around a little. This is one freaky old house. I mean, can you say time capsule or what?"

Allison stepped back into the hall and answered the phone.

"Hey, Gillian told me that you'd called while I was in class. Something I can help you with?"

His too-innocent greeting reignited her earlier anger. "More like something you could have clued me in on," she snapped. "How long have you known that the committee had already decided, hearing or not, that I wasn't getting my variance request?"

"What?" That one word spilled over with alarm and surprise, enough to tell Allison that she wasn't far off the mark.

"Well? They have, haven't they?"

"Not the *whole* committee, Allison. Just one or two…" He sighed. "Okay. Three. And with me, that's four. But it's not a foregone conclusion yet. I'm still trying to work out a compromise—"

"A compromise? A compromise would be that I could put a coat of paint on this house before it rots into the ground. You know it's overdue for painting—long overdue. I'd think you'd want to see it not peeling at least!"

"Allison…it's complicated, okay? The way the laws are written, it ties my hands—"

"Well, the way the laws are written are wrong! And, Kyle…" Allison stepped back so that the pink-streaked pixie cut of the reporter was back in her line of sight. "Those laws? They may be written…but they're not written in stone."

With that, she stabbed the disconnect button and marched back into the living room. "Why don't we start with me, and I'll talk to my grandmother about whether or not she'll be willing to have her photo taken with the house?"

Gwen took the last bite of her burger and wadded up the paper wrapper. "Sounds like a plan. Sounds like a plan, indeed."

CHAPTER SEVENTEEN

KYLE WAS SLIDING the last stack of papers to grade into his portfolio case when a knock came on the doorjamb. He looked up to see Lorenzo Adams standing there.

"Councilman! Whatever's on your mind, can we walk and talk? I need to go see someone—"

"Would that someone be an..." the tall lanky man flipped a card out of his pocket and squinted "...Allison Bell?"

Hearing Allison's name come out of the city council member's mouth jolted Kyle. "Why?"

"Oh, my hide's been turned into hamburger meat with the chewing out she's just given me. You have one unhappy neighbor there, Kyle."

Kyle let the portfolio case's flap close, and shook his head. "Why...what did she want with you?"

"Well, turns out, I'm her city council representative. You know, that part of the downtown that got squashed into my district after the last census to make the numbers come out right."

"Yeah. I'd forgotten that the district line falls right behind her block."

"That reporter buddy of hers hadn't. They showed up at my dry cleaners and ambushed me. I would have appreciated a heads-up from you—"

"Reporter? What reporter?" Kyle froze in the midst of strapping his portfolio shut.

Now it was Lorenzo shaking his head. "Man, Kyle, I came here to get answers from you, but it looks like I'm the one filling you in. That new girl, Gwen Chapman. You know? Pink hair—at least it was pink this week, but who knows what color it will be next week. Nose ring? Tattoos? Wilson hired her a few months ago, and she's done nothing but file Freedom of Information requests in hopes of turning up a scandal. Looks like this time she's got a story with some legs."

Kyle sagged against the table. Had he heard correctly? Allison had gone to the paper? Without even giving him a heads-up? Was that what her phone call had been about? The idea knifed through him.

"So what—what exactly was Allison asking?" Kyle phrased the words as carefully as he could to keep from revealing the feeling of betrayal coursing through him.

"Asking? She wasn't asking. She was demanding. Demanding that we either repeal the historic section's preservation ordinances or pass a hardship exemption."

"Well, that's not going to happen." Kyle let the tension flow out of his body and started to pick up his case. Then he caught sight of the councilman's face. "Right? Lorenzo, you aren't seriously considering caving on this, are you?"

The man shrugged. "She's got a point, Kyle. An old lady? On a fixed income? And you historical guys won't budge on paint colors? You know I'm the new kid in that part of my district—I barely squeaked by in the last election. I can't afford to look insensitive to my constituents' needs and problems in this economy."

"I'm working on it, Lorenzo. I am. But we struggled too hard to get those ordinances passed in the first place—and look what a powerhouse we've made of the downtown section. Thousands of visitors every year come to tour those homes, and they spend money here…in the restaurants, in the gas stations, in the bed-and-breakfasts, in the antique shops. Think about the needs and problems of those people if suddenly anybody could do what they want to their historic home."

"This is just one almost ninety-year-old woman…and the house is a shambles as it is. It would look better with a fresh coat of paint in any color, wouldn't it? Surely you can make this problem go away for me."

Kyle grimaced. "Like I said, I'm working on it. But I'll tell you what I've told her…the way the laws were written, we don't have any wiggle room. I'm trying to get other committee members to, uh, more loosely interpret the timing of when a project has to be completed—that would let Allison start the job and finish it as she got the money."

"Well, now, that sounds like a good compromise." Lorenzo beamed. "See? I knew I could count on you to work something out."

"It's nowhere near a done deal. To be honest…" Kyle rubbed his eyes. "To be honest, I haven't convinced even one committee member yet. They remember when I suggested the original language, and they keep reminding me that if we let one project slide, we'll have to let others do the same."

"But with a variance request, isn't that giving you the elbow room you need? On a case-by-case basis?"

"No, it's not what it was designed for. Usually the only time we would ever pass a variance request is for something structural that wouldn't show."

"Gwen, the pain-in-the-neck reporter, reminded me that a lot of towns don't have ordinances that govern paint colors…and that a state law prevents towns from passing laws to do that now. So is it even legal for us to tell people what color they can paint their houses?"

Kyle resisted the urge to glance at his watch. He wanted to find Allison, not stay here explaining—once again—the rationale and legitimacy of the city's historic ordinances. "Uh, yeah. The law grandfathers in towns like ours. Lombard started their historic preservation committee up the year before the law went into effect. The committee just didn't press the issue, not until…"

"Not until you came to town." Lorenzo finished Kyle's sentence. "Listen, I get what you're saying. Tourism is a big deal here, one of our main industries, especially now that we've lost a couple of factories."

Kyle jumped in eagerly to push home that thought. "Yeah. A lot of those displaced factory workers started businesses to do with the historic section—sandwich shops or tearooms or antiques shops or souvenir stores. It may not be profitable all year long, but come the high season, they make money."

"I get that, Kyle. I do. And I'll help you all I can. But you've got to understand…I can only do so much, and I can't control the rest of the council. If it comes before them—like she's wanting it to—you never can tell what they'll do. So my advice? Give her what she wants. Compromise. Because once those ordinances are repealed, you may never get them back."

With that, Lorenzo clapped Kyle on the shoulder and headed down the hall for the door.

KYLE SWUNG OPEN the side gate of Belle Paix's wrought-iron fence and spotted Allison kneeling over a paint tray at the outside faucet.

She looked over her shoulder at the clang of the gate. "Well, well. Look who finally has the nerve to show his face."

"Allison, you don't understand—"

She scrambled to her feet and switched off the faucet. "Me? I think I understand perfectly. You never had any intention of turning in that variance request, did you? You thought you could sweet-talk me into borrowing big money, and I'd swallow your complicated paint scheme just like I swallowed Jerry's song and dance about the plaster."

Her choice of words irritated Kyle. "Now, that was not a song and dance, and you were free to do whatever you liked—"

"Yeah, and you know Jerry would have walked out on the project. And you knew I couldn't get anyone else to do it. What? Did you blackball me or something? Warn contractors off? Tell them, 'Let her get desperate and she'll agree to anything you want'?"

Did Allison for one minute think he was that low-down and dirty? That corrupt? "That's not true and you know it!"

"I don't know anything. Because you've kept me in the dark!"

Their raised voices must have attracted the attention of a passerby, because someone called out from the sidewalk, "Hey, everything all right there?"

Allison craned her neck around Kyle and called back, "Oh, yeah, I'm just giving him a piece of my mind."

But she beckoned him into the house, leaving the half-washed paint tray where it was. For a moment, Kyle wondered at the wisdom of prolonging the conversation. She was too angry right now to even to listen to his side.

Lorenzo's warning about losing the ordinances forever echoed in his head, though. If he could just explain to her that he'd tried everything, maybe then she'd back off?

Kyle followed her up the side porch steps and into the kitchen. He stared at the yellow walls and crisp white metal cabinets.

"This looks great—"

"Don't try to soft-soap me, Kyle Mitchell!"

Allison snapped. "Don't you try to get on my good side."

"I don't have a clue where you've hidden away your good side," he muttered. Louder, in what he hoped was a reasonable tone, he replied, "If you'll just hear me out without jumping down my throat, we might actually accomplish something besides both of us losing our voices."

She folded her arms across her chest. "Fair enough."

He swallowed. "I warned you that your request was pretty much pie-in-the-sky when you first started on it. I told you about the city ordinances. But you insisted on doing it and I promised you I'd help. So…I tried. I sent it to a few of the more influential committee members—"

"Oh, yeah. The ever-so-open-minded Herbert. He'd like nothing more than to make choosing the wrong paint color a federal offense."

"You said you'd listen," Kyle pointed out.

She had the grace to blush. "I'm sorry. Go on."

"What I was trying to do was to, er, work out an extension. A timeline for you to paint the house in stages. Or…maybe even get you something like a hardship waiver."

"Now why didn't you mention the possibility of a hardship waiver to begin with?" she demanded.

He frowned. "Because it doesn't *exist.* There's nothing in our ordinances that would give us the flexibility to do that—"

"Well, gee, that was forward-thinking of you, wasn't it?"

"You're not listening," he growled.

"Because I'm not hearing anything I haven't already heard from you at least a dozen times."

"Because it can't be changed, okay? There's nothing that I can do to change it."

Allison stared at him, then sank into a kitchen chair. "You mean to tell me that nobody ever foresaw this possibility when you and your fan club were busily writing up these laws?"

"You have to understand, Allison…the downtown section here was in a mess. We couldn't require people to put things back to rights at the drop of a hat—they didn't have the money. So what we did was take a long view. If we changed the restoration ordinances, then when they did renovate, they'd have to keep things historically accurate. Voila, things improve, bit by bit. And nobody has to do it overnight. The town gets a tourism engine, people's home values increase, historic structures are properly preserved and renovated…everybody's a winner."

Kyle pulled out a chair to sit beside her. "Don't you see? It was a good, common sense approach."

"Not for people like Gran." Allison's chin jutted out stubbornly.

He ran his fingers through his hair. "You're right. You're absolutely right. We never thought about people who were cash-strapped and had a house as big as Belle Paix. But your grandmother could have been part of that discussion. She chose not to be. If she'd weighed in back then, if she'd participated in the process, maybe we would have seen the need to write in some flexibility."

"Well, you see the need now, so hop to it."

Kyle closed his eyes. "It's not that simple and you know it. If we give you that variance request, then we're setting a legal precedent of favoritism, and we could open ourselves up to a lawsuit. I've asked our attorney about it, and he said that we have to go by the letter of the law. I'm sorry. I wish there was a way around it, but if we say yes to you, we have to say yes to everybody else, and before you know it, Lombard will look exactly like the mess it was before."

"I grew up in this town, and it wasn't a mess, Kyle. Maybe it wasn't postcard ready, maybe it didn't meet your high standards, but it wasn't a mess."

"Oh, you would say that, wouldn't you? You of the 'let's just fix it the quickest, easiest way we can, and hang the right way' school of thought," he retorted.

"There's something to be said for pragmatism. I don't have the money to fund your fantasy of what Belle Paix should look like, okay? And maybe, just maybe, I think it's a really bad idea to sink that much money into appearances, anyway. Maybe that money could be put to a better use than paint!"

"Belle Paix is a treasure—don't you realize that? Don't you understand what you have here? Your great-great-great-grandparents built this house! Your family has *always* owned this home," he retorted. "You say so many things that make me think you don't understand what a jewel this house is."

"It's Gran's home, that's what it is. It isn't a museum or a…a national park, Kyle! We have to live here—don't you get it? And to do that, we actually have to have money left over to live *on*! Of course I want to take care of the house—what do you think I've been doing? I've been busting my backside trying to get it into shape for Gran to come home, spending loads of money, every cent I've saved. But it's never going to be good enough for you until it matches the little picture you have in your head, is it?"

"That 'little picture,' Allison?" Kyle was on his feet now, too angry to sit still. He paced back and forth, taking in all the touches that made the kitchen authentic: the Chambers stove, the metal cabinets, the marble countertops, the subway tiles. These things were the threads in the tapestry that all Allison's ancestors who'd lived in this house had woven.

He closed his eyes and pictured the awful travesty his own family's home place was now. Allison would regret letting Belle Paix slip away. Maybe not immediately, but when she saw the end result, she would. And so would Gran.

Kyle opened his eyes to find Allison staring at him, waiting for him to go on. "That little picture is just as important to your grandmother…and you know that, don't you? Because you painted the kitchen yellow, just like she remembered from being a little girl. And I notice you didn't really balk about saving the upstairs bathroom fixtures—because you knew how important that was to Gran."

Allison stared down at her clenched hands, so he continued. "If you really acknowledged how important this house is to Gran, you'd want to do it right—for her sake. Wouldn't it be something to have it just as she remembered from her childhood? Wouldn't that make her homecoming that much more special?"

Allison flew at him. "What don't you get? This house is a home! Not a scrapbook! It's a living, breathing and, oh, yeah, dying thing, this place. I know what I have on my hands, believe you me—a hundred twenty-six years of someone else's problems, someone else kicking the can down the road and not making any of the necessary repairs. You couldn't have done a thing about it if Gran had had the money to replace those windows five years ago, could you? But she didn't—and you know why? Because she used her money to put me through school. It wasn't enough, not nearly enough, Kyle, and I had to borrow tons more to pay the bills. No, what you don't see is all the junk I have to work around—a century of somebody's leftovers stuffed in the attic and the basement, things nobody ever got around to throwing away."

"If it's that much of a problem, then why not sell the house? Sell it and move to a brand-new house where the floors creak because they use strand board for the subflooring, and the walls are thin but by God they have easy-to-patch drywall, and the windows might have all the charm of a fake Christmas tree, but, hey, they're double-paned. Because at least then somebody who *really* appreciated Belle Paix would own her!"

With that, Kyle slammed out of the kitchen, not bothering to wait for her reply.

CHAPTER EIGHTEEN

ALLISON COVERED A yawn with one hand as she used the thumb of the other to scroll through a website on her tablet detailing various city ordinances for historic districts. She glanced around, just to make sure that no one needed her, feeling guilty for using the tablet even though she was on her supper break.

The ER had been strangely deserted, save for a kid with a tummy ache in bay three. After an impossibly busy late afternoon and early evening, the department had turned as quiet as a graveyard. That was good; it had meant she could do research and actually sit down to eat her sandwich during her break, even if it meant enduring the staff room's smell of burned popcorn.

Allison yawned again.

"Don't do that!" Laurel Wells, one of the ER physicians on staff that night, told her. "You'll tempt me into sneaking off and taking a nap, and then I'll just feel worse than I do now. It's too quiet. Gives me the creeps. Something is bound to cut loose any minute now. So if I were you, I'd go ahead and get that sandwich in while you've got the chance."

"Sorry...I didn't get much sleep last night." Allison liked Dr. Wells, who was nice to the nurses and didn't stand on ceremony. "It *does* feel weird for the ER to be this slow. I keep thinking I've forgotten to check in on a patient or three. And the time just drags by." She picked up her sandwich and absently took another bite as she tried to make sense of the complicated legal jargon the ordinances were worded in.

"Yeah, I saw the paint in your hair. How many rooms have you got done?"

"Paint?"

Dr. Wells gestured to a particular corkscrew curl, and Allison examined the strand to find a telltale streak of sage green she'd painted the living room and library.

Dr. Wells seeing the paint in her hair made Allison think of Kyle and the day they'd stood outside his house. Since their argument last week, he hadn't called. Or dropped by.

And she didn't want to focus on how sad that made her feel. No, regardless of what her best friend, Melanie, kept telling her, she did *not* miss Kyle. Really, it was that he'd completely given up on her—on Belle Paix. She'd been proved right, she guessed. Now that she'd drawn a line in the sand and declared, "This far and no farther!" he'd written her off.

Belle Paix's restoration had been his only interest in her.

"Want some coffee? It might keep you awake. What are you researching, anyway? From the way your eyes are glazing over, it could be my old advanced-molecular-biology textbook." Dr. Wells pushed her chair back to cross over to the coffeepot.

"City ordinances about historic districts. I'm trying to see what most cities with historic sections have in place. If I'm going to convince the council to repeal that stupid paint law, then I need some ammunition."

"What's the fuss about paint, anyway? I mean, how expensive is a bucket of paint?" Dr. Wells asked. "So, coffee? Or no?"

Allison looked up to see thick, tarry hospital coffee glugging out of the carafe into Dr. Well's mug. She shuddered. "I'll pass, thanks. That stuff resembles toxic waste. And yeah, one pail of paint isn't that expensive, although you'd be surprised—sixty bucks a gallon for custom historic colors. But Belle Paix is huge, so it will take lots of buckets of paint. Plus, how many shades do you have on your house?"

"Well..." Dr. Wells squinted and slurped the coffee. Her responding shudder matched Allison's, and she promptly dumped two packets of sugar into her cup. "You're right. Definitely toxic waste. Pity that's the only source of caffeine around here. Somebody stole my cola out of the fridge. As for my house, it's two tones—the main color and the trim. I did talk Mike into painting the door a different hue, but he wanted the shutters to match the trim."

"City ordinances here state you have to choose a paint scheme that matches the—and I quote—historical accuracy of the home's original era. And since Belle Paix is a Second Empire, really high Victorian, that original paint scheme calls for five colors."

"Five? Get out!"

"Yep. Different portions of the trim were painted different accent colors to highlight the architectural details."

"But nobody does that anymore," Dr. Wells protested. "It would cost a fortune in labor, because you'd have to paint the trim one color, then wait for it to dry and break out another one."

"Exactly." Allison was gratified by the woman's quick grasp of how the paint scheme ratcheted up the labor costs. "I mean, I've gotten quotes, and some of them said they wouldn't do it for less than twenty thousand bucks. I've even looked at trying to paint the house myself."

"Oh, no. Trust me. It took Mike forever to paint our house, and it's just a normal-sized deal. He started out all gung-ho, with a ladder and a paintbrush. Climbing up and down that ladder got old in a hurry, let me tell you. But, man, renting the scaffolding was expensive, and every day, it was another trip to the hardware store. Oh, no, if your house is as big as you say it is, well, it's well worth the money to hire someone to get it done."

"I know. I figured up the scaffolding costs myself. I even looked at *buying* a set of scaffolding. But then there's the question of having to move it, you know? Still, twenty grand? I can't afford that." Allison stared down at the table and its coffee stain rings that hadn't completely come up with an earlier swipe of a damp napkin. Her sandwich suddenly held all the appeal of a bucket of sawdust.

"So tell the city they can cough up the money if they're so fired up about wanting your house to be historically accurate," Dr. Wells suggested. "Sounds to me like it's almost a tax on people with historic homes, an unfunded mandate."

"Amen. I've got to remember that—it's a great argument."

Just then another nurse popped her head into the room. "Dr. Wells, I know you're on break, but we've got a multicar pileup on the interstate, with at least one unrestrained passenger ejected from a vehicle. EMS is bringing them in now and says they need at least two trauma bays."

Dr. Wells nodded and gulped down her coffee with a wince of displeasure. "Better put down that tablet, girlie," she told Allison with a wry smile. "Because it looks like we complained too much about it being quiet."

THE CAR ACCIDENT had been the signal for the floodgates to open, because after that, Allison didn't have a chance to grab anything beyond her half-eaten sandwich. By 11:00 p.m., every bay was full, the waiting room overflowed with crying babies and at least one raving drunk, and the last of the car accident victims was either out the door and to a trauma hospital, or upstairs on the floor.

Dr. Wells saw her coming out of a bay and tapped her on the shoulder as Allison shuffled through a sheaf of papers in her hands. "Hey, help me out here...I've got Sheila making calls to find a bed for one of our lovely guests, but she's left Melba the frequent flier in bay four, and a hand laceration waiting in another bay. I've got to get that cut stitched up, but it needs to be cleaned first. Gotta warn ya, the hand's a beaut. But if you'll do that, I'll go handle Melba in the meantime."

"Oh, all right. I don't mind a little blood. And Melba doesn't like me very much."

Dr. Wells laughed. "It's just that you called her out last time on mixing herbal remedies and her prescription meds."

"It's gonna kill her one day, but she won't believe me. What's the deal with the laceration?"

"Get this…guy was carving some sort of decoration and slipped with a chisel. A pretty deep gash."

"Ouch." Allison pictured a grizzled old lumberjack type, complete with a plaid shirt, a beard and a baseball cap—and probably an attitude to match. "Just stitches?"

"Yep, thankfully, because we'd have to transfer him out if he needed hand surgery. He'll require something for the pain—I've got the orders in, but Sheila didn't get a chance to give the medication to him. You got it?"

"Consider it handled. Let me go irrigate the old coot's wound."

"Nope, not an old coot, he's very much swoon-worthy. Name's, er—Kyle? Yeah. Kyle Mitchell, a professor over at the college. Shh… don't tell Mike about the swoon-worthy bit. He'd never understand I'm just window-shopping." Dr. Wells pointed at a unit down on the end. "He's all yours. I'm off to lecture Miss Mabel about how herbs really can screw up meds."

Outside the bay, Allison drew in a deep breath, then pushed aside the curtain. There indeed was Kyle, sitting on the edge of the bed, holding up a tightly swaddled hand.

"Oh," he said, spotting her. His face tightened, but she couldn't translate what the expression meant. "I forgot about you working here... So you're the one who's going to stitch me up, huh?"

"Nope, that's Dr. Wells's job. I'll just get things started."

Allison forced herself to plaster a professional smile on her face, as though Kyle was just another patient, not the man who hadn't spoken to her in a week.

She didn't want to, though. She couldn't get past the anger that ate at her. He'd told her to sell Belle Paix, as though she was some inferior owner who Kyle had totally given up on.

Allison swallowed back the words she really wanted to say, and concentrated on doing her job. The quicker she did it, the quicker he'd be out of her sight and...well, back to wherever he'd been for the past week.

She accessed the computer screen that would let her begin inputting things. She was grateful that Sheila had done the actual intake. It would have felt odd to have to ask Kyle the standard battery of questions. While she'd wound up taking care of friends before, she'd never taken care of a person she…

What? What do you feel for Kyle?

Pushing the thought from her mind, she crossed the room to examine his hand. "So what happened?"

Just taking his hand in hers and unwrapping the gauze felt hugely intimate. Sure, they'd worked side by side before…

And admit it, every time, it takes your breath away.

"I…" He ducked his head. At first she thought he was averting his gaze from the fairly spectacular laceration across his palm; he was lucky he would just need stitches. A few millimeters more and he would have required a hand surgeon to repair tendons.

"Yeah?"

Then she saw him stare down at his hand without the slightest bit of squeamishness, but more than a little guilt. "It will be okay?" he asked. "I need my hand for typing…and, well, working. I've never met a one-handed carpenter."

"You very nearly ended up being one—or at

least losing the function of your fingers," she retorted. "What on earth were you thinking?"

He drew his brows together, the corners of his mouth digging deep into his cheeks. "Obviously, I wasn't thinking, or I wouldn't have hurt myself, would I?"

"What, trying to recreate some arcane historical detail to make your house ultraperfect? News flash, Kyle—whatever money you saved on trying to do it yourself, well, you've blown that here in the ER."

"I couldn't *find* it to buy it," he snapped. "Or else I would have just bought it."

She irrigated the wound with a little more force than she might have, and felt only a small twinge of guilt at his wince. "I thought by now you would have had your house perfect—oh, except for the digital clocks."

"I wasn't working on something for the house, thank you very much. I was working on something for you—"

He broke off and clamped his jaw tight, the muscles in it working hard to control whatever words he might have wanted to say.

"For me?" More than a little shame permeated Allison. Her hand trembled as she squirted antiseptic into the wound. "What—"

"There's a piece of the detail missing on the front staircase. I noticed it the day we did the tomatoes, and I'd tried to find a replacement piece. But I hadn't had any luck."

"So…you tried to whittle it?" She gaped at him, stared down at the angry gash on his hand and felt sick that he'd done this to himself on her behalf.

"I've done carving before, lots of times," Kyle said. "Ow! That stings! Could you take your anger out on something else?"

"But I didn't ask you…" She knew the piece he was referring to. It was high up on the inside corner of the stairs, just at the turn of the landing. "Leave it to you to notice it."

"It was just…something I was fooling around with. For you. I'd found a pattern in a book, and it didn't look that hard. Plus you had your hands full with…" He trailed off.

Now she was the one overcome with guilt. He was hand-carving a piece for her? When she was trying to take down his precious ordinances?

Maybe he's changed his mind, she thought. *Maybe this is his peace offering.*

Gently, she laid his hand on the table. She was astonished at how bereft she felt at the lost connection once her fingers slipped from his. She turned so he couldn't read her expression. "Let me get you some pain meds."

"Now that you've stopped torturing me, I'm okay," he muttered.

Allison glanced over her shoulder and chuckled. "If you think *that* was torture, wait till Dr. Wells starts stitching you up—especially without meds."

"Oh, all right. But don't give me anything that will make me too loopy. I drove myself."

"What, Herbert or some other fellow committee members wouldn't come to the aid of their comrade-in-arms?" she sniped.

"I didn't ask them. I'm sure Herb would have, but I didn't feel the need. It was just my hand."

She stood at the opening of the bay, gripping the curtain in exasperation. "Kyle, that's a bad injury. Historical accuracy is not worth getting hurt over."

He shrugged. "Maybe not to you. But it bugged me…the missing piece, I mean. And it was in my power to fix it." Now his eyes held a challenge she couldn't mistake. "My hand will get better. And I'm almost finished with the carving."

She shook her head and snatched the curtain closed. She couldn't talk with him, not with any success at getting him to use sense, anyway. Didn't he see the costs of being such an idealistic stickler for detail? Money and time and now his hand?

Dr. Wells saw her as she was signing out Kyle's meds. "Wow. I should have given you Mabel. You look positively steamed."

Allison compressed her lips. "I know him, that's all. He's a—a neighbor."

The doctor lifted an eyebrow. "And he seemed so nice..."

"He's...he's just..." Allison glanced at her helplessly. "He got hurt because of me. He was making something for Belle Paix."

"Aww...now that's better than chocolates, in my book. Can I send Mike over to get him trained? Hey, look, let me just give him a local. That will get in his system faster than the other. And since he lives alone and you're obviously his favorite neighbor, why not check on his stitches and dressings in the morning for me?"

Allison was speechless at first. But then she saw the doctor waiting expectantly for her answer, so she gave a grudging nod. "Sure, if he needs me."

Dr. Wells punched her on the shoulder. "That's the spirit, girl!" And then she turned and headed toward Kyle's bay.

CHAPTER NINETEEN

THE MORNING SUN spilled golden pools of light over Kyle's front lawn as Allison put her car in Park at the curb. She stared at the house for a few minutes, trying to decide why she was even bothering with this.

And don't con yourself with the idea that it's because Dr. Wells told you to, she ordered herself. It had been a long and busy night in the ER, and Dr. Wells clearly didn't expect her to go out of her way for a wound that was probably okay on its own—and on a patient who had all the appearances of good common sense.

If he'd had common sense, he wouldn't have been whittling that thing in the first place, Allison groused to herself. But there was a secret part of her that thrilled to the idea that he'd made her something with his own hands...even when he hadn't been able to bring himself to pick up the phone and call her.

It took him a few minutes to answer the door, and when he did, he didn't look at all like Kyle. His face still held the shadow of a beard, his button-down shirt was open, revealing a V-neck T-shirt, and a little cowlick stuck up on the crown of his head.

"Oh! Hey! I—is something wrong?" Kyle asked.

She held up the kit where she kept gauze and tape and scissors. "Thought you might need some help with that dressing."

He glanced down at his hand and colored slightly. "Uh, yeah, probably. Since I soaked it in the shower this morning. Stupid, huh?" Kyle opened the door and gestured her in with his bandaged hand. "Thanks. I hadn't got that far along, but I knew trying to bandage it one-handed was going to be a challenge."

His house, just as it had the first time, surrounded her with that back-in-time sensation. And just as before, it awakened all her feelings of inferiority about her own plans for Belle Paix.

As she followed Kyle through the dining room he called over his shoulder, "Come on… I've just got the bacon started, and I did manage to get coffee on."

And there was that picture-perfect kitchen. This time, it had a slightly more lived-in look, with a coffee cup on the butcher-block worktable and a frying pan on the stove. "Oh, shoot!" He muttered something else under his breath.

She closed the gap between him and the stove. "What?"

"I burned the bacon. Well, not exactly burned, but…"

Allison stared down into the pan and saw that it held a curious mix of raw and burned-to-the-point-of-charcoal bacon. "Sit," she ordered him. "You've rescued me enough times. Now let me pay you back."

He dragged out a stool from under the table and sank down on it. "I think, just for this morning, I'll let you. Unless you tell me it's a highly addictive choice and I'll never want to cook bacon on my own again."

Allison laughed in spite of herself. "I think you know you can resist me."

An awkward silence followed her words, broken only by the sound of the scrape of fork against pan as she raked out the burned bacon. Now why had she said that?

It's true, she thought as she busied herself with finding more bacon in the fridge—which was hidden behind decorative panels to match the cabinetry. *He hasn't called me in a week. He's never once tried to kiss me without hesitating first.*

When he did speak, it was on a totally different subject. "Did you—did you come by here to see the medallion? I can get it for you."

She looked up from the bacon she was adding to the pan. "No…I just…" Somehow she couldn't bear to tell him that she'd wanted to see him, so she fell back on Dr. Wells's request the night before. "The doc suggested I come over and look in on you."

His crestfallen expression, which he altered in a matter of seconds, heartened her. Had he missed her in spite of not phoning?

"Oh, I see."

"But I wanted to come," she hurriedly told him. "I figured you could use some help."

"And here I was, thinking you'd come just to borrow my modern stove," he joked.

"I have to say, it cooperates better than Gran's."

"Oh, you just have to know how to talk to old things," Kyle said. "Cajole them out of their cantankerous ways. Smooth out their bad moods and let 'em know you appreciate them even when nobody else can see their value."

A sudden longing to be loved by someone who was that patient, someone who could appreciate a person or a thing despite how it could let you down at the worst possible moment, filled her. Kyle was that sort of man. He wouldn't let his head be turned by a trendy, fashion-forward younger woman if he'd committed himself to someone. Allison felt that in her bones.

Now he was up again, busy moving around the kitchen. She heard plates and silverware rattle as she concentrated on the bacon—and tried to block out her confusing feelings for him.

This was a guy who wouldn't see reason, who wouldn't use his considerable influence with the committee to help her grandmother. So why on earth would Allison want him to be the guy she came home to?

"If you'll hand me some eggs…" she started, more to get her mind off her thoughts than real hunger.

But even before she'd finished the sentence, Kyle had the carton of eggs on the counter by the stove. "And you'll need a bowl…or did you want to fry them? Up to you, as you're the chef for the day."

Did he always have to be so considerate of the little things? she mused. That he could be so thoughtful in so many ways magnified the one thing he couldn't be flexible about.

"But you're the wounded warrior." Now she took out her frustration on the bacon in the pan, jabbing it with a fork until the grease in the pan splattered up and just missed her fingers.

"Keep that up and you'll be joining me. Can't

paint as well with a burn on your fingers." Kyle leaned against the counter by the stove.

She felt his eyes on her and tried not to wonder what he was thinking. It shouldn't matter what he thought of her—just her variance request, just what he could do to help Gran get home.

"I'm almost done painting." She couldn't meet his eyes, for some reason, so wound up staring at his uninjured hand, which was propped against the counter. Suddenly, unbidden, came the memory of a time he'd used those hands… He'd been helping her paint, and had put down his roller. With his strong fingers he'd massaged her neck and shoulders until all the knots were out.

But that had been before, when things were easy between them, conversation had never flagged and she'd thought he was really going to help her—not just with the house, but also with getting that variance request. When she'd thought she could count on him.

Allison took up the bacon and cracked two eggs into the pan. "I figure fried eggs," she told him. "Easier."

"Yeah. That's you…simplest, most direct solution. No fuss, no muss," he said. There was no sting in his voice, though, no accusation. It was almost…wistful.

With the eggs done, she started to pull out the stool at the butcher-block table.

He stopped her. "No! C'mon. Let's eat in the breakfast nook." Despite his sore hand, he picked up her plate. "Grab our cups."

She followed him to the butler's pantry and slid into the seat across from him in the nook. The morning sun spilled onto the table and lit the glass doors of the built-in cabinets. She could see that the panes were old, the glass wavy and rippled, distorting the blue-and-white china stored behind it.

"So you really eat here, huh?" she asked.

"Only with very special breakfast guests who come by to doctor my wounded hand. Not just any riffraff." He smiled at her over his cup of coffee. "So what do you think of it?"

"It's…it's a tight squeeze," she admitted. But maybe it felt that way only because she was so keenly aware of how close he was. This was no wide table in a restaurant, designed to hold huge platters of food. This was a tiny table that left her no more than a breath away from Kyle.

"Yeah. Made for little ones, I suspect."

"To give the mom breathing room," Allison suggested.

But she wasn't picturing a pair of kids now… she was picturing newlyweds eating their first breakfast together after their honeymoon, and she couldn't help but wonder if that woman, so many years ago, had felt as aflutter as Allison did now.

They ate their bacon and eggs in silence, though she did notice that every time she sneaked a glance at Kyle, he was sneaking one at her.

"Kyle—"

"Allison—"

At that, they both laughed uneasily. "You go first," she said, all at once not certain what she would have said.

"Well...it's just...I've missed you," he blurted out.

Instead of giving her pure and unadulterated comfort, his statement perversely reawakened her earlier irritation. She started to retort that he'd been the one who'd slammed out her back door, and that he'd known where she'd been the whole time, if he'd really missed her all that much.

Kyle's pinched and miserable face, though, shut that thought down before she could utter it. Maybe he'd used this week to think things through, to come up with a strategy to help her.

"Oh...I—I figured you missed all that work on Belle Paix like a hole in your head." Her attempt at a joke fell flat.

"I assumed you'd had enough of me." With

his forefinger, he traced a ring on the vinyl tablecloth with its retro kitchen print. “But I thought about you a thousand times a day… what were you painting? What colors did you choose? Did you need help? What sort of complications were you running into…?” He lifted his gaze to meet hers.

Okay, so no heartfelt declarations of undying love, and maybe secretly he really missed Belle Paix more than he did me. But...maybe I should take what I can get?

She chased the last bite of fried egg with her fork. “Sage.”

“What?”

“I painted the living room and library a sage green.” She flicked a corkscrew curl up for his inspection. “See? I even have a handy paint swatch for your viewing pleasure.”

Kyle reached over and twirled the sage-hued lock around his index finger. “That’s—that’s nice,” he said, but without conviction. “How’d you choose it?”

“I chose it because I liked it on the swatch, the same as anybody else, I’d think.” She snatched the curl back and tried to tamp down her irritation. “Let me guess. It wasn’t a popular color back then.”

Kyle wrinkled his nose and shook his head.

"Nope. Not that particular shade. But it's what you like."

She laid her fork across her plate and traced the simple lines on its handle. She would bet that silverware pattern that could have been found in the drawers of the kitchen or here in the butler's pantry when the house was brand-new. "The wallpaper that was in the house when it was new was particularly gosh-awful, you know. Hideous stuff with big cabbage roses printed on it."

"Doesn't surprise me at all. Victorian wall-papers could be…garish. But people liked them like that."

"No, they didn't, not everybody. Davinia complained in her journal that Ambrose ordered the wallpaper without even asking her. She hated it. In fact, it was Davinia herself who gave me the idea about the sage green. She wrote that if it had been left up to her, she would have painted the entire downstairs the color of the underside of a sage leaf."

Kyle sat back, his eyebrows lifted in surprise. "Really? You'd mentioned journals, but I thought they were probably fairly dry… Many women were circumspect with what they wrote in their diaries back then, as their menfolk were apt to inspect them. Davinia's journal might be a perfect primary source—"

Allison shook her finger. “Nope. Don’t even think about it. Gran is very opinionated about keeping Davinia’s journals private. One of the worst times in my life was when she caught me and my friend Melanie giggling over one of them. They aren’t for public consumption.”

Kyle’s face fell. “Oh. Well. It’s so rare that we historians tumble on anything new.”

“Well, yeah. I mean, after all, you study *history*, and what’s anything but old news about that?” she teased. “Have you always been a history buff? Always liked old things?”

“I’ve always liked a good story,” he said. “That’s what I’m a sucker for, a good yarn.”

“And old houses? You got into that because of your love of history?”

He frowned. “Not exactly.” He stood and picked up her empty plate. “Let me—”

“Wash dishes? I don’t think so, not with that hand.” Allison took the plates back from him and headed into the kitchen. “You didn’t answer my question. What made you the patron saint of old houses?”

She’d begun to fill the sink with hot, soapy water before she realized that, though he’d followed her into the kitchen and stood beside her, he still hadn’t answered her. Allison turned her attention to Kyle’s face and was surprised to see genuine pain there.

"What?" she asked.

"You know, I didn't always appreciate old houses. As a teenager...shoot, even in college, I just sort of thought they'd always be there. I'd grown up in my father's home place...nothing fancy, just a folk Victorian that had been built about the same time Belle Paix was."

Restlessly, he began to prowl around the kitchen, straightening canisters and bringing the frying pan to the counter by the sink. Allison scrubbed a dish twice in order to give him time to put the memory into words.

Her patience paid off. As the frying pan clattered to the counter beside her, Kyle picked up the story. "And then my parents decided, since I'd told them I wasn't interested in staying in our hometown, that they'd sell. The guy who bought the house...the stupid idiot ruined it. First thing he did was put cheap aluminum siding on it—white, mind you, which turned this awful grayish color. He ripped out the windows, stripped off every inch of the gingerbread trim, tore down the chimneys."

Allison couldn't ignore the pain in Kyle's voice. She let the plate slip into the sudsy water and dried her hands. Turning to face him, she said quietly, "Oh, Kyle. So that's why..."

"The last time I saw the house, I barely recognized it...and you know what? All those 'improvements' he did? They're falling apart now. That house had lasted over a hundred years with nothing more than a good coat of paint every few years, and now it looks like it's ready for the junk heap. He could do what he liked—and I couldn't protect it."

She reached up to touch Kyle's shoulder. "That must have been awful, to see your family home so mistreated."

"My dad regretted selling that house for the rest of his life. If I'd only appreciated what I'd had…if I'd agreed to move back—"

"You wouldn't be here—or the person you are today, Kyle."

Now he jerked away from her. "That's as good as telling me I had to sacrifice my family's home to gain a little wisdom. Well, I won't let it happen again, that's for sure."

His emphatic words reminded her of the variance, and she wondered if he thought of her plans with the same contempt. Kyle would never be able to judge her choices about Belle Paix as anything but terrible. She turned back to finish the dishes, her hope fading away just like the soapsuds in the sink. "No, I don't imagine you would."

He seemed to realize what he'd said and how she'd taken it. "Don't—don't let me have spoiled a good morning with you," he told her. "And we've had a good one, right?"

Her heart twisted. She shook the water droplets from the now clean frying pan and began to dry it off. "Yeah. When we can tiptoe around me wanting a variance request, we're okay—more than okay," she admitted. She set the frying pan on the draining rack. "But can we really keep doing that?"

She thought about the story that Gwen was working on, and her own plans to harass every one of the city council members until they saw her point of view. If she succeeded, she'd be allowing people the opportunity to wreck Kyle's accomplishments.

But if she didn't try, the historical preservation committee would turn her down. She'd be stuck in limbo for another year—a year Gran might not have—before Allison would be allowed to submit another proposal.

And Gran's house would continue to fall apart.

Kyle ducked his head and avoided meeting her eyes. Part of her was glad he seemed to be really considering this, not just tossing off words he thought she wanted to hear.

"Maybe," he said finally. "I'll try if you will. You do what you have to do. And we'll…we'll let the chips fall where they may."

Tears sprang to her eyes. It wasn't what she wanted to hear him say. No, what she'd really hoped he'd tell her was that he understood her reasons, trusted her judgment, and knew that Gran was more important than some poky old ordinances.

But it was a sign he was trying. Maybe if he could manage to move that little bit from his position, there was some hope he could meet her halfway. "Okay!" she said brightly. "Okay, then. I guess I'd better take a look at that hand."

CHAPTER TWENTY

ALLISON STARED AT the chairlift installer, knowing she was gawking at him in disbelief.

"But your salesman assured me that one chair was all I'd need. Now you're telling me that we really need *three* on this back stair? Your coworker told me that you could make the chair negotiate both turns! In fact, that's the reason that I chose your company, because he said you could do that."

The cost and aggravation of the one thing Gran had to have in place before she could come home had just tripled at the worst possible time.

Allison wished that she'd spent the past few days, since Kyle's ER visit, rushing the chair lift installer, instead of painting and sanding.

And let's be honest, thinking about Kyle.

Not for the first time did Allison wish Ambrose had put at least one actual bedroom downstairs.

But no. Gran had her heart set on her own bedroom, with no way up besides this flight of stairs or the main staircase. She was tired of making do in the library.

Allison dragged her attention back to the long and complex explanation the workman was giving her.

He stopped, wrinkled his mouth a little and then said shortly, "Well, yeah. I mean, it's on a track, see?" He indicated where the track would lay along the stairs. "So it ends here. And then your granny would have to move to another chair over on these three steps." He crossed the first little landing and demonstrated. "And then, boom, she moves over to this flight and the last chair. So not ideal, but way better than no lift at all."

"I could probably put in an elevator for the cost of this!" Allison muttered.

"Hey, we do that, too. Just rip out these old stairs and I'll put you in a fine elevator, big enough for a wheelchair. Lots of old folks are doing that these days. And we could do it, hmm, for about fifteen."

"Fifteen *thousand?*" Now she was gawking again.

"Yeah. But cheap, ya know, in the long run because it will help the resale value of the house."

Allison laughed as she pictured Kyle's reaction to an elevator. He'd had to physically lift her grandmother up and down these stairs himself before he'd even begun to consider a chair lift a good idea. "I don't think so. The only person willing to buy this house would be someone who's a purist, and I've met one or two of them."

The worker shrugged. "Suit yourself. But that's the nuts and bolts. Three rails, three chairs."

Allison sighed. She walked to the front hall and stared at the sweeping curve of the staircase there. Her eyes lit on the missing medallion detail, and it bugged her that the design seemed a bit snaggle-toothed without that piece of carving.

Gran would kill her for putting the chair lift here. And Kyle would swear she was ruining the entire effect of the entrance. But needs must…

"What about in here? On these stairs?" she called.

The worker loped into the front hall, squinted up at the stairs and shook his head. "I can do it. But those curving steps up there? See?" He pointed at the gentle curve at the top. "That's gonna be a problem. And pricey. It will be as much as the three simple rails."

Allison groaned, but in an irritated flash, she realized she was glad of the news. She didn't want the chair lift on these stairs—and not because of Gran or Kyle. She didn't want them because *she* knew they'd spoil the effect.

I have to stop letting Kyle ruin me, she thought. *I wouldn't have given it a second thought before I met him.*

"Okay, well, I guess I don't have a choice. I've gotten bids from three different companies, and you're still a bit cheaper than the other two. Plus, the rehab facility that Gran is in recommended your work."

"Won't be that much more to put in that elevator for ya," he told her. "What's another five grand, huh? And you'd have peace of mind and handicap access."

She pictured shiny stainless steel doors closing off the back staircase, felt the gnawing pain at the anticipation of a part of her childhood gone.

Kyle really has *ruined me*, she thought. "No, we'll go with the chair lift. Can you get it done today?"

"Nope. Sorry, but I've got to order those other two chairs. If I'd known at the start I needed three of 'em, I would have brought them with me. I've got enough track—at least that idiot measured right. Our sales force..." The guy shook his head. "I tell you, wouldn't it make more sense for the people installing this stuff to actually come out here and quote you a price? But no. Corporate geniuses, the lot of 'em."

"So…how long?"

The man cocked his head to one side. She saw pity on his face, but she was beyond pride. Maybe if he felt sorry for her, he'd move a little quicker.

"Let me make a phone call or two," he said. "If the chairs don't absolutely have to match in color, I might be able to scrounge them up from some of our other installers in this area. That would mean we didn't have to wait for them to come from the warehouse."

He went off to his van to make the calls, leaving Allison to wander outside to the front porch, where she sank onto the steps.

In the harsh daylight there was no mistaking the peeling paint and porch boards that needed replacing. The furniture looked wispy and ragged, as if the basket weave was coming undone, but it had been on that porch for as long as Allison could remember. Gran had managed to have it patched and recaned a time or two, and they had repainted it every summer…but it was long overdue for some serious repair.

I'll get her home and she won't even be able to venture out onto the porch. Allison let her chin sink into the palm of her hand. She would not cry. She was tough. She had Davinia Shepherd's blood in her veins, and she was better than the wimpy, whiney thing this house had reduced her to. She just had to focus on why it was so important to do this.

Gran made the sacrifice for you, when she was already on a fixed income and retired. You have a job, a way to earn money, and all the overtime you want. So this is a piece of cake. Just work harder.

She reached in her pocket for her phone, but just as she was about to see if Melanie was free during her planning period, she heard the front gate clang open.

"Hey, there. Communing with nature?" Kyle asked as he strode up the walk toward her.

Allison felt her heart rat-a-tat in her chest with a ridiculous amount of pleasure at seeing him.

"No, trying to get over the shock of having the chair lift guy tell me it was almost as cheap to install an elevator."

Kyle stopped short. His mouth literally fell open before he said, "You're not serious."

She waved off his slack-jawed reaction. "Don't worry. I'm not about to rip out the back stairs and put in an elevator. The historic preservation committee really would burn me at the stake for that sin."

But Kyle had closed the gap and now sank

down beside her. "No, I wasn't even thinking about that—although elevators in that day and age weren't unheard of, and some larger homes had them. We could make it work, aesthetically speaking. What I was so blown away about was the cost."

"I don't think you could get a pretty elevator for the price he quoted me. Besides, we all know that when you start ripping things out, you're in for a lot of 'jumpin' Jehosaphats.'" She dropped her chin into her palm again.

Kyle put an arm around her. "The end is in sight..."

"Kyle, it's not. Gran's rehab facility called me this morning. I had a choice. I could either switch her to self-pay status or use up the precious little remaining of her benefits before her long-term care insurance maxed out. And it's a lifetime cap, so once it's gone...well, it's gone."

"Oh. Wow. How much?"

"They're giving me a discounted rate, since her health insurance is still covering a portion of her therapy. But it's still nearly five grand a month. I have to get her home. I can swing two weeks, maybe a month more...but that's it. Besides..."

"She's ready to come home, isn't she?" Kyle asked.

"Yeah. She is. And even the admissions person at the facility told me that she's reaching the end of whatever in-patient physical therapy can do for her. They want to switch her to outpatient occupational therapy and start working with her here."

"That sounds good, though. You get the chair lift in and—"

"Look at this place. I wanted it so much nicer for her." Allison sprang to her feet and faced the house. Every bit of peeling paint and dry rot seemed to accuse her. She couldn't help but shake her fist at it, melodramatic as she knew that was. "Cursed old house!"

The installer rounded the corner and came to a halt. "Ma'am? You…you okay?"

Allison managed a tight, grim smile. "I will be if you tell me you found those chairs."

"Well, actually…I got an installer about an hour away, and he's upgrading the standard chairs in a house with our deluxe model. People do that, ya know, they go the cheap route, and then they realize they should have— Well, anyway," he interrupted himself. "Long and short of it is if you don't mind some gently used chairs that are the basic model, I can drive over and get 'em today. We'll give you a good deal on 'em, too."

"Great! That's really good news."

"All right, then. I'll go get 'em and be back this afternoon to start work on it."

With that, the installer loped off in the direction of his van.

"See? Things are looking up," Kyle told her.

She turned back to him. "Maybe. Until the next jumpin' Jehosaphat leaps out from around the corner."

Kyle didn't say anything to that. He regarded her with so much caring and patience she thought her heart would twist in her chest. What could she do for him that would tell him how much she appreciated his kindness? His willingness to stick it out with her in spite of her attack on his precious ordinances?

You're just feeling guilty.

"Come on, before I change my mind," she said.

Allison led him up the two flights of stairs to the third floor. "This was to be extra guest rooms—oh, and the billiard room, too, but since there was no bathroom on this floor, the space was too inconvenient for people to use. I think this floor has pretty much always been used as a huge dumping ground for junk. Mind your step...you've got over a century of clutter to negotiate around."

"And that's a lot of stuff." On her way to what would have been the front third-floor bedroom, she heard Kyle clattering behind her, and knew he'd run afoul of a big, chunky wooden carving of a Native American in full regalia that Gran had stashed up here. "Is that a…"

"It supposedly stood outside a tobacco shop at one point, and my grandfather—biological, not Pops—won it at a card game. But who knows? You're addicted to stories, right? Well, there are a thousand stories up here. It's in this room, what I wanted to—"

"Wait! These are records!"

"Well, yeah." She turned around to see him pawing through a stack of vinyl records. "Some of 'em go with a Victrola that's up here somewhere. But the rest of them are Gran's."

"Wow. These are almost mint-condition albums from…looks like Frank Sinatra and Dean Martin and…" Kyle was flipping through them. "These could be worth some money."

"Oh, Gran won't sell them. I've tried to get rid of them at yard sales—"

"No, Allison! I mean real money. Collectors love these sorts of things."

She stared around at the mountains of junk. For a moment, she wondered if any of it could be sold to raise money. Gran would kill her. She'd held on to all these treasures with white-knuckled intensity every time Allison had even gently suggested they clean out the third floor.

She shrugged. "Doesn't matter. As long as Gran is alive, she's not willing to part with anything up here. And hey, it's her stuff, and...really, when you think about it, she has managed to purge a good bit. I mean, this is it—this floor holds all the detritus we've saved from a hundred twenty-six years."

"Wow. How did she decide what to keep?"

"If she could remember a story about it. If she couldn't find it anywhere else. If it belonged to Davinia or Ambrose or her grandparents or her parents. She's a little more ruthless with her own stuff."

Allison stepped around dusty trunks and boxes to clear a path to a set of bookshelves crammed with leather-bound volumes and old college textbooks. Interspersed among them was a hodgepodge of ticky-tacky porcelain shepherd boys and girls, broken lamps, and more than a few vases of stunningly atrocious colors.

She moved a couple vases to reveal a set of slim, leather-bound books in various muted shades of green. "Voilà," she said.

Kyle peered over her shoulder, so close she could smell the clean scent of the soap he used. She recognized it. It was the only soap Gran would allow in the house—Kirk's Natural Castile Soap, in production since 1839.

"What…what are these?" he asked. He reached around her, then drew back his hand before touching one of the books.

"Davinia's journals. I have one downstairs—I figured it would be interesting to read about the time the house was being built. See? You've turned me into one of those renovation fanatics." She craned her head back to look at him, then wished she hadn't. His mouth was a mere two inches away, and even though he wasn't touching her, she could feel the heat from his body.

But Allison couldn't turn away. The light in his eyes, the O of surprise that touched his mouth, mesmerized her.

It took an inordinate amount of effort—made just a bit easier because Kyle was focused on the books as firmly as she'd been focused on him—to break the spell she was under. She reached out and handed him a journal.

He stepped toward the light spilling in from the front window to examine it. "I shouldn't even be handling these without gloves—and they really ought not to be up here…"

Now the spell was really and truly broken. "Leave it to you to fuss over how we keep these journals," she muttered.

He lifted his eyes from the page just long

enough to skewer her with one of his famous know-it-all expressions.

"Don't." Allison held up a hand, palm out in warning. "Don't start lecturing me on the proper way to keep historical artifacts, because I know it would either involve giving them up or spending a whole lot of money that I don't have."

With that, she shook her head and headed for the stairs. When would she learn? With Kyle, it seemed she could never do anything right.

CHAPTER TWENTY-ONE

KYLE EASED HIS way down the stairs, listening intently for any sounds of Allison. He hadn't meant to offend her—again.

She just never seemed to value what she had.

Simply because something had seen better days didn't relegate it to the dump, or mean it couldn't give you enjoyment—just like the items he held in his hand.

He found her in the living room, sitting at the gleaming black grand piano, Cleo the ninja cat beside her. Allison held a photo in a heavy ornate frame, staring at it as though she was listening to it issue important, sage advice.

When Kyle approached her and asked, "Who's that?" she jumped slightly. She put a hand to her chest and blew out an embarrassed breath.

"Sorry. A tad anxious today, I guess." She glanced back at the picture. "It's Gran, when she was young. Her first wedding day. Pops never minded that she kept it—said she was beautiful, and it would be a shame for her to put it away."

Peering closer, Kyle noted the old-fashioned dress with lace sleeves—clearly out of the 1940s despite a swooping sweetheart neckline. "Wow...that neckline—"

"Scandalous for the time, wasn't it?" Allison set the photo back on the piano. "Gran loved Rita Hayworth and wanted a dress just like one she wore in that old movie—what was it? *You'll Never Get Rich*? Gran said her father very nearly didn't let her walk down the aisle with that much skin showing. If her fiancé hadn't been leaving that next week for basic training, my great-grandfather might have called off the wedding. And then, who knows? I might not have even been here. What have you brought down?" She dipped her head to indicate what he was carrying. "I thought you'd have the journals already boxed up, to take them to a proper home."

"I..." Kyle was confused. Had Allison meant for him to take them? "But you said Gran had strong feelings about them. I didn't want to plunder until I had asked her permission. But I might bring you an archival box to put them in. That would at least protect them a bit better. But these..." He held up the 45-rpm records he'd chosen. "You looked so depressed and overwhelmed. And I remembered seeing a turntable down here. Does it work?"

"Sure, though even Gran has an iPod these days."

He lifted the lid, placed the record on the turntable and gently set the needle down. It pleased him to no end how big a smile Allison rewarded him with when the strains of "That's Amore" filled the living room.

Cleo wasn't as pleased, skittering out the door as fast as her sable paws could carry her.

"Come on," he said to Allison. He drew her off the piano bench into the middle of the floor. "You can't just listen. "

"I can't dance—look at me—"

When she would have pulled away, he held her gently but firmly in his arms and shook his head. "I am looking at you," he told her.

And he was. Her eyes were still a little shiny from some unshed tears, and they glowed green and bright in a face nestled among those beautiful red curls. She wasn't wearing a scrap of makeup, but she didn't need to. In fact, he thought she looked wonderful just the way she was.

The blush that touched her cheeks entranced him. For a moment, he found it hard to breathe, until he spun her away from him. The breathing problem came back as soon as she returned to his arms.

Why was it that, when she was next to him, he could forget about all the things that made the two of them such a mismatch?

She laughed as he swung her around and Dean Martin sang about the moon being like a big pizza pie, the accordion swelling to its crescendo. Now her eyes were bright with happiness, not tears. Being with her like this felt effortless and easy. If he could always make her feel this way…

The song ended and the next 45 made its characteristic clunk as it landed on the turntable. The needle fell, unleashing Sinatra and "The Way You Look Tonight."

"I should be wearing a big swirly skirt for this, not old jeans," Allison protested.

"Close your eyes…pretend," Kyle told her. "No, I mean it, close 'em. Close 'em up tight—no, you're peeking!" He swung her around in a foxtrot. "You're very good at this."

Allison's eyes flew open. "You sound surprised! I'll have you know Pops taught me how to dance. He said it would come in useful someday to know how to do an actual dance that had an actual name and that you actually needed a partner for." Her mouth quirked, and she closed her eyes again.

"Have you visualized me in a dinner jacket yet?" Kyle asked.

"I'm still struggling with transforming my outfit, much less yours," Allison told him. "No, I'm thinking of Gran and Pops, and how much they loved each other. They were two peas in a pod, you know."

Suddenly she went still in his arms. Was she thinking what Kyle had been pondering just a few short minutes ago? How different the two of them were in their views of life?

The record changed again, and soon Sinatra was crooning about flying to the moon. Kyle couldn't bear for her to pull away now. He bent down, with no hesitation, no thinking, just going on impulse, and kissed her.

The blaring brass of Sinatra's band couldn't outblast the pounding of Kyle's heart as Allison kissed him back with an unmistakable intensity. Now they weren't dancing. They stood in the living room, on Gran's ancient faded carpet, wrapped in each other's arms, hanging on for dear life.

Forgetting everything. And he allowed himself to do that, let himself focus on the here and now rather than the showdown that was coming, the possibility that the city council would even consider repealing his ordinances, the idea that Allison couldn't bring Gran home to the house she'd hoped to—and that he was the cause of that.

No. He just drank in her nearness, the warmth of her, how she made him feel.

The kiss ended, began again, then was interrupted by the ta-chunk of the needle skipping, as it had no other record to start on. Allison backed away from Kyle. She put her fingers to her lips almost protectively, and stepped over to the turntable to rescue the record. She didn't face him when she broke the silence, and somehow that spoke more loudly than her words.

"Wow." Her voice was strained, husky. "That—you're not just a great dancer. That was amazing."

"It's easy with the right girl."

He made a move to close the gap between them. But he stopped when he saw her wince as though in pain.

"Allison?"

"Kyle—what happens?"

"What do you mean, what happens?"

"Don't be obtuse. What happens when either I convince the city council members to change their ordinances or you convince them to keep them as they are? Aren't we lying to ourselves?"

"I think—"

But she obviously wasn't interested in his answer, because she cut him short. “We are, aren’t we? I am, anyway. I like you. No…maybe more than like. But…I can’t do this, okay? Can’t we just wait until…well, after?”

“So you know the city council will definitely take up the question of the ordinances?” All his early warm, fuzzy feelings had faded, and he felt as though he’d been doused with cold water and awakened from a dream.

She turned now, finally, to face him. “No. I don’t. But if they don’t, it won’t be from my lack of trying. I have to do this, Kyle. I have even less money than I did before, now that I’m footing Gran’s stay at the rehab facility.”

“And you honestly think I can simply snap my fingers and make all this go away, don’t you?” Her face was answer enough. “Well, Allison, I can’t. I wish I could, and I’m sorry, but those ordinances were as carefully thought out as we could make them, and they’re there for a purpose. And as much as I want to, I can’t bend them for you—or for Gran—or even for myself.”

And without things devolving into a shouting match—something he didn’t want at all—there was nothing left to say. He spun on his heel and walked out the front door.

KYLE TAPPED HIS foot while he waited for Lorenzo Adams to make small talk about the weather and summer vacations with his latest customer. Finally, just as Kyle had decided to leave, Lorenzo handed the woman her dry-cleaned clothes. The plastic bag enclosing them flapped in the breeze as she headed out the door.

Lorenzo's big, toothy smile died as he regarded Kyle.

"What? Just because I didn't bring any clothes to be cleaned?" Kyle attempted to joke. But the uncharacteristic sober expression on the man's face worried him.

"If I depended on you to keep me in business, I'd be bankrupt," Lorenzo told him. "You have got to be the most self-reliant bachelor I know."

"Go fuss at my mom about it. She's the one who insisted I learn how to look after myself," Kyle retorted lightly. "So if it's not my lack of patronage, what is it?"

Lorenzo reached under the counter and pulled out a newspaper. "I was hoping you'd come by to explain this." He slapped the paper down on the counter.

At first Kyle didn't see how he could possibly be expected to explain the main headline, Factory Announces More Job Cuts.

But then his eye slid down the page to the far left corner. There it was, in a box, with a picture of Belle Paix: Local Octogenarian Challenges Historic Ordinances.

"First of all, it's not Gran herself—and second, it would be historical, not historic—"

"Get off your nitpicky self and read the story, won't you?" Lorenzo tapped the article with a stubby index finger. "Much as I hate to admit it, Gwen wrote a zinger of a story, clunky headline or not."

Kyle ground his teeth but picked up the paper. It was all there, a well-worded retelling of Allison's woes, with even a quote from Gran saying she'd already warned her granddaughter how the committee would stonewall her on her requests. That was the tone of the article. Allison was reasonable; the historical committee was hysterical.

"Not one quote from our side," Kyle pointed out. He threw the paper down. "She didn't even try to get a response from me."

"Just as well. You would have come across all professorial and rattled on for three paragraphs about the need for historical accuracy." Lorenzo folded his arms across his chest. "Now am I right or am I right?"

"Lorenzo! Whose side are you on, anyway?"

"Side? I'm not on either side—I'm on my district's side. Whatever the folks who elected me want, well, I'm obliged to deliver."

"That's not true, and you know it. Every person in your district would *want* zero taxes, but you can't give that to them, now can you? Because it wouldn't be in their best interest. Same here."

"Listen, Kyle, half of my constituents think all those people living in the historic district are rolling in money—and having it on the record that you expect those folks to dish out twenty grand to paint a house just reinforces that. Don't you get it? A lot of the people I represent don't make twenty thousand dollars in a year."

"I don't expect people to pay twenty thousand dollars to paint their house—"

"Oh, yeah? Well, that's what the costs were when this Allison bidded it out. Says so right here." Lorenzo tapped the newsprint again.

"That's on the high side. I know that guy. He doesn't want to fool with Belle Paix, anyway, so he quoted high to discourage her. She can get it done more reasonably than—"

"How much? Ballpark?"

Kyle stared down at his shoes. Why did he feel so guilty about this? Yes, owning a historic home meant extra sacrifices, but it was worth it. And if it wasn't, nobody forced you to live in one.

"A paint scheme like Belle Paix's, in the shape it's currently in...ballpark, ten to fifteen thousand." He saw the I-told-you-so forming on the council member's mouth. "But that's because Gran let it go so long, and it's going to need a ton of scraping."

"So you're telling me to explain to my people that it's right and fair to demand that an old lady with a broken hip pays out ten thousand dollars to get her house painted to suit you?" Lorenzo shook his head. "It's not going to fly, Kyle. And you know it."

"You're going to consider repealing those ordinances, aren't you?" Kyle's throat went dry. He recalled what the historic district had looked like just a few short years before, and he knew it would take just half that time to see his work undone.

"I've already had three council members call me, demanding we at least have a hearing on it, and the ink's still smearing on this paper. I get you, Kyle. I get why you're so fired up about the historic district, and I know why you wrote the ordinances the way you did—no!" Lorenzo shook his finger when Kyle would have spoken. "Don't say the committee, because not a person on that committee would have been able to draft those ordinances without you. And we passed them as a whole, just like *you* asked me to."

"And it's paid off, hasn't it?" Kyle protested.

"Look at the money we've brought in. At the tourism dollars. One person complains—"

"No. One woman tells a very convincing, very easy-to-relate-to story about her grandmother, who has lived in that house all her life. She points out a real flaw in your ordinances, a consequence you hadn't considered. So, Kyle, if I were you, I'd be practicing my best arguments about why the city needs such restrictive ordinances. Or better yet, make this whole headache go away and work out some compromise with this woman. So go on." Lorenzo made a shooing move with his hand. "Beat it. Because me? I'm not the one you have to convince."

Kyle turned for the door. "Could have fooled me, Lorenzo. You sure could have fooled me."

CHAPTER TWENTY-TWO

THE CLANG OF the wrought-iron gate snapped Allison's attention from Melanie's tale of classroom woe and the tall jug of lemonade they'd been sharing on Gran's front porch. Allison looked over to see Herbert stomping up the front path.

"Who's that?" Melanie asked. "He seems as fierce as any mad parent I've ever encountered."

"That would be Herbert, a zealot from the hysterical society." Exhaling, Allison rose slowly and took the porch steps to head him off.

He shook the newspaper in her face. "Young lady, just what do you think you're doing? You're ruining everything!"

"I beg your pardon—"

"This story! You don't deny you're hounding the city council to repeal our ordinances? Do you want Lombard to look like the mess it did before Kyle turned things around?"

"Sir..." Allison struggled with her temper. She hated being talked to as though she were a wayward ten-year-old. Not even Pops had spoken to her like this in his worst scoldings.

"Well? Answer me!"

"I will. When you calm down."

The old man compressed his lips, but still nearly trembled with anger. "I am calm. But I will apologize. I wish I could maintain my cool like Kyle does. I just get so…so—"

Yeah, right, well, at least with you, I know where I stand. Kyle makes you think he's on your side and then lets you down.

"Mr.—"

"Just call me Herbert." Again, she could see him making a valiant attempt to rein in his temper. But his anger was visible in the way his throat worked and his chest heaved.

"Herbert, would you care to sit down and have some lemonade?" She waved a hand in the direction of the porch and Melanie, who was hanging on to every word with round eyes.

"No, I don't want any fool lemonade!" Herbert shook his head again. He took a handkerchief out of his back pocket and wiped his brow. "Have mercy," he muttered. "Look, could we just cut the small talk and you tell me why you're bent on destroying Lombard's historic district?"

"I assume there's a story in there about Belle Paix?" Allison gestured toward the paper.

"As if you didn't know." His mouth took on an even more pinched, sour crimp.

"I'm not trying to ruin the historic district. I'm just trying to get Gran's house painted. Don't you think it needs a coat of paint?"

Herbert stared up at the big Victorian. "Young woman, that house *has been* needing a coat of paint. Now it needs pressure washing, sandblasting, two coats of primer and at least another two base coats. And that's just to get it started. If your grandmother hadn't been so stubborn, she could have gotten this done much more reasonably years ago."

"She wasn't stubborn." Allison insisted. "She was broke. Not everybody has a fat pension to help feed their historic house habit."

"And you think I've got a fat pension?" He drew himself to his full height. "No, ma'am, I don't. I've saved, and when I see something that needs fixing, I fix it…because if you ignore it, it just gets that much more expensive."

Allison pressed the heels of her palms to her eyes. If this man didn't get off her front lawn in five seconds…

She dropped her hands, marshaled her thoughts and stared him down. "Sir. I won't dignify with a response your implied accusations about my grandmother. I will say this. I will be happy—more than happy—to entertain any sort of compromise you and Kyle and the rest of your happy band of historic OCDers can work out. If you can't help me address this very real problem that I have—no money, a falling-down house and an unbending ordinance that you helped pass—well, I'll exercise my civic right and go before the city council. Maybe there, cooler, more reasonable heads will prevail. Until then? Have a very good day, sir. A very good day."

With that, she turned and stomped back up the porch steps. She wasn't quite sure what she'd do if he dogged her heels.

So she was glad when she sank back into her chair across from Melanie and saw out of the corner of her eye that Herbert was storming toward the gate.

Her friend let out a low whistle. "I'd forgotten what that redheaded temper looked like when it got unleashed."

"Oh, he didn't see the half of it." Allison picked up her lemonade. To her irritation, the glass shook. She steadied it and took a long, welcome sip.

"You told him off but good. What was all that about, anyway?"

"Oh, a story that was in the paper about those stupid ordinances."

"Wait. I have the paper—today's?" Melanie

rooted around in her huge sack of a purse until she came out with a rather battered edition. She smoothed out the pages across her lap. "Here it is—on the front page, wow!"

She skimmed it in silence, her smile dimming into a thoughtful frown.

A knot of apprehension formed in the pit of Allison's stomach. She hadn't expected Melanie to give a raving cheer of support. Still…

"What is it? I haven't read it, so I don't know what it says." Allison crowded beside her on the love seat and peered over her shoulder.

Wow. Gwen hadn't pulled any punches. She'd called the ordinances draconian and repressive. While she'd quoted Allison accurately, somehow on the page, in that unforgiving ink, Allison sounded more partisan.

And Kyle and the historic preservation committee wound up looking like an unfeeling bunch of pencil-pushing bureaucrats.

Well, the ordinances are unfair, she thought.

"You said all this?" Melanie folded the paper and laid it on the table. "You really think the ordinances are a tax on home owners of the historic houses?"

"Well…" Allison shifted uncomfortably in her seat. "We pay to keep a main attraction polished to perfection, and other people profit from that. We don't get a dime from all those businesses that make money off the historic district—"

"But, Allison! You do! You save on taxes because of sales tax dollars that flow into the community. And we have higher employment, and less crime, and better schools. But then, my own mother owns a tea shop that caters to the tourists, so of course I'm biased. But the historical society has done a lot of good in this town, given the place an identity, something to be proud of. And my students benefit from the name recognition Lombard has now—not to mention the projects the historical society has done on behalf of the school."

Allison sank back against the love seat, astonished at the vehemence in Melanie's words. If there was one thing she could count on from their years of friendship, it was that Melanie would always call it like she saw it. And she saw it, Allison had to admit, pretty much like it was.

"I'm not trying to turn back the clock, Melanie." She fumbled for the words. "I just want Kyle to—to work with me. I have to get this house in shape. Gran's not getting any younger, and I really, really have no more money."

Her friend reached over and squeezed her hand. "I know. I know how much you love Gran. But somehow..." She gave the paper a gentle shake. "This feels personal—no, not to me. It feels like it's something between you and Kyle, not something that needs to spill out and affect the whole community. Your actions have consequences—consequences that could cost people their livelihoods."

Anger flared up in Allison. "So I should take one for the team? Pay at least ten grand to some house painter so this place will match Kyle's dream-house ordinance?"

Melanie shrugged. "I don't know. It's not fair. But there's got to be a solution that neither of you has considered." She rose to her feet, clearly ready to leave. "Because it sounds like you two could be a pair of puppies fighting over one bone, and not bothering to look around to see that there's another bone just waiting to be had."

AT THE END of the boardroom table, Eunice took off her glasses. The rhinestone-bejeweled chains attached to the earpieces clacked together as she held the spectacles aloft. Her brow furrowed.

"Kyle, I just don't know." Eunice slipped her glasses back on and flipped through the stack of papers before her. "This doesn't quite seem legitimate. We're holding a meeting about a home owner's request without the person being here. It feeds, I don't know, extralegal."

Her response evoked nods and grunts of agreement all around the table.

Kyle planted his palms on the mahogany finish, the beeswax polish satiny to the touch. It reminded him of the feel of Allison's cheek—

Who was he fooling? *Everything* reminded him of Allison these days.

The board had agreed to meet, all the members shaken by the previous day's news article. He didn't have to spell out the consequences to them.

But he could see he needed to connect the dots.

"We're not considering her particular request. I just thought you should all have in front of you exactly what she's asking for and why she felt she had to go to the city council," Kyle began.

Herbert interrupted. "See, now, it sounds like you *agree* with her, Kyle!"

"No—well, yes—not exactly." How to explain the emotions running through him? He took a deep breath. "I don't agree with the particulars of her request—and we won't consider that request now, as Eunice is perfectly correct in saying that we would need to follow protocol. But I can empathize with Allison's situation."

"We all can," Shelby Calvertson said. She

was slightly older than Kyle, and the most recent addition to the board. She and her husband had really struggled to restore their 1930s Craftsman bungalow, but they'd finally accomplished it.

Still, if Kyle had expected that Shelby would be the thin edge of a wedge to work out a compromise, his hopes were quickly dashed with her next words. "We've been there. We know how it is to run out of money before you run out of a to-do list. But that's why you go to the bank and borrow the money. It's not the end of the world. Besides…she and her grandmother haven't had to deal with a house payment for years. What if they had been like us, with the mortgage *and* a construction loan?"

"Guys, I don't want this to end up before the city council. If it does, given the way it looks now, we may well lose these ordinances. And that means—" Kyle broke off. He could hardly bear to view their faces. They all had the expectant look of someone waiting to be told what to do—while he was hoping *they* would pull a rabbit out of their hats for him.

"Yes. All that money we borrowed? All that sweat equity? It was for nothing," Shelby said flatly.

"More than that, the downtown business owners feel safe in plowing money back into their companies because we hold the neighborhood's feet to the fire," Eunice interjected. "They know they can count on us to be sure the tourists have something to actually come and see. Five years ago, there wasn't one antiques shop downtown. And now how many are there? Three?"

"Four." Kyle's quiet correction felt to him like an admission of guilt. They were right. Of course they were.

But so was Allison. And that couldn't be, could it? Both of them couldn't be right at the same time.

Those faces were fixed on him again, waiting, expectant. "As I was saying…we need to work out a compromise. Find some loophole we haven't spotted. Some fund or tax break Allison has overlooked—that I have overlooked. Because if we don't, she *will* go to the city council. And they'll hold a hearing on the ordinances."

"Then you have to convince them not to repeal them!" Herbert slammed his fist down on the mahogany table. "These ordinances protect our investments, our property values, and we've all had enough of a hit from the recent housing bubble. Home prices are just beginning to edge up in the district—and you know we count on that equity to borrow money for the repairs we have to do."

"Those are all good points. And yeah, a representative from the committee should present all those to the council—" Kyle began.

Herbert didn't wait for him to finish. "A representative? That would be you, Kyle. You're our chairman. And you've got great public speaking skills—plus, you can keep your cool with that woman. Me? The idea of what she's trying to do? It just puts a bee in my bonnet, let me tell you."

Kyle suddenly envisioned Herbert in a frilly bonnet, and had to struggle to keep a laugh choked back. He gradually registered the fact that Herbert's idea was being met with great enthusiasm.

"Oh, no—" Kyle tried to contain the wave of excited responses that were being volleyed around the table.

Herbert spoke up again, his stentorian voice ringing out. "I make a motion that Kyle serve as our representative to the council about this whole mess."

Kyle barely heard it being seconded, and the chorus of "ayes" over the pounding in his head. Go up against Allison? At a public meeting?

To her, it would be the ultimate betrayal. She'd never forgive him for that.

So why couldn't he focus on how *she* had betrayed him?

ALLISON SPOTTED GWEN CHAPMAN practically skipping down the steps of City Hall, her hair now sporting kryptonite green streaks in the place of its formerly hot-pink ones. She danced to a stop on the sidewalk.

"Just got a copy of the agenda of the meeting." Gwen waved the sheet of paper in the air. "And guess who's on it?"

Allison's stomach churned. "They really called the meeting?"

"Yep. Isn't that why you're here?"

"Well, the city manager asked me to stop by. I was honestly hoping they'd worked out some sort of deal."

Gwen shook her head decisively. "Can't do that. It has to go before the council for an open vote. They actually *did* try to pull a fast one and get Lorenzo Adams—he's the chair of the subcommittee over downtown development, and the historic preservation committee falls in his wheelhouse—to just run it through his group. But I put a stop to that."

"Why?" Allison's skin prickled. She reached out to take the agenda from Gwen. But a look at its fairly vanilla wording didn't reveal the source of Gwen's hyperhappiness.

"Sunshine laws, baby! They can't push me out of that boardroom unless they call an executive session, and they can't do that except for personnel and real estate. So they've got to wash their dirty laundry in public."

"I—public?" Allison could barely croak out the word past a dry-as-dust throat. "You mean…it will be open to the public? People will be there?"

"As many as I can squeeze into that hearing room—shoot, I'm hoping that the fire marshal will have to order it moved to the auditorium."

The prospect of speaking her piece before a packed auditorium made Allison feel faint. "You think that having people there will help my case?"

"Sure, sure," Gwen said. Her phone vibrated, and she started tapping away on it. "Oh, wow! Lots of social media buzz! This thing *does* have legs! And the story's above the fold! This is great!"

"Buzz?"

"Yeah! Yesterday I got some irate calls from downtown businesses, saying I didn't have the full story. So today's front page story featured their side, and my boss finally pulled his head out of his… Well, anyway, he put the story above the fold. You know. Of the front page. Only really punchy stories go there. I may get a Georgia Press Association award out of it. Plus…" Her eyes danced. "I got a full-time beat—city hall! And a raise!"

Gwen pointed one zebra-striped fingernail sporting an image of a cupcake to a fat green rhinestone in her nose. "Like my new nose ring? That's how I celebrated! Hey, gotta go! See you at the meeting!"

And with that, she left Allison standing alone on the sidewalk, feeling as though she had unleashed a tornado on an unsuspecting town.

Allison dug out her own phone, but no. There were no messages or missed phone calls from Kyle. He was back to radio silence again. How could she ever have considered a relationship with someone who wouldn't stick around and talk through the hard stuff? He couldn't just vanish every time they had a disagreement.

He can if he values being right more than being with me.

Shaking off her misgivings about Gwen, and her tumultuous thoughts about Kyle, Allison climbed the steps to City Hall.

She was shown into the city manager's office. He looked harassed and busy, tapping out a message on a cell phone while he had his office phone jammed to his ear. "Yeah, yeah, I got that—no, I assure you, we will hold an open meeting, and you are definitely welcome to come, but the agenda's already set," he said. He stabbed the touchpad on his cell with ferocious effort, set it aside and rang off with the person on the other phone.

Staring at Allison, he shook his head. “Ma’am, you have opened one giant economy-sized can of worms, did you know that?”

She folded her hands and willed them to stay still. But of course, two seconds later she was unclasping and refolding them. She redoubled her efforts to betray no nervousness. “If you mean that other people share my concerns about these ordinances—”

“Oh, sure,” he said. “They do. Approximately half the people who have called me today share your point of view.”

“Really?” A surge of relief went through her. This wouldn’t be so bad, then—people would be supportive of her, and Kyle would see she wasn’t asking for the moon. Maybe he’d cave before the meeting could even take place.

“Oh, yeah. The other half? The local businesses? They want me to run you out of town on a rail. But I told them it’s your constitutionally protected right to make trouble.”

She crossed her arms over her chest. “That shows me how wonderfully objective you are about this case.”

“Ma’am…” The manager ran a hand through his hair, then pinched the bridge of his nose. “First off, I apologize for being a little hasty with my words today. Your newspaper stunt has really…I mean, Gwen Chapman? Of all people to sic on me! That woman is just out for a story…I know her kind. She'll be here for a few headlines and then she'll leave for greener pastures. But when she does, Lombard will be left with chasms of division that weren't there before."

Allison had a sick feeling that he was right. Gwen *was* only out for the story—hadn't their exchange on the sidewalk just now proved that? Still…

"Would the city council have even entertained the prospect of a hearing on these ordinances if I hadn't pulled my—what did you call it? My newspaper stunt?"

He pursed his lips. "Probably not. The council has been content to leave the historic preservation committee to work out the details. After all, there is an appeals process in place. You are entitled to a public hearing about your variance request—which I have since discovered you haven't even formally filed with the committee."

"Because if I do, they'll turn me down, and I'll have to wait a year—a whole year—to file another proposal. You've seen my grandmother's house. It can't wait another year for paint and repairs."

The city manager leaned back and closed his eyes. His chair squeaked as he rocked in it. "You know, I agree with you? No, really. I know you think I'm just saying that to patronize you, but it's the truth. Paint is the absolute least permanent thing in the world you could do to that house, and it would look a sight better painted—painted purple, even—than the peeling mess it is now. Your grandmother came to me a year, year and a half ago, trying to get the historic preservation committee to see some sense. But no…they wouldn't."

"So…what's the deal, then? If you think I'm within my rights and the committee is being unreasonable—"

"Frankly?" He pushed forward and leaned on his elbows. "The committee has the downtown businesses convinced that changing one iota of those ordinances is the beginning of the end."

"But you don't really think that, do you?" She watched the man carefully.

He shrugged. "Doesn't matter what I believe—or even what should theoretically be the case. What matters is if those businesses start to lose faith in Lombard. If they think this is a lost cause, that it's simply a matter of time before the historic district fades into oblivion because of less-than-historically-accurate renovations, what happens then? They stop expanding their trade and services, stop encouraging tourists to stay longer and spend more dollars. We have fewer tax dollars to plow back into downtown development. The city core suffers. The whole thing becomes a self-fulfilling prophecy."

"All because I want the freedom to paint my grandmother's house the way I can afford to?" Allison stood up. "Don't. Don't try to guilt me into dropping this. Because that's what you're doing, isn't it? Well, I won't. I won't go away, not until Kyle Mitchell himself tells me that Gran's house is exempt from those ridiculous rules."

The manager's face sagged even more, and she realized that she had hit the nail on the head. "So I guess..." he said.

"I will see you at that meeting."

"Your constitutional right, that's for sure." With that, he picked up his cell phone and start punching on it with his thumb, while he stretched out his other arm for the office phone. "We'll see you there. Now if you'll excuse me, I have a crisis or two to manage."

CHAPTER TWENTY-THREE

ALLISON SMOOTHED THE fabric of her summer-weight wool skirt with a damp palm as she wished desperately for a drink of water to ease her parched throat. She craned her neck and twisted in her hard folding chair. People of all sorts packed the city council's meeting room, their conversations a hum that vibrated through the confines of the large room, their competing aftershaves and perfumes and colognes assaulting her nostrils.

She didn't, however, see Kyle.

With a whoosh that made Allison jump, Gwen Chapman collapsed in the chair beside her. "Well, shoot. It didn't get moved. I'll have to rewrite my lead," she told Allison.

"You've already written the story?"

"Started on it. We've got an early deadline tomorrow, so I wanted to get a head start. This is another front-pager." She rooted around in an oversize canvas bag and produced a reporter's notebook and a pen with a silk flower on the end. She looked up at Allison.

"The flower's to keep people from stealing my pen. Oh, and also to help me find it faster. So? Are you ready?"

Allison's stomach lurched again. "No. You know, I was picturing something a lot less… publicized."

"You'll thank me when you get the city council to change the ordinances. They wouldn't even dream of doing it without all this public outcry."

Allison didn't see incensed people around her, though. The men and women who were milling around, searching for a seat, seemed more curious than angry. And the members of the city council, now making their way to their places at the front of the room, didn't wear panicked or nervous expressions. Instead, they seemed implacable and resolute.

She suddenly had a very bad feeling about her prospects.

Gwen jabbed her in the ribs with an elbow. "Hey, didn't you hear me? I asked if the historical guys had been in touch. Heard a peep out of that Kyle Mitchell?"

"No," Allison replied.

She hoped that single word didn't reveal the private agonies she'd gone through as she'd waited for her phone to ring or her doorbell to peal. But Kyle had kept up the silence. He hadn't called. He hadn't come by.

And she could be sure that no news, in this case, was not good news.

Then she spotted him, elbowing his way through the crowd, with the city manager tagging close behind. Herbert and other familiar faces from the historical society followed in their wake.

Her palms were sweaty again, and Gwen was being obnoxiously annoying as she cracked jokes about what people were wearing. If the reporter would just shut up for two minutes, Allison might get her thoughts together. Should she speak to Kyle?

He had spotted her now. His brows drew together, not in an angry frown, but more in bewilderment, as though he wasn't really sure how he and Allison had ended up in this situation. She'd pushed up out of her chair as he neared the front when the bang of the gavel sounded and the mayor, a woman wearing a navy suit, her blond hair in an upswept do, brought the meeting to order.

She came to the point quickly, recapping the reason for the meeting. "In the interest of time, I'm allowing Ms. Bell to present her request to the council, and a representative from the historical society to add his input. Other interested parties have been invited to submit written responses, which have been reviewed by the council members already and will be—"

An unhappy rumble of protest rippled through the crowd. The mayor banged her gavel again to restore order. "Those responses will be entered into the record. Now. Ms. Bell? Would you care to address the council?"

Allison's knees nearly buckled as she stood up. But it wasn't Gwen's squeeze on her arm that gave her strength and steadiness to approach the podium. No, she thought of her grandmother. She thought of her bank account. And she reminded herself, *You've been part of a team that saved lives and responded to natural disasters. You've got this.*

At the podium, she pulled the mic down, cleared her throat, then couldn't resist glancing over at Kyle.

Who, though he had a tense expression on his face, gave her a thumbs-up.

It nearly undid her. How could he be rooting for her and so unyielding at the same time?

"Ms. Bell?" the mayor prompted.

"Thank you, ma'am, for allowing me to speak." The words came out croaky at first, but then Allison gathered confidence and started her story. "I am here not just on behalf of my grandmother, but on behalf of everyone who might find themselves in my grandmother's situation. All she wants to do is restore her home to a livable condition, nothing fancy, just safe and sound and solid—and to do so without having to go into debt at her age of eighty-nine years."

Allison took the next few minutes to relate Gran's plight. She told the council how she'd moved home to help her grandmother and how her own funds had been sucked into necessary repairs.

"Just today," she said, "I received a letter from Gran's insurance carrier. They stated that they would be canceling her policy unless she could have the exterior painted and brought up to their minimum standards for coverage. She's never missed a payment, never even been late—and this insurance is very expensive because it's designed for historic homes. Regular coverage isn't available for Gran's house, since it's more than a century old. I have—" she smoothed out the letter "—sixty days to get Gran's place painted or she will be without the security of home owner's insurance. I am hoping that you ladies and gentlemen will either repeal the ordinances that demand we paint the home in historically accurate colors, or at least provide my grandmother with a hardship waiver. Thank you for your consideration."

She turned from the podium and was about to sit down when the mayor stopped her. "Hold on, Ms. Bell. Council…do you have questions now for her? Or would you rather hear from the historical society's representative first?"

The councilors talked among themselves, then Lorenzo Adams spoke into his mic. "Madam Mayor, I move that the council be allowed to ask any questions now."

When his motion had been seconded and passed unanimously, the mayor leaned forward. "Ms. Bell?"

Allison returned to the podium and gripped the sides with hands she wished weren't so sweaty. She stared at the faces of the council members and prayed they wouldn't ask her any questions.

But of course they did.

Lorenzo Adams started off, smiling at her with a kindness that eased her nerves. "Now, Ms. Bell, you've told us a good deal about your grandmother's situation. Do you feel that you've explored every option to help fund the exterior renovations?"

"Yes, sir, I do. My grandmother doesn't want to go into debt at her age, and from what I understand from local bankers, it might not be an easy loan to get, given her age and income. And I am still paying off student loans."

Adams chuckled. "My daughter is, too—grad school's a killer, isn't it?"

"Yes, sir," she said, breathing easier. Maybe she had really convinced them.

But the softball question was quickly followed by harder ones, in rapid succession.

"But the house has been in need of a paint job for several years, right?" This question came from another council member. "I mean, it didn't just get like this overnight."

"Uh, yes." Allison cleared her throat again. "But as I said, my grandmother spent a lot of her savings raising me after my parents died, and putting me through college."

Another question came at her, this one from a council member at the end of the table. "Do you think that your grandmother is more important than the family members of those who own small businesses dependent on the historic district tourists?"

"Why—why, no." Allison bit back a furious answer and tried for a calm reply. "I'm just saying that anybody in my grandmother's situation should be allowed a little flexibility."

Now a more sympathetic council member leaned forward. "You called this a tax, didn't you, in the newspaper article? A tax on people based on where they live in our city? Do you still agree with that?"

"Yes," she said firmly. "I understand that the historic district is an important part of Lombard's economy, but it rests to a large degree on the backs of the people who own these homes. What if they can't afford to keep them up?"

"So you're asking the city for the funds to paint the house?" another council member asked, obviously confused.

"No, no…I'm asking…I'm just asking for permission to paint the house without having to use five different colors. Without having to match the idea of what the historic society thinks is best for the house. It might be pretty, but it's not pretty to my pocketbook."

This got a laugh from the spectators and the council alike. The mayor gave a light tap of her gavel and stared around at the council members. "Are there any further questions for Ms. Bell? No? Well, then. Thank you, Ms. Bell. We appreciate you bringing this to our attention. Now…" She referred to some paperwork in front of her and then looked up again.

"Dr. Mitchell? I understand you are representing the historic preservation committee?"

Allison shouldn't have been surprised. After all, he was the chairman and practically ran the historic society. But still, it was a sucker punch. She'd expected Herbert to be the one blasting away at her.

Now Kyle was glancing over at her, but somehow she couldn't manage a thumbs-up for him.

Gwen hissed in her ear, "Wow. Are you two...are you guys seeing each other? How did I miss that? What an angle! So how long—"

Allison leveled a drop-dead stare at the reporter and was surprised that it shut her up immediately. But perhaps Gwen's sudden silence had been due to Kyle introducing himself and beginning his speech.

At first it sounded like a rehash of everything Allison had already heard: the economic impact of the historic district, the unjustness of giving one home owner a break, the possibility of setting a precedent and opening the city and the historic society up to a lawsuit.

But when he started on the importance of historical accuracy, he surprised her.

"I know—" he smiled at Allison again "—I know that some people think that the historic preservation committee is all about external appearances, and that such a focus is purely superficial. But if you'll allow me to share with you a brief PowerPoint presentation, you can see the difference yourself."

He waited for the mayor to nod and for the city manager to hand him a remote control. Then a screen came down and Kyle's slides flickered to life on it. Allison felt unprepared and amateurish in comparison to Kyle's very slick, professional presentation.

He's a college professor. What did you expect?

Kyle started off with before-and-after photos of the neighborhood. Allison hadn't really remembered how dingy and run-down the houses had looked before the ordinances had been put in place. Some of them had been far worse than Gran's was now. All the "after" photos showed beautifully restored homes that currently graced the historic district.

He came to a recent photo of Belle Paix, impressive despite its peeling paint and shabby condition. For a long moment, Kyle said nothing, just stared at the picture. "This is what Belle Paix looks like now."

He clicked the remote and the next slide came up. It was an old sepia-toned photograph he'd dug up from somewhere. "As you can see, Ms. Bell is correct in stating that the paint scheme for this beautiful old Second Empire would be more complicated than your average home. This is what it looked like when it was about ten years old, in 1898. You can see the various shades that were used—five including the main color, even though this is a black-and-white newspaper print."

He clicked the remote once more. The Belle

Paix of the present came to life again. Allison wanted to shrink down in her seat at having the old house revealed in all its tatty tiredness. *It isn't my fault*, she thought grimly. She was trying.

"Now." Kyle swiveled back to face the council members, who were staring at him with an intent focus. "The question before you is simple. Does it matter how this house is painted? Wouldn't anything be better than what we have now? Well…yes. And no."

The next slide filled the screen, a doctored version of the house with a simple base color of pale yellow. "I've taken the liberty of using photo-editing software to show you what the place would look like. This is the house with a monochromatic paint scheme."

It was improved, but even Allison had to admit it looked nothing like the 1908 photo.

"Oh, you say, a home owner would use at least one trim color. Okay. Let's try one more."

The next slide showed what the house would look like with the trim in a dark hunter green.

"Nice, right?" Kyle's words held a steely edge. "Good enough, right? What difference would it make if we just let this one house slide?"

The picture on the screen dissolved, to be replaced with another version.

And even Allison gasped at the difference. Belle Paix…glowed. The various trims seemed to gel together, not in the tacky, atrociously bright way she had secretly feared, but with a genteel and polished air.

"Ladies and gentlemen," Kyle said, "I give you the way Belle Paix's first owner—Ambrose Shepherd, the man who designed her, dreamed her into existence, watched over every nail and screw and board and drop of paint—intended for the home to appear. And with that, I rest my case."

CHAPTER TWENTY-FOUR

ALLISON KNEW THE council's decision as soon as Kyle's rendition of Belle Paix flashed up on the screen. Every single one of the members' mouths formed surprised little O's that didn't soon go away.

Sure, the council had debated the request, but it had been halfhearted, almost pro forma in nature. They'd referred to their notes, to the submitted letters of support both for her and for the ordinance.

But it hadn't really mattered.

No, they'd seen Kyle's beautiful picture, saw what a difference it would make to the historic district, and their minds were made up.

Because in all honesty? Kyle's picture had been beautiful. It hummed with the same authenticity that his own Sears kit home did. His artistic rendition could have been a color plate straight out of a book of Victorian house plans.

It made her want to weep, because she could never, ever afford to transform Gran's house into the showplace it should be. And what would happen if she did manage to get the blasted thing painted? In ten years' time, the same paint scheme would require even more money.

But the council didn't seem to care about that. They just saw what a difference a restored Belle Paix would make to the historic district, and they wanted it as badly as Allison did.

After all, it wasn't their money they'd be spending.

Lorenzo Adams summed up the council's position after the unanimous vote had been made to uphold the current ordinances.

"Ms. Bell, I am sorry for your grandmother's situation. But we have to weigh her circumstances against all of the business owners and their families who depend on the historic district. And honestly? I can't believe you have explored *every* option. Yes, the money may be hard to find. Yes, debt is never a good thing, and not even always possible to secure. But I wouldn't vote to uphold these ordinances if I didn't think that somewhere, somehow, a woman as determined and resourceful as you couldn't come up with a solution to your grandmother's dilemma."

Afterward Allison remained in her chair, the hubbub around her working into a furious uproar that mostly ignored her. Not even Gwen had stuck around. The reporter had dashed off to get quotes from historical society members and, twisting the knife even deeper, "Gotta see if Kyle Mitchell will give me a copy of that picture of your granny's house. Didn't it look fab?"

What to do now? It was all well and good for Lorenzo Adams to compliment her by describing her as determined and resourceful, but it didn't solve her problem.

Allison hadn't shaken off the numbing shock of the council's decision, hadn't yet managed to stand and negotiate her way through the crowd to the door, when she felt the lightest tap on her arm.

Kyle.

He stretched out a hand to assist her to her feet. "Can we talk?" he asked.

Anger rocketed her from her chair. She knocked aside his hand and snatched up her purse. "Somehow I don't think you'd feel much like talking to me if the decision had gone against you, Kyle. So spare me the added misery of having to be a gracious loser. I've got to get a house painted to suit *you,* with no money and in the next sixty days. I don't have time for pleasant civilities."

"Allison, I—"

She didn't let him finish. "In fact, you know

what? I much prefer the past few days, when you didn't talk to me at all."

The remark obviously stung. He jerked his head back as if he'd been slapped. For a moment, his lips compressed and the earlier warmth in his eyes cooled. Then, saying nothing else, he turned and walked off.

As she watched him go, Allison hated how that momentary surge of pleasure at wounding him had faded into an all-encompassing heartsick loneliness.

KYLE'S SHOULDER SMARTED from all the backslapping he'd received from historical society members. Or maybe he was just numb from Allison's words.

"I much prefer the past few days, when you didn't talk to me at all." Her tone, her eyes, had held so much venom.

He'd spent those precious few days ahead of the meeting desperately trying to swing a compromise, while at the same time preparing a defense to save the ordinances. And she hadn't even missed him when he wasn't around?

No. She'd *preferred* it.

Todd White, the city manager, chucked him on the arm, breaking into the tight circle the historical society members had formed around him.

"Kyle, I have to say, you saved our bacon on this one. If you hadn't given such a stellar presentation, we'd have been here all night, and those council members would have surely voted to repeal the ordinance." He stretched out a hand, which Kyle took unthinkingly, resulting in his being pumped with enthusiastic energy. "Yes, sir, that PowerPoint speech was inspired. You really hit it out of the ballpark with the picture of what that old house would look like painted up properly."

"You got that right, buddy!" Herbert nodded his head vigorously in agreement with the city manager. "Kyle, you've earned a steak, boy! Woo-wee, but that was some kind of speechifying you did there. Saved our neighborhood, you did! How about it, folks? Y'all want to head out to celebrate with a steak?"

Kyle's eyes weren't on Todd or Herbert or Eunice or any of the other members. His gaze slid past the reporter with her green hair, which shifted and mixed with another blue streak until it reminded Kyle of nothing so much as the exact shade of a bluebottle fly.

His attention was wholly focused on Allison. She had edged through the crowd, her back hunched, her arms folded tightly as though she were trying to become invisible.

Her face revealed none of the pinched anger

that had spilled out just a few minutes earlier. In its place was pale misery, with eyes he could see even from this distance were shiny with unshed tears, defeat in the way her back was bowed.

"Oh, I'll be the one to buy Kyle a steak, I will," Eunice was saying. "It would be my pleasure, now that we've put that Bell woman in her place. I am so pleased, Kyle, just ever so pleased! Why, to think I ever worried about..."

Kyle didn't listen to Eunice prattle on. Instead, he focused on a tall man in a dark suit who materialized out of the crowd and touched Allison on the elbow. She whirled around. The man began talking earnestly. After a minute or so, the misery in her expression began to lift.

The dark-suited man gestured toward the door and began to lead Allison outside. She in turn was suddenly animated, smiling, her back straight and the defeated air magically gone.

Kyle would have killed to have been that man in the dark suit, with his ability to make Allison smile again.

"No, Eunice, *I* was going to pay for Kyle's steak—" Herbert had reverted to his quarrelsome, competitive ways, arguing down Eunice about the privilege of who would treat him.

"Herbert," Kyle interrupted, more harshly

than he'd intended. "No offense, but the last thing I feel like doing tonight is celebrating. Now if you'll excuse me, I'm going home."

CHAPTER TWENTY-FIVE

GRAN'S WALKING STICK struck the floor with a hollow clack.

"Now, that doesn't sound like real wood." She squinted down at the floor of the house they were viewing. "When I walk over it, it sounds like that time all those squirrels ran amok on the third floor. Remember that awful racket? And it doesn't even look like real wood, either."

Allison drew in a deep, calming breath. "It's not, Gran. It's laminate. It's a modern replacement of wood."

Gran frowned. "Yeah, I heard of that stuff. Buckles when it gets the slightest bit wet, and it's slippery to boot. Gladys Horton fell and broke her hip because she slipped on some sugar she'd spilled. Nope, this is not for me. We can move on to the next one. No, I want good old-fashioned wood, thank you very much." She turned and headed for the door.

Allison closed her eyes and gripped the doorjamb. "Gran, you've barely looked at any of the houses we've seen today—"

Her grandmother stopped, her back rigid. She carefully turned to face her. "Because they're not quality, Allison. Not at all. They've all got these plastic floors—" she thwacked the laminate once more for good measure "—and plastic cabinets and that icky Berber carpet, and if I see one more wall painted—what did you call it? Contractor beige? I'm going to lose my appetite forever. I never *did* care for oatmeal."

"Gran..." Allison crossed the laminate floor, which to her chagrin did indeed put her in mind of that nest of noisy squirrels from her childhood. She wrapped an arm around Gran, noting how bony her shoulders were. "I know this is hard for you. But I don't know what else to do. I can't afford to paint the house. You can't afford to paint the house. And we have someone who is willing to pay us top dollar for it. We'll get you a nice, new home that's just the right size—"

"I don't trust that Greg Draper," Gran said. The corners of her mouth were tugged down, her face more drawn than Allison could ever remember. "We don't need to sell Belle Paix to some man who wants to turn it into a boardinghouse!"

"Gran...it's not a boardinghouse. He's an investor, and he wants to make it a bed-and-breakfast. A very nice hotel. He'll paint it like it's supposed to be painted, and it will look just like it did when it was new. He promises. And think—it will be filled with happy people—"

"A boardinghouse." Gran's face wrinkled with contempt. "My mother didn't resort to taking in boarders even in the midst of the Depression, after my father lost all our money, Allison. And I just can't see us doing that now. Why, Davinia Shepherd would turn in her grave!"

The Realtor, who'd been in the next room, rushed in, her own heels clacking on the floor. "Mrs. Thomas, if you're not happy with this home, I'm sure you'll like the next one better. It's an older home, with, er, more character—"

"Does it have thicker walls than this? Because I could hear every word of the conversation you were having on that cell phone—*both* ends of the conversation. These walls could be paper!" Gran spun around again. This time, the slick floor almost did her in—would have if Allison hadn't been there to catch her.

As Allison steadied her, she noticed a tear trailing down her powdered cheek.

"Oh, Gran..."

"I just want to go *home*, Allison. Home to the only place I've ever called home. I don't want these newfangled houses with their plastic floors. Why, my bed wouldn't even fit in the living rooms, much less the bedrooms, of most of these houses. Are you going to make me sell my bed, too?"

Allison wanted to weep. Confound Kyle Mitchell. *He should be here, so he could explain to Gran why she can't go home.*

"Let's—let's call it a day, Gran. You're tired, and we've looked at a bunch of houses—"

They hadn't, not really, because Gran had refused to set foot in half the ones on their list. Allison had been coaxing her to look at homes for two weeks now, desperate to find one that would suit her.

But Gran had made it nearly impossible. First of all, she didn't want to live in a house that was too small. Then she didn't want to live in a house too large. Then she'd declared that if she couldn't go home to Belle Paix, she wanted to move away from Lombard altogether.

So not only were they looking for a home that would suit Gran, they were also searching for a town that would suit her. It was quickly becoming clear that no town stacked up to Lombard, and no house stacked up to Belle Paix.

Allison gently guided her grandmother, who was now making a vain attempt to hold back more tears, to her car. She settled her into the seat.

Gran fumbled in her purse for a tissue. "I know it. I'm an unreasonable old woman. I should start using that pragmatism I tell everybody else to use. Tell that nice lady that maybe I can come back tomorrow and look at this house again and give it a fair shake, all right, Allison? I am sorry. I know—I know. It's got to be done."

"It's okay, Gran. We'll find the house for us. I promise. I know this is hard."

She closed the door and turned to face the Realtor.

"I'm sorry for wasting so much of your time today. Please don't give up on us. I really do have to find her a home," Allison said.

"I'm the one who's sorry," the woman replied. "I thought for sure some of the houses I'd picked out would at least interest her. You must live in a fairly spectacular house now."

"Oh, you could say that." Allison was suddenly swept up in visions of Belle Paix's beautiful, mellow pine floors, the high ceilings, the cheerful brightness of the kitchen now that it was painted yellow. "It's a Second Empire Victorian built in 1888."

"And you're selling that? Oh, my. No. None of these houses would ever live up to what you have now." The Realtor's tight brow remained smooth and unfurrowed despite her frown of concentration. "Tell you what, I'll go back to the drawing board and see what other homes might…well…" She trailed off.

"Thank you. I appreciate all your efforts." Allison choked on tears of her own. The idea of Gran selling Belle Paix had seemed like such a godsend when Greg Draper had first approached her at that meeting. The more houses they looked at, though, made Allison all the sadder.

She'd be uprooting Gran from everything she'd known, from the support system of friends and acquaintances, and even doctors and merchants that Gran had counted on for years. This couldn't be good. Gran couldn't really mean that it would hurt worse to live near Belle Paix.

In the car, Gran was swiping her eyes with a tissue, no doubt wishing for a proper handkerchief. She straightened up and fixed her eyes straight ahead of her on some point far off in the distance. Her usually smiling mouth was pinched, but her head was high, and Allison detected a resoluteness that she found herself in envy of.

Maybe Gran knew better. Maybe it was best to sever all ties with the place that would haunt her.

Honestly, could you ever drive by Belle Paix without the car wanting to turn in and park on its own? Could you ever live in Lombard in any other house and not grieve for her home?

Now another memory flooded Allison's brain: of a neat little white house with blue shutters and a bench by the matching blue door. A kitchen with a swing-out stool under its farmhouse sink, and a console in the living room to hide the big screen TV.

And there, in her vision, was the man who was part and parcel of that house, who'd made it what it was. In her imagination, he was smiling, holding out his arms—not being stubborn and unyielding about stupid standards that sounded logical on paper but caused so much grief in the real world.

Now how can I miss Kyle when he's the reason we have to move in the first place?

She shoved the thought of him away, down into the deeper darker recesses of her mind. She'd cry tonight, alone where no one could hear her, as she had the night before and the night before that. She'd cry for lost chances and could have beens, and maybe even a few should have beens. In any other circumstance, she and Kyle might have had a chance.

But for now Gran needed her, and Gran came first. Allison's own heartache would simply have to wait.

CHAPTER TWENTY-SIX

"It's good of you to meet with me, Dr. Mitchell." Greg Draper extended the hand not holding a roll of blueprints out toward Kyle.

Kyle took it, impressed with the man's firm handshake. "I understand you're interested in buying one of the historic homes here in Lombard and turning it into a B and B? There are several homes that would be perfect—"

Draper's mouth twitched in a suppressed smile. "Not to worry. I've already picked it out. Belle Paix."

Kyle sank into his desk chair. "Then I'm afraid you've wasted your time. Belle Paix isn't for sale."

Now Draper's smile broadened. "Oh, but it is. I spoke with Allison Bell after the meeting, and with her grandmother the next day. They could see selling to the right person…for the right price."

Draper's words took Kyle aback. To regain some measure of composure, he shifted a stack of exams off his desk to the credenza. Gran? Sell Belle Paix?

He recalled the dark-suited man at the meeting, and realized too late that Draper must have been that man. So for all her passionate talk about her grandmother not wanting to leave her home, Allison had started negotiations not five minutes after the council's vote.

"I see." He didn't. But he wasn't going to share that with Draper. "So what can I do for you?"

"I'm interested in closing on the house before the current home owner's insurance is revoked. It's much harder to find insurance if you don't have evidence of prior coverage, you know, and historic homes can be a nightmare. So I thought I'd cut to the chase and bring my plans to you. That way, we could review them, make sure they are in compliance. I have to have your written approval before the bank will issue the loan." Draper turned to Kyle's small table and chairs. "May I?" Without waiting, he spread the blueprints out on the dark wood.

Kyle couldn't resist the siren call of unfurling house plans. He rose from his chair and rounded the desk to inspect them.

What he saw was impressive. The top sheet was a color drawing of the house in the requisite five colors of paint, coordinated even better than Kyle's own color scheme had been in his slide at the meeting.

"That—that's something," he said. "You work fast."

"Well, I admit, I'd been looking for a while now for a property large enough to turn into a B and B, but none had been on the market. So when I saw the news coverage and the photo of Belle Paix, I got out my drafting tools. I'm an architect by trade, but my father was in real estate…so I've been able to blend the two vocations together fairly well." Draper tapped the drawing. "Now, as you can see, I intend to restore the exterior to the 1888 paint scheme, or as close as I can manage. You were exactly right the other night when you talked about the importance of historical accuracy. It really bugs me to see a Victorian painted lady swathed in white."

Kyle surveyed the meticulous drawing and marveled. The front elevation even included historically accurate landscaping. No doubt about it, Belle Paix would look every bit as good as the day Ambrose had first turned the key in the lock. "You've done a fine job, Mr. Draper."

"You approve. Excellent! That's a good omen. Now, if you'll bear with me—" Draper set aside the first drawing to reveal a detailed sketch of the interior.

"So as I understand it, the house is not on the National Register, right? Even though it's over a century?" he asked Kyle.

"No…it's an oversight, really. The family just never got around to requesting it, but it would be a shoo-in—"

"Oh, no, actually the omission works in my favor. If it were on the register, then I couldn't do the renovations I plan."

Kyle wasn't sure he'd heard Draper correctly. "I beg your pardon?"

"It's going to be quite a job to transform a private home into a structure to serve the public. For one thing, we'll need a bigger commercial kitchen. And for another, even though the rooms are generous, I'll need larger public areas on the main floor."

Kyle pushed back a chair at the table and dropped into it. With a sinking heart, he examined the plans in earnest.

Gone was Gran's charming 1930s kitchen with its Chambers range. In its place was a dining area that joined the original dining room, the wall between them replaced with load-bearing columns. Draper's version had the space jammed with eight-foot round tables.

"So I'll use the daylight basement as the

commercial kitchen, and we'll put an elevator in place of the back stairs," Draper was explaining. "I'd thought perhaps I might add a kitchen onto the back...but the basement is such a generous size. This way, the house can be open to the public for restaurant meals. It would be a perfect place for historical society meetings, mind you." The man winked. He actually winked at Kyle.

"That's...that's quite a change," Kyle said.

"Very necessary, I'm afraid. Now for the upstairs..." Again the pages of the blueprints made their familiar rustling sound as he rolled away the proposed first floor. "As you can see, I'll have to do some significant renovations, as one bathroom will not be sufficient at all. So each of the rooms will be made just a trifle smaller to incorporate a small but well-appointed private bath."

Kyle bent closer to the page. "Is that—are those hot tubs? And...and wet bars?"

Draper beamed. "Good eye for detail. Yes, indeed. We'll be catering to a, shall we say, special sort of patron. This is the wave of the future for Lombard, Dr. Mitchell. Our other properties all have at least a three-and-a-half-star rating, and we are striving to bring those up to four-star accommodations. You've worked so hard to bring Lombard up to snuff, to attract the right sort of attention, and this will be your reward—wealthy tourists who come to Lombard for a week to take in the sights."

Even on paper, seeing Belle Paix's generous rooms carved up like this, its kitchen gutted, seemed like a nightmare to Kyle.

He smoothed a ripple out of the blueprints, almost hoping the move would erase the offensive plans. The outside of the home was the only good and decent thing about Draper's proposal.

It was inconceivable that such a travesty might move ahead—and it could. It would. There was not a single, solitary thing the historical society could do to prevent Draper from having his way with the house once Gran sold it to him. Their purview ended at the threshold…and Draper had been careful to keep the patina, the skin, of the old house intact.

But inside? If Draper did this, the house's very soul would be ripped out.

How could Allison do it? She could stop Gran… Heck, maybe it was even Allison's idea to begin with.

But she loved that old house. He knew it. And Gran wouldn't be happy anywhere else. So why…

Because Allison had given up. She'd thrown in the towel. She wouldn't—or couldn't—paint the house to match the historical society's criteria.

"Do you mind my asking..." Kyle framed his words carefully. "What was the deciding point? What made them move ahead with the sale?"

Draper blinked. "The council's decision, of course. And you were apparently very persuasive. Allison went on and on about your presentation and how the house ought to look. She said she couldn't...how did she put it? Do right by the house. That Belle Paix ought to be in the hands of someone with the funds to look after her properly."

"You mean 'it,'" Kyle muttered, returning his attention to the atrocious proposal before him.

"Oh, no. Allison was quite charming as she referred to Belle Paix in the feminine. 'I can't do right by the old girl anymore,' she said. 'We just don't have the funds. But you'll look after her, won't you?' Yeah, it was sweet—as though the house were an actual person."

Kyle's stomach twisted, and he found himself clenching his fingers into fists. He had done this. He'd finally convinced Allison that Belle Paix deserved a proper exterior renovation... and she was selling the house in order to provide it.

He pictured the rooms filled with boxes, imagined Gran overseeing the packing of her family's treasured belongings. That third floor—so jammed with the things she'd salvaged over the family's history. What would become of all of it?

The sick lurch of his heart transformed itself into a quick double beat. Yeah. That third floor…

CHAPTER TWENTY-SEVEN

ALLISON KEPT HER head down, her broom in motion, as Kyle strode up to Belle Paix. She had less than sixty times left to sweep the old girl's front walk, and she wouldn't let the man who'd caused her to lose the house distract her from the task at hand.

The broom straw caught on a cracked paving stone. The jagged break split the stone smack-dab between the "18" and the "88" underneath the paver's name. Allison jerked the broom free.

"Allison. I've left you about a dozen messages."

"Obviously you failed to get the larger message then," she snapped, and turned her back to him under the guise of her sweeping.

"You can't sell Belle Paix." Kyle told her. He circled around so that she had to face him. "You can't!"

She stared at him. Where has this come from? "Weren't you the one who said if I couldn't properly take care of her, then I needed to sell her to someone who could? And oh, for the record, it's Gran's house, not mine. She's the one selling it."

"You said 'her.'" Kyle jabbed a triumphant finger at Allison. "You *don't* want to sell her, do you?"

Allison went on with her sweeping. She would not cry. Not in front of this man. "Of course not. But what choice have you left me, Kyle? Where on earth am I going to find another fifteen thousand dollars—and that's the cheapest bid I've found—to paint this house before the insurance is canceled? If you'd just worked with me—"

"But you can get that money. The attic, Allison!" Kyle wrapped his fingers lightly around her upper arm to stop her from sweeping. His touch reminded her of other times, sweeter times, when she'd thought she could trust him. "Don't you see? All those things in the attic."

She shook his hand off. "So what now? You want me to hold a yard sale and sell all my gran's sentimental favorites and family heirlooms?"

"Not a yard sale—we could go through it together, auction them off online, raise the money that way."

"Right. Let's just put the whole thing on eBay." Allison hated the acid-laced tone her words held, but she couldn't shake off the regret and sick guilt she felt.

"Not eBay—well, maybe eBay, but there are other sites designed for collectors. And if you didn't want to do it yourself, I know of a few auction houses that handle estate sales—"

Kyle had held her focus until he uttered the words *estate sales*. That reminded her of Gran—Gran, who barely spoke these days and who had insisted she be allowed to come home to enjoy "the last days I'll ever be happy."

"No."

The flat refusal caused Kyle to take a step back, his eyebrows raised in surprise. "Why not? You said you didn't want to sell Belle Paix. I thought you'd be excited about this."

"What happens, Kyle? What happens when we sell part of Gran's stuff—or even all of it—and it's still not enough money? Then what?"

"It would be less to borrow!"

"Get it through your head," she said through gritted teeth. "I can't borrow the money. No bank will do it, not on a house I don't own. And the bank won't even think about loaning money to someone as old as Gran unless she either takes out really high priced credit life insurance or if she does a reverse mortgage. Gran can't afford the first one, and she's not going to do the second. And I don't blame her, Kyle."

"So...so you checked, then?"

She gripped the broom to resist the urge to thrash him with it. "Did you think I didn't? Did you think I just said, 'Well, gee, I think I'll sell the only house Gran's ever lived in?'"

"I think you're really scared and really panicked and you're not thinking through all your options—"

"Yeah. I'm scared. But no, I'm not panicked. Determined? Yeah. Resolute? You bet. And as far as options, I've spent many a sleepless night—or day, because, gee, I still have to work—thinking, thinking and thinking. There's just nothing. And you know it. You knew it when you were standing in front of that council. You could have petitioned for a hardship waiver to be created. You could have backed me up. And you didn't."

"You know why..."

He had the nerve to look at her with such patient innocence, as though it had really all been beyond his control.

"Your precious ordinances? Your precious historic district? Well, you got 'em, Kyle. You protected them. And you know what else you managed to accomplish?" She drew in a deep breath. "You landed one nearly ninety-year-old woman out on the street." Tears threatened to overwhelm Allison, and she knew she had maybe thirty seconds before she was sobbing. She whirled away from him, determined to get in the house before he could have the satisfaction of seeing her cry.

"No. No, I *haven't* put your gran out on the street," Kyle insisted. "You still have an option that you haven't tried, Allison! You could at least let me look at some of those things in the attic and—"

Her anger incinerated her tears. She spun back around to face him. "No. You won't put a foot—not a pinkie toe—inside Belle Paix. If I had followed Gran's practice of running off the likes of you to begin with—" She bit off her words and shook her head.

He gaped at her. "That's—that's ridiculous. What did allowing me to see inside Belle Paix have to do with you not wanting to spend the money on a proper paint job?"

Now Allison was the one gawking in astonishment. "Me? It's not a question of not wanting to *spend* the money, Kyle—it's a question of me not *having* the money. And if I'd never let you in, then—then..."

Suddenly all those memories of working side by side with him on Belle Paix flooded back. His strong, capable hands holding a paint roller or a spackling knife. The day they'd spent canning tomatoes and beans. All the pep talks he'd ever given her. The million little things he'd done for her that had made her think he cared and she could count on him…

"Then what?" he retorted. "If you hadn't let me past the front door that first day, how would this be better?"

"This wouldn't hurt so bad!" And with that, she dashed for the sanctuary of the house, slammed the door behind her and wept.

CHAPTER TWENTY-EIGHT

A LOUD *THWACK* sounded over Allison's sobs. She hiccupped and took her hands from her eyes, to see Gran's walking stick planted in front of her.

"May I ask what all this ruckus is about?" her grandmother demanded. "I haven't seen you reduced to a ball of tears since…well, ever."

Allison let her eyes follow the dark wood of the walking stick up to Gran's face. At least Gran was talking. She hadn't said more than two words at a time to Allison since she'd come home.

"N-nothing, Gran." How could she tell her that her heart was breaking over the man who'd rained down all this trouble on them?

"Kyle didn't want to come in?" Gran asked. "Get up, child. That floor is hard. You'll get lumbago if you sit there all balled up like that."

She extended a hand to help her, but Allison hitched herself up to her feet. She swiped away her tears as she leaned against the banister to regain her composure. She'd almost wrestled her emotions back into their bottle when her eyes lit on the missing medallion on the staircase.

Had Kyle finished carving the section he'd been working on? Would he give it to Greg Draper to replace the missing one?

"Allison, did you hear me? I asked you what Kyle said that could have reduced you to this gibberish mess."

Allison had to chuckle in the midst of her tears. Her grandmother had resurrected her old "teacher" voice. This was the no-nonsense woman she'd grown up with, the one who liked to remind Allison not to spill the milk to begin with if she didn't want to cry over it.

Her grandmother's acerbic tone served its purpose, and her words rekindled some of Allison's anger at Kyle. "He was saying we shouldn't sell the house."

"Well, that's true enough," Gran snapped. "Has he come to his senses about that paint job?"

"Kyle? Of course not." She rolled her eyes. "No, he was telling me to sell off everything on the third floor to raise the money."

Gran's shoulders sagged, and Allison realized with fresh pain that her grandmother had been hoping Kyle had shown up to grant them a reprieve.

"Half that junk probably needs to be taken to

the county landfill," Gran murmured. She settled slowly into an armchair Allison had moved near the foot of the stairs to give Gran a halfway point between the kitchen and the living room. Her gnarled fingers clasped her walking stick and she at its marble head as though it were a crystal ball. "I hadn't even thought about all that. We'll have to pack it up. Oh, dear. It's just…"

Allison reached over and laid a hand on her arm. "I'm sorry, Gran. I'll pack it up for you. Don't worry about it."

Gran's back bowed with despair, a feeling Allison knew all too well. "No, girl, I'll have to help you. You wouldn't know what to keep or what to toss. I haven't been up there in years. Why, that huge Indian carving will have to go—no room in those dinky houses you've been looking at for such as that. And all the books on those shelves…" Her rheumy blue eyes took on a faraway look.

Allison refused to succumb to tears again. She would not. She could do this. She could find a house Gran would be satisfied with, get this monstrosity cleared out and…

Now images of Belle Paix's rooms, empty and echoing, haunted her. She closed her eyes and let herself be tempted, just for a moment, that Kyle could be right and those attic treasures could bring in enough cash for them to paint the house. Allison could worry about the next paint job later.

The thump of Gran's walking stick on the oak floor dragged her back to cold, hard reality. Gran had lost enough. What if she sold everything, and it wasn't enough to cover the paint? Then they'd still have to sell Belle Paix, and Gran would have nothing left of her old life.

Allison opened her eyes to see her grandmother negotiating the hallway toward the kitchen. Seconds later, she heard the whir of the chair lift on the back stairs. Gran must be retiring to her room for a nap—or a good cry.

When the chair lift's motor quit, Allison turned toward the door, planning to retrieve the broom she'd dropped when she'd dashed inside. That's when she heard the telltale thump of Gran's walking stick on the main stairs—going up to the third floor.

Allison flew up the staircase and rounded the landing, to see she had managed four steps.

"Oh, there you are," Gran panted. Her knuckles were white with effort as she gripped the banister. "Good, you can help me."

"Gran, I'll do it. That third floor's too hot for you, and these stairs—"

"Nonsense! There's something I want to see, a vase that my father bought in Paris." Gran ignored her and hefted herself up another step. "Spent a pretty penny on it—my mother was furious, especially when the crash came not two months later and we lost all our money. That thing has to be worth something—"

"Gran!" Allison scampered up in front of her to stop her progress. "I'll get it later. Come back down!"

But her grandmother didn't listen. Instead, she grumbled, "It's still my house, at least for now. I'll go where I please, thank you very much, with or without your help!"

And she let go of the banister.

Tried to sidestep Allison.

Lost her footing.

Tumbled.

Kept tumbling.

All Allison could do was stare at her outstretched hand, which had missed the fabric of Gran's blouse by a fraction of an inch. Then watch in horror as she slid to a soundless heap at the bottom of the stairs.

"Gran?" she gasped. And when her grandmother didn't so much as moan in response, Allison scrambled down to the landing beside the frail, broken figure, screaming, "Gran! Gran!"

KYLE HAD MADE it up the street to the post office when Herbert stopped him.

"So are you satisfied that this Draper guy will do the house up right?" he asked. "I mean, I don't want the same mess we've had in the past with the current owner."

"Herbert, I really don't want to—"

"And I'm not real fired up about a B and B that close to my place. It's not the *ideal* solution—"

Still agitated by Allison's refusal even to listen to his suggestion, Kyle interrupted him. "You can't have it both ways, Herbert! Either we build in some flexibility in the ordinances, or Draper will buy that house and gut it. And it's not just a B and B. He wants to put in a full-scale restaurant."

Herbert's eyes popped. "But the parking will be a nightmare. Kyle, we can't have *that*. There's got to be some solution."

Kyle's neighbor waved as she skirted around the pair of them, and he nodded an acknowledgment and exchanged a brief greeting. Turning back to Herbert, he conceded, "I thought I had it, actually."

"What was it?" Herbert perked up considerably.

Kyle found his anger heating back up at the thought of Allison's stubbornness. "They've got over a century's worth of stuff squirreled away on the top floor of that house—all manner of things collectors would pay top dollar to get their hands on. So I went over there just now to try to talk Allison into selling it."

"That's a great idea! Why, I'd bet it would work! You could get probably half the money they'd need—maybe even more. So you think she'll do it?"

"Not in this lifetime. Allison swears she can't borrow any money."

"Won't take the risk, you mean." Herbert pursed his lips. "Talk about wanting it both ways. Her idea has always been to do what she dang well pleases with that house and hang our ordinances. Doesn't she understand what we've worked so hard to accomplish?"

"She doesn't value it, Herbert. If she did, she'd fight for it. But she just sees that old house as something that's—I don't know. Too much of a sacrifice."

Just then, the cool morning quiet was rent by the scream of a siren. Kyle watched as an ambulance rushed by, then focused more intently as he saw, two blocks down, the brake lights glow red in front of Belle Paix. For a moment, the vehicle just sat there, lights flashing, siren screeching. Then a head popped out of the passenger window, craning up and down the street.

It hit Kyle all of a sudden that the EMTs couldn't figure out how to get around the wrought-iron fence.

And if an EMT needed to get in…

Kyle started sprinting down the block as fast as he had back in his college track days, yelling and waving like a madman as he went. "Go around! The driveway's on the side!"

Either they heard him—impossible, he knew at that distance—or they saw his gestures, because they backed up to him as he closed the distance.

"Hey," the EMT on the passenger side said, "you know how—"

Kyle gasped, "On the side… Driveway…" He was too winded to get more words out, but he pointed.

The tires screeched as they backed around to the side street and through the Belle Paix's wide, open gate. Kyle bent over, chest heaving from his gut-busting two-block sprint. The ambulance doors clanged open and the gurney clacked over the driveway's paving stones as the EMTs wheeled it toward the house.

The front door flew open and Allison rushed out. "She's upstairs! Hurry!" she called, and beckoned the EMTs up the porch steps and into the house.

But she must have caught sight of Kyle, because the fear on her face dissolved into white-lipped rage.

"Allison—"

Saying nothing, she spun on her heel and slammed the door closed.

CHAPTER TWENTY-NINE

"SHE'S LUCKY, ALLISON," the radiologist told her. "I mean, lucky. That could have been bad."

"An eighty-nine-year-old woman with a concussion *is* bad," Allison insisted. She peered over the radiologist's shoulder and squinted in the darkened room at the computer screen.

"A mild concussion," the radiologist corrected. "And as you can see, that hip joint is fine. No problems. And no signs of fracture in the ribs or the other hip. I'd say clean living has paid off again."

Allison's skin felt clammy, with fear and relief battling for control. She shook it off, knowing it was the aftereffects of the adrenaline that had been buzzing through her. "I'll take it," she said. "But this is a clear sign. Gran needs to be in a house with a single story."

"Yep," the radiologist agreed. "I see more old folks with broken bones because of steps. They're a killer."

Allison retraced her way back to Gran's bay in the ER. She'd left her grandmother in good hands with another of the nurses while she went to check out what the radiologist had found; being an ER nurse here had its perks. Now, at least, she didn't have to worry for the length of time it would take the doctor to report back.

When she yanked aside the curtain to Gran's cubicle, she saw it wasn't a nurse with her grandmother.

Kyle Mitchell and Gran were engrossed in a deep, low conversation, their heads together in an almost conspiratorial manner.

"What are you doing here?" Allison snapped.

"They let me in," Kyle told her.

"Well, they can let you out. My grandmother could have died because of you. She would have never tackled those steps if she hadn't heard about your harebrained scheme—"

"Allison!" Gran's protest was weak and tired, but still held an edge. "I asked them to let him in."

"They shouldn't have. If you don't mind, I want a word with you." She gestured for Kyle to follow her.

As he rose from the chair by the bed, Gran reached out to him. "Kyle…you'll tell her, right? You'll see to it?"

He patted her hand. "I'll try, Gran. But…" Now he met Allison's eyes. "It doesn't look like she's in the mood to listen."

Allison marched outside to a small courtyard where she could give Kyle a piece of her mind out of earshot from coworkers and patients.

Before she could open her mouth, Kyle folded his arms across his chest and said, "She doesn't want to sell."

"Well, duh, genius, neither do I."

"She was describing this vase to me. It may be a Jean Dunand, could be worth a considerable amount of money—"

"Kyle. Stop." Allison warded off his words with outstretched palms.

He fell silent. The only sounds in the courtyard were the trickling of the fountain and a noisy pair of mockingbirds trying to outsing each other.

Allison tried to frame her words carefully, without anger, so that he would be sure to understand. This wasn't about him or her or the stupid paint job. This was about Gran, and what was best for her.

"She could have died today. She could have been killed. All because of that house."

"It's her house, Allison. And she wants to keep it."

"You're filling her head with nonsense, with false hope. We could sell everything on that third floor and still not have enough—"

"She's willing to risk it. She's ready to fight

for her home. The question is," Kyle said as he regarded her, "are you?"

The mockingbirds were joined by a third, their screeching driving Allison crazy as she tried to focus on what to say to make him finally get it.

"That house isn't safe for her—"

"Yeah. You *aren't* ready to fight for it. You're just too chicken." Kyle's words brimmed with contempt. "You want the safe way, the sure bet, the easy out. I'm not like that. I'm not that guy. And I never will be. How I could have *ever* thought you might be someone who would understand me, I don't know." He stared off into the distance. "Well, if you change your mind, go look upstairs. Not for me. Not for Belle Paix. For your grandmother. It's a black vase with gold stripes, very art deco."

He turned, started to walk away. Then over his shoulder, he tossed another question. "And you tell me. How sick would you feel if you sold the house out from under your grandmother and then found that vase was worth more than enough to pay for the repairs?"

"You want me to believe in a fairy tale, Kyle? One where we're sitting on a gold mine and don't even know it? Next you'll tell me Gran's got a Picasso or two tucked away up there. That's junk in the attic. Junk that I've got to move and store and cry over. Leftovers from somebody else's life. A hundred and twenty-six years of leftovers, to be precise."

"History..." Kyle said it sadly.

"What?"

"Your leftovers? That's my history."

"Well, it's pretty clear that your history is more important than me, Kyle. If you cared for me one whit, you'd realize that history isn't as important as real living, breathing people. History is *gone*, the past, yesterday. And I'm here now. Doesn't that matter?"

He said nothing, but when he ran his fingers through his hair, she saw that his hand trembled.

"History isn't just the past. It's *me*, Allison. It's who I *am*, what I've devoted my life to." He focused on her face. "You know what? I should look at the bright side. When you sell Belle Paix for half of what it's worth, because it's too much trouble and because it's full of someone else's 'leftovers,' at least you'll be gone, and I'll know. Maybe I'll really get it then."

"Get what?" She was perplexed, couldn't follow what he was saying, though a sick feeling of loss was already permeating through her.

"You're not for me. You can't be. Not if you can't understand what I love. Heck, half the time, Allison, you don't even pretend to respect it. So it's good I found out what you were—or rather, what you weren't—before this went too far."

He didn't wait for her reply, just stalked off.

The finality of his words, the sad resignation, even the fact that he didn't look back as he rounded the corner, echoed through her. It was the same feeling she'd had whenever she'd broken something precious and irreplaceable, only ten times worse.

He was gone.

And he wasn't coming back.

SHE FOUND HER grandmother where she'd left her, but in a totally different mind-set.

Gran's arms were folded across her chest, her chin jutted out. "You can call that Draper man if you'd rather, or I can do it for you. I am not selling Belle Paix."

"Gran, that house could have killed you today—"

"Not that house. My stupidity. My stubbornness. And if I'd died there, well, at least I would have died *there*. I'd rather die there tomorrow than live another ten years somewhere else. Get it through your head, Allison. I'm not selling."

"Great, so you tell me how we'll get the money to paint that monstrosity."

"Kyle says—"

"Kyle—" Allison banged around the claustrophobic bay, relieved that her anger was back, numbing her to the heartache swirling through her. "*Kyle* is the reason we're in this mess, Gran. And the reason *you're* laid up in that bed."

"Very logical, Allison. First you blame the house and then you blame Kyle."

"Well, it's both," she insisted. "And it's high time we stopped depending on someone else to rescue us or bend the rules or—or whatever. We have to face this, Gran. Isn't that what you always taught me? Not to wish things were different, but face them and deal with them?"

Gran's face crumpled. She wouldn't meet Allison's eyes. "I'm not selling."

Her voice was low, but firm, and brooked no argument.

Great. Another one of Kyle's lovely complications. Allison had just got Gran reconciled to the fact that the house would have to go.

Arguing now wouldn't work. She patted her on the shoulder. "Sure, Gran, whatever you say. Just don't cry, okay? I can't take it when you cry." With that, she wrapped her in a gentle hug, and they both wept, anyway.

CHAPTER THIRTY

NOT EVEN CLEO greeted Allison when she arrived home after dark one night later that week. It was as if the cat knew Gran was back in the hospital, and put the blame squarely on Allison.

It had been a tough few days, with Gran developing a hospital-acquired infection and having to go on another round of IV antibiotics. Allison had not been able to do much more than run back and forth between work and Gran's bedside.

And Kyle hadn't left a single solitary message.

Oh, she'd heard through the grapevine that he called Gran every day, but never when she was around. And Allison's phone had rung, all right. Right off the wall. Apparently Gran had called Greg Draper from the hospital and told him the sale was off.

Apart from that, Gran wouldn't even talk about the house.

Still, Gran was doing better in body, if not in spirit, and responding to the antibiotics. This was the first night that Allison had dared spend the night at home in bed.

Home. She looked around the bright, cheery kitchen with the Chambers stove that Kyle loved so much. Belle Paix wouldn't be home for much longer.

The old house was silent. The absence of sound smothered Allison. She'd gotten used to Gran's thumping and banging, and now the place seemed even larger and emptier than it ever had.

She wandered from room to room, finally ending up in the living room by the turntable. The 45s that Kyle had played were still on the machine. She picked up one in the stack that he hadn't played, read the title. It was Frank Sinatra's "High Hopes," way too cheerful for her current mood. She flipped it over, saw that the B-side was "All My Tomorrows," but she couldn't remember how it went. She shrugged and put it on the turntable.

Sinatra's doleful voice about luck passing him by moved her to tears—but it was more than that. This person Frank Sinatra was singing about had stuck by him.

No, what made her cry was the thought of Kyle giving up on her. And he had. Because she wasn't a fighter.

Okay. So she'd give him that. And she'd give

him the fact that she didn't always treasure "history" as he did.

But he'd made history come alive for her. No, he'd made *her* come alive.

And she'd called it leftovers.

The record came to a halt. She considered replaying it. Changed her mind. No point in wallowing in self-pity.

The stairs sparked another battle within her. She found herself loathing them for the near disaster they'd brought on Gran. But at the same time, Kyle's words came to her.

"How sick would you feel if you sold the house out from under your grandmother and then found that vase was worth more than enough to pay for the repairs?"

It wasn't. She knew in her heart that it couldn't be that easy. Surely if it was as valuable as Gran thought it might be, the family would have sold it during one of the many times they'd needed money in the past.

But it certainly couldn't hurt to look.

Besides, it might show Kyle that she had a little bit of fight left in her.

Upstairs on the cluttered third floor, the jumble of possessions pressed in on her. These bits and pieces were all that was left from someone's life, a person's treasures—her family's treasures. She found herself totally understanding how someone could turn into a hoarder. Letting these go—even the silliest oldest trinkets—would hurt, mainly because she didn't know the stories that were attached to them.

She'd never wanted to live in the past, because it was too painful. It was where her parents had died, where life as she knew it had suddenly been wrenched away from her. The future, now, *that* she could control. The future was safer, less likely to hurt her, if she just didn't take too many gambles.

Right. And that had worked out so well with Kyle.

She headed for the shelves of books and porcelains. Davinia's journals tempted her at first. Had Ambrose ever wanted to give up on his Davinia? Had they managed to make a real go of it, despite how different they were? Oh, yeah, they'd stayed married, but that's what people did back then.

The real question was had they been *happy*?

Allison forced her eyes away from the journals and scanned the shelves. At first she saw nothing but one ugly little shepherd boy after another—someone had really been into shepherds.

Then she spotted it. High up on the far shelf, dully gleaming despite a layer of dust, it was just as Kyle had described it: black with gold stripes arranged into overlapping triangles, looking straight out of the 1920s.

Allison dragged a stool over to the shelf and clambered up to retrieve the vase. When she lifted it, she found it was at once lighter and heavier than she'd anticipated. The vase would have virtually no weight at all if it wasn't for the heavy base. And the finish! Silky and mesmerizing, it was nothing like any porcelain or ceramic vase she'd ever seen or felt. She flipped it over to find a manufacturer's mark. A piece of paper fluttered out and landed on the floor. She ignored it for the time being and squinted to read what was on the base.

Inscribed into the bottom was a scrawled signature: Jean Dunand. And a date: 1928.

Incredible.

Gran had been right. It was made at the height of the Roaring Twenties, before the crash that had changed their family fortunes.

Allison stepped off the stool, carefully holding the vase. The scrap of paper caught her eye and she stooped to pick it up.

It was a receipt, a bill of sale from an art gallery in Paris, with a description in French of the vase in her hand, along with the astounding price paid for it.

No wonder her great-grandmother had been furious. And no wonder the vase had been banished to the third floor. After the crash, there'd probably been no way to convert such a piece of art into cash for anywhere close to the amount her great-grandfather had paid for it.

Allison's heart began to race. Hope surged through her. What if Kyle had been right? What if this vase could help her grandmother keep Belle Paix?

She fished out her cell phone from her back pocket and did an internet image search of Jean Dunand vases.

An eBay listing of a squatter, uglier vase filled the tiny screen. She drew in a breath at the price: $25,000.

Allison stared at the object in her hand. Would such a vase be worth that much? The finish was still shiny and lacquered, but the detail of the stripes in their triangle pattern had a spiderweb of light lines in the glaze.

Her pragmatism fought back. A collectible was worth something only if someone else wanted it. And likely as not it might bring only a few hundred bucks.

Allison returned to the internet images. A famous auction house listing popped up now—and when she saw the amount paid for it, her knees went weak. She collapsed onto the stool.

Nearly a million dollars.

For a vase?

It might not even be the vase Gran had been talking about.

But there was only one way to find out.

GRAN HELD THE vase in her hands in the dim light of the hospital room.

"Well, now. That's it. That's the vase that nearly got my parents divorced."

"Gran! You never told me that. You said your parents lived to see their fiftieth wedding anniversary and then some."

"Ah, but they nearly didn't. And it was all because of this." Gran tapped the black vase. "Came from Paris, it did."

"I know. I found the bill of sale."

"Yep. Mama stuffed it in there when she took the thing upstairs, and told my father in no uncertain terms that she never wanted to see it again. I'd forgotten about it until I started thinking about what all was upstairs. All those stories, Allison... Every piece up there has a story to go with it, you know."

Allison rolled her eyes. "You sound like Kyle."

"I do. Because it's the truth."

Her grandmother went back to staring at the vase, and Allison could tell she was a million miles away—no, eighty-five years away.

"I don't really remember it," Gran said. "I

was only, hmm, three or four at the most when the crash came. I only heard about it later. Whenever money would get tight, and it was always tight back then, my mother would bring that vase up. My father…my father was never the same after the crash. He'd lost it all, you see, and hadn't even seen it coming. He went to Paris for some business deal in the summer of '29, and my mother had wanted to go."

"But she didn't go with him?"

"No…she hated to leave me. I'd been sick with—oh, I forget what, but some childhood disease, chickenpox maybe, or measles. And so she stayed."

"And your father bought the vase while he was there?"

Gran chuckled. "He called it an investment. My mother called it expensive junk. She didn't like it the minute she laid eyes on it." Gran's smile faded. "And then, of course, the fall came, and the crash, and all the fights about money. So one day she marched it up to the third floor and told him she didn't want to see it ever again. My father didn't argue. I guess he didn't want to think about all the money he'd wasted on that vase, either." Gran waved away the memory. "Do you think it's worth anything?"

Allison hedged. True, someone somewhere had thought a Jean Dunand vase was pretty valuable, but she didn't want to get Gran's hopes up.

"Maybe, Gran. But I don't have a clue about how to find out." She leaned forward in her chair. "Besides, just because this vase might sell for enough to paint Belle Paix doesn't mean it's a good idea for you to keep living there."

Gran narrowed her eyes and clutched the vase all the more tightly. "Now why do you say that? I've told you. It was my stubbornness, not anything else, that caused that accident. Belle Paix was where I was born and where I want to die. Spending nearly three months away from it in that rehab facility convinced me of that."

"But, Gran…you should have someplace safe and new and easier for you to get around in," she protested.

"Allison…come here. Sit." Gran patted the bed.

She heaved a sigh and obeyed. Gran reached up and traced her cheek, and it instantly brought Allison back through the years to when Gran would tuck her in bed. She swallowed past the lump in her throat.

"Gran…I know you love that old house," she murmured, before her grandmother could speak. "But I'm just…not good at it. I'm not patient enough with it. I get frustrated too easily. I'm made for new houses that aren't falling apart around me."

Gran squeezed her hand and nodded. "I thought it was more about you than me," she said. "Do you remember when you went off to college?"

Allison blinked, failing to find any connection between Belle Paix and college. "Yes, ma'am."

"You came back at Christmas, remember? And swore you weren't going back?"

Allison pressed her fingers to her forehead and cringed at the memory of the fight she'd had with Gran. She'd made C's on all her final exams and nearly died of mortification in the process.

"I remember. But I went back."

"You weren't going to. You told me then that you just weren't cut out to be a nurse. And what did I tell you?"

"That if it wasn't hard, I wasn't working at something worth having."

Gran beamed at her. "Now look at what a good nurse you are! And you almost weren't, because you nearly gave up on yourself. Don't do it again, Allison. Don't give up on anything that you really, really want, just because it's hard at first."

It wasn't Belle Paix that filled Allison's mind at those words.

It was Kyle.

What had he wanted?

A fighter. Someone ready to fight.

He hadn't just meant for Belle Paix. He'd meant for each other.

Allison put her fingers to her mouth. "Oh, Gran. I think it's too late."

She pressed the vase into Allison's hands. "Child, you take this vase and give it to Kyle. And tell him that you're not ready to quit. Not on Belle Paix. Not on me. And not on the two of you. Because if you don't, if you let him get away…why, who knows what tomorrows you'll be giving up?"

KYLE BALLED UP yet another piece of paper and threw it in the trash can. It bounced off the metal rim and landed on the floor. The hour was late. He should give up and call it a night.

He stared at the silent phone on his desk and willed it to ring.

He would not call Allison. Not until he could offer a solution to help her save her grandmother's house.

The mound of crumpled paper balls attested to how far he was from that goal.

He'd been working on a number of different

ideas—a hardship exemption for people over sixty-five, a revolving loan fund that residents could pool their money in. As of yet, nothing had gelled enough to take to the board.

But something would, eventually.

If he couldn't have Allison, then at least he could make sure that she didn't lose Belle Paix to a man who'd gut its soul to make way for a soup of the day.

Kyle picked up all the crumpled paper and put it the trash, then realized the can was overflowing with bad ideas. Blowing out a dispirited breath, he toted it to the kitchen.

The memory of very nearly kissing Allison here came back to him. Had he really passed up that opportunity? He wished like mad that he hadn't. He wished he had more memories of kissing her, holding her.

Face it, buddy. You were smart to end it. She's just like the others. You saw how that wound up every time. You and Allison would never make it, not without her realizing how important history is to you.

Another voice whispered back, *And not without you being able to give in a little. She was right. You could have argued for that hardship waiver. Isn't that what you're doing now?*

It was. Because it just hurt too much to have her gone.

The doorbell rang, a timid half ring that made him think it was probably the Turner boys down the street up to their double-dog-dares again. An irritated glance at the clock told him it was almost 10:30 p.m.—they'd sneaked out their bedroom window yet again.

He crossed through the dining room and into the hall and flung open the door. "Boys! You should—"

It wasn't the Turner boys.

In the pool of illumination from the front stoop's light, Allison sat on the bench by the front door, a black lacquered vase in her arms. She stared up at him. "I know it's late," she began. "But is it too late?"

Kyle's throat went dry as the Sahara. He had so much he'd wanted to say to her, and now he couldn't utter a single syllable.

"I mean..." Allison stood up and scooted backward. "If it's too late—"

"No," he rasped. "No. It's never too late for you. Why don't you...er, why don't you come in?"

He watched as she walked from the front door to the dining room to the butler's pantry. It was only when she stopped at the green baize and asked, "Aren't you coming?" that he was convinced she wasn't an apparition of wishful thinking.

In the kitchen, she carefully set the vase on the worktable. "It's a Jean Dunand," she said simply.

Kyle didn't care. More precious to him than any old vase was having Allison here, in his kitchen, when he'd wanted her so.

When he'd believed she would never darken his door again.

"Kyle..."

"I'm sorry," he blurted out. "I'm so sorry, Allison. I get it. I'm trying to draft a proposal so that your grandmother can have more time to paint the house—or that we can create a loan fund. I think that's got a shot, actually. That maybe the downtown business owners would chip in, as well. It wouldn't be cheap interest, but it would be—"

Allison came around the worktable and took his hands in hers. "Kyle. You didn't hear me. The vase. It's a Jean Dunand."

Now her words sunk into his brain. "What?" He stared first at her, then at the vase, then back at her.

"A 1928 Jean Dunand, with the original sales bill," she said. She pulled a slip of paper from her pocket.

"You didn't crease it, did you? Because even that bill of sale might be valuable if it's actually signed by him..."

Allison laughed. It was a beautiful sound that filled the room with music, and Kyle realized it was just that sound that his perfect house had been missing.

"I did, actually. Will you forgive me?"

Kyle breathed out a long exhalation. "Oh, Allison, will *you* forgive *me*?"

"Done. So done." Her throat moved as she swallowed. She ran the tip of her tongue over her lips. "Kyle, I…this vase…it might be worth fifty cents or fifty thousand dollars or even a million bucks. I don't know. But I'm ready."

"Ready?" His heart seized in his chest. Ready for what? To move? To leave? To sell Belle Paix?

"To fight. For…" Allison dropped her gaze. "For Belle Paix. And…and us, if you think there's still a chance. I can't…I can't promise that I will always get how important history is to you. I can't promise that I won't secretly long for drywall and modern plumbing and a house that isn't falling apart around us. But…I can't see my tomorrows without you. Or without Belle Paix."

She dug into her pocket again, pulled out five little pieces of cardboard and dropped them into his hand. Hunter green and pale butter yellow, autumn gold, a deep burgundy and a black as dark as the Jean Dunand vase on the table beside them.

"Paint swatches?" He squinted at her, bewildered.

"Maybe this vase will sell for enough. Maybe it will take everything on that third floor. Maybe it will even mean I have to sell my car and walk to work. But whatever it takes, you're right. The old girl deserves new clothes. And I…I want to do it right."

With a hand that trembled, he set the paint swatches beside the vase.

"You. You are more important than things. Or paint. Or even history. History is about yesterday, and I know what yesterday was like, Allison, because you weren't in it. And…" He stroked a finger along her cheek, marveling that she was back, marveling that she was saying all the words he'd longed to hear. "I can't face tomorrow or the day after that—or the day after *that* without you in it."

She wrapped her arms around him, and he buried his face in her hair. He pressed her close determined not to ever let her go. "So…I guess it's not too late. I was so afraid I was too late Kyle."

He laughed and swung her around the kitchen. "Not even close."

"Whoa! Wait! Don't knock over that vase!" Now Allison was laughing, too, her eyes bright, her beautiful mouth curved into a smile. He leaned down and kissed her. Her mouth was warm and sweet, and he was bent on making the kiss last as long as he could.

She broke away, smiling shyly.

"But…you know, we *do* have another problem."

Kyle froze. His brain frantically searched for her meaning. "Huh?"

"Well, you have your darling little house here." Allison swept a hand to encompass the kitchen. "I can't ask you to give it up for a run-down heap like Belle Paix."

Kyle grinned. "Honey, you and Belle Paix are more than worth giving up this house. You alone are worth that. Besides…" He winked. "I need to keep my DIY skills honed and at the ready."

She pressed her mouth to his again in a mind-blowing kiss that Kyle never wanted to end. "Okay. But don't say I didn't warn you. I mean, we *are* going to fight, you know."

"I know. You'll want that modern plumbing."

"But you'll convince me that history has its charms." She laid her palm against his cheek.

"You're the one," he told her.

"The one what?" Allison asked.

"The one with all the charm. You're the one for me." And with that, he stopped talking and went back to kissing.

* * * * *